AUGUST HEAT

AUGUST HEAT

A Novel

BETH LORDAN

1817

HARPER & ROW, PUBLISHERS, New York

Cambridge, Grand Rapids, Philadelphia, St. Louis,
San Francisco, London, Singapore, Sydney, Tokyo

FIRST EDITION

Designed by Cassandra J. Pappas

Library of Congress Cataloging-in-Publication Data

Lordan, Beth.
  August heat.

  I. Title.
PS3562.073A94   1989   813'.54   88-45917
ISBN 0-06-016094-2

---

89 90 91 92 93 CC/HC 10 9 8 7 6 5 4 3 2 1

For my mother, Emily Kathleen Spicer,
and in memory of my grandmother, Ora Maye Spicer

PART I

C H A P T E R 1

ll down the winding length of River Street, the invisible women are hanging out the wash, filling the sweet morning with the *skreek-skreek* of their clothesline pulleys and the high faint smell of bleach. The back yards grow thick with sheets, white sheets and flowered lifting free in the breeze as they are pushed off past the back stoop railings. Shadows dance among the brilliant bedclothes and flick across the flower beds and sandboxes and high grass of River Street's wide back yards. In less than an hour the sheets will be dry, hauled back and gathered in through those open back doors, and the towels will be sent out in proud unison, pale or white, announced again by the raucous pulleys. Today the lines will be filled again and again, and after the bedding and the towels, the street's true variety will begin to show. Drizzling rain for a week, and now such a day for drying! Diapers, housedresses, starched white shirts, chinos and dress pants and gray work pants and dungarees on stretchers; Sunday dresses, undershirts, slips and petticoats; blouses, nightgowns, socks sorted and unsorted, underpants of every style and every size, corduroy overalls two feet long, girdles; throw rugs, dishcloths, table-

3

cloths, tea towels, dresser scarves, bath mats, dust mop heads, slipcovers, crocheted antimacassars and doilies: there is no end to what the women on River Street will wash on a day like this.

Tonight their arms will glow with weariness, and their hearts will be soft and warm. All unaware, the husbands will come home, and start up their singular and eccentric lawn mowers. When they go to bed, something will rise up and they will act as if that something is desire, but it will be only the sun-dried sheets around them, and the languorous satisfaction they barely saw in the faces of their happy wives, and their own glad triumphs over the high-grown grass of their back yards and front yards. Only! The wide generosity of the day's breeze will roll on in the bedrooms: grave and voluptuous, as if they danced alone in moonlight in their summer nightgowns, the women will turn and produce the sweet favors and secret acts of lovemaking they keep saving for the men of their dreams. And their husbands, astonished at how plentiful the dark world has suddenly become, will sigh, finding endurance in sheer curiosity about what could possibly come next.

There's more. The grass is already growing again, and between the moment when a hand reaches surely and gently in the dark to find a smooth shoulder and the moment when a thigh slides one inch to the left in response, five leaves on the nearest maple tree have increased their individual areas by one tenth. Seven moths are born in that moment. The bats begin carousing above the night yards, daredevils. The darkness is filled with things that swoop and alight only for an instant at a time. Not a single child, all down the dark length of River Street, so much as coughs between ten o'clock and dawn. All that still to come. All that assured and mysteriously assumed in the bright sweet beginnings of this washday in July, in the throaty jubilation of the clothesline pulleys shouting like blue jays in the morning sun.

But it's a one-day revel. This breeze isn't going to stop for another four days, and even then the sun will keep shining most days; no long rains are coming. There won't be a need for any such common celebration of drying weather for the rest of this summer. River Street's women will do their wash alone, or only by chance at the same time. Even tomorrow, a little lame in a

4

muscle here and there, and blaming it all on hanging out those heavy things, the women will have subsided. They'll take the stiff shirts from the ironing baskets, wet them down with water from a saucepan sprinkled off their fingertips in sharp flicks or shaken from old soda pop bottles fitted with tops designed just for that. They'll roll the damp shirts into cylinders as heavy as pieces of pipe and stack them at the ends of their ironing boards. They'll iron and fold and hang and replace all those clean things tomorrow, efficient and mildly disapproving, like costume mistresses after opening night. Next time, washday will arrive because clothes are dirty.

Today the women are distracted by their own sober delight. They answer the children as if the house were full of company; hours later they wonder for a moment where the children have gotten to, and vaguely remind themselves. It will be all right. Nobody's lost. A stranger with a blue overnight bag gets off the Greyhound bus in front of the grocery store, and the bus makes its instant's pause and goes on, without being noticed. The stranger walks right through the village to the bridge where River Street becomes Bridge Road and the town ends, crosses over and passes out of sight down the dip the road takes to the bridge there. Not a one of the women on River Street has seen her in the ten minutes it takes for her to arrive and disappear. They eat scanty lunches between loads, standing in their back doorways beside empty laundry baskets, watching the first or second loads of colored wash drying before their eyes. They don't notice how they tap a foot or move their shoulders to the beat of the washer's agitator; they see nothing but their own clotheslines, the narrow strips of grass between, the gardens or garages at the backs of their own yards, and the sky. They put the babies out to nap in the shade between the lines, and the babies sleep lightly in the smell of drying wash, wake in the tunnels of dancing clothes to the racket of the pulleys above.

In the front room of the first house on Bridge Road, Jacob Wilcox naps too, his mouth a little open. Three small boys crouch outside, hidden from the house and the road by an ancient privet hedge that has grown tree-high. Just beside the back door, a blueberry bush wears Jacob's three pairs of undershorts, his other shirt, and a navy blue bandanna. From the maple sapling, a few steps closer to the garden, Jacob's two sheets dangle. Jacob's gray trousers lie folded over the high back of the old front porch rocker that sits right next to the garden, his nightshirt lies over one arm and his two undervests over the other, and seven socks, all black silky gentlemen's dress socks, take up the narrow rush seat.

When Jacob goes to town, he's the town's madman. He's stork-tall and stork-thin, and he walks like a pack of dogs was worrying at him from all sides. Every step he's cursing, and not a word can anyone understand in the noise he makes. He swings his head, and he wraps his arms tight over his chest and throws them wide in helpless fury, all the time swearing vengeance, he'll get them all: it's not decent, the rhythm of his rage, it's every cadence that joins filth with all that is dearest and most vulnerable. When he must go to town, the shouting comes around him and he moves within it, protected as if by invisibility, for when he shouts no one speaks to him, no one touches him, and he is invulnerable. But here, in the silence of his mother's house, he is his mother's son. Here he keeps himself safe in his mother's ways: with the silence that fell years ago from her death, and with the tricks of sleeping he learned from her example when he was young, right here in this house. He feels the drowsiness approaching from so far off that when it draws close he has forgotten it, although he has been preparing for it all the time. Today, called like the others by the high free breeze, he went about the house gathering what was washable. He washed the clothing and the sheets piece by piece, with yellow soap, by hand, stooping over the bathtub to dunk and worry every inch of each garment between his fisted knuckles. The drowsiness began as he waited for the water to fill the tub for the first rinse, but it was far off, a pleasure of the distance. He rinsed them all, the heavy sheets first and the elegant socks last, wringing them out one by one, and stacked them on the board he had put across the toilet lid just for them. Then a second rinse drawn, one by one the wet wads blooming out in the clear water to become shirt, vest, trousers, sock. He remembered that he would lift each of these again, out there in the wind, and the creeping drowsiness was not in his mind a bit. He worked, rinsed and squeezed and stacked and waited for water again, and took pleasure again in the sudden weightlessness of the heavy hanks of clothing as he fed each one into the bath and it became itself again. He sloshed the sheets mightily. He lost all thought of ever being sleepy. The trousers he dipped with respect, as if they were a gentleman; with the socks he was dainty and playful. Like the women on River Street, he celebrated, he indulged himself for the day's own sake. He is crazy and they are not, but in the joy of today's wash it doesn't make much difference: they are all mad or they are all fine.

His basket fills with wash he has squeezed almost as well with his long hands as a River Street wringer would have. He carries it to his back door and out into the sun. Jacob is fifty-eight, and he has never in his life alone in his mother's house had so many things to drape in the sun at once. Some days he washes his underclothes, some days a pair of trousers, once in a while a sheet. And some days Jacob cowers before the necessity of deciding just where to dispose of even a single pair of dark socks; or he grows angry with the height of the young maple before he even tries to arrange his sheet on its limbs; or the impossibility of choosing between the identical arms of the rocker leaves him helplessly confused and he stands with a sock in each hand until both are dry. Not today! Today is made for drying laundry. Jacob feels how humorous and plentiful the wind is, and the places he hangs his wash stretch eagerly toward him, and in no time at all the basket is empty and Jacob's wash lies gratefully open to the wind's steady caress.

The drowsiness arrives as if in the wind, a full hour ahead of the stranger, who is his sister coming to rescue him after all these years from his life of mad drowsing and shouting. Sleep passes like a dry, kind hand, enormous and thin, over Jacob's narrow forehead and up through his fine white hair. Jacob smiles. He lets the basket drop to the ground, where it rolls over once. Jacob goes into his house holding lazily to the wall as he drifts through the kitchen and the back hall and drops into his parlor chair, already deep asleep, the very image of his long dead mother.

*

The three boys crouched outside are from the village, so they
have come across the bridge, down in the dip. At the top of the
rise out of the dip they cut cross-lots to Town Line Road, above
Jacob's house, and follow that back down, to come at the hedge
from the far side, as if they had come from out on one of the
farms. When farm boys come to watch for Jacob, they come
down Town Line one way or the other to a certain place, cut
cross-lots to the bridge, and sneak up through the tall grass to
come at Jacob's house from the town side. There is hedge on
both sides. The cross-lot paths are various, but behind each
hedge is a nest, three or four boys wide, where the grass is so
worn it seems to be a different plant from what fills the meadows
around it.

Two of the boys are Allen and Tony Darcy, and the third is
Chris Blandell. Allen and Chris are older and taller than Tony,
and they aren't wearing shirts. Their ribs show and their bel-
lybuttons still pout like flower buds. Tony's does too, but he's
wearing a shirt, his striped pullover shirt that he wears and
wears until his father makes him take it off. Tony walks behind.
At the bottom of the dip, on the bridge, he says, "I'm getting
a bike for my birthday."

Allen keeps looking straight ahead. "You are not."

Tony smiles shyly, a beautiful soft smile, but no one is looking
at him. "I am too," he says, sweet, placative.

Allen pulls air in through his teeth, cold air pulled in over the
canker sore in his cheek. His face seems to be grinning, but his
eyes are narrow. It hurts like crazy when he isn't pulling air over
it.

"Yeah, what kind of bike," Chris challenges. He might be
putting up with the brothers or he might be tagging along. He
is paler than they are.

"I don't know yet."

"You are not getting any bike," Allen insists.

"That's the only part I don't know yet, what kind of bike it's
going to be," says Tony, happily puzzled.

"I got a Schwinn Starfire," Chris says.

8

"Your birthday's in January, Tony. You don't get any bike in January," Allen says.

"What color?" Tony asks Chris.

Allen listens to see if Chris will answer Tony again. He grimaces, sucks the air in cold. It sounds like a gasp. They walk at the side of the road, in the first weeds beyond the gravelly shoulder, going up the rise now.

"Huh?" Tony reminds, very quietly and patiently from behind.

Chris says, "Green," and Allen would say, *Hunh, you haven't got any green bicycle you old liar,* because he knows Chris is lying, but if he said that, he'd have to keep saying more things, and every time he talks it hurts that canker sore. They walk without speaking just long enough for Chris to begin to understand that even Tony might not believe him. He pulls the head off a Queen Anne's lace and throws it into the field. "You going to cut here?" he asks Allen.

Allen sucks again, satisfied. "Not yet," he says. He scratches the back of his neck, then up behind and over his ear, like his father does. They go a little farther up the rise, past the usual place four strides, five, seven. Allen cuts away from the road, through the high grass and chicory, and the others follow him, Chris blank-faced in submission, Tony beaming with pleasure at the green Schwinn Starfire his parents have leaned against the coffee table for him, and a choir of voices like Christmas carols at church when the fathers sing too fills his ears with *Happy birthday, dear Tony, happy birthday to you.* They come out onto the side of Town Line Road just as a county road truck roars by.

"Has it got streamers?" Tony asks.

Chris looks hard after the truck. "I wrecked it."

Tony tries to remember Chris riding his green bike before it was wrecked. He tries to remember Chris riding any bike at all. It troubles him. "That old Jacob Wilcox," he begins, to comfort himself, "that old Jacob Wilcox, one time he threw all his cans out the front door and they went rolling all over the road and made a bunch of cars have an accident." He shakes his head in mild disapproval of such craziness.

"He did not," Allen says, evenly.

"He did too. All his cans of soup and stuff, because of that encyclopedia guy."

Allen turns around and glares at Tony, who waits with the serious face of a true scholar. Allen speaks slowly, pausing carefully. "What he did was, he threw every, single, can out his upstairs, front window. Right through the glass. That's what he did."

Tony doesn't even blink. He waits for Allen to see that Chris has started across the road without waiting for Allen to go first.

Allen doesn't have to see it, any more than he needs to see inside his mouth to know where his torture is coming from. He puts a gentle ragged fingertip into his mouth and presses the burning sore. His eyes close. He breathes slow and steady after the first blunt touch. Almost pleasure, the exchange of that surprising hurt for this steadiness, this true throbbing pain.

One spring night almost thirty years ago, when Jacob was still quite a young man and Allen's father a baby, a short German man on Spare Avenue threw from his bedroom window a middling quantity of canned food. The cans damaged nothing but the window of the German, who had a goiter and believed his daughter was promiscuous.

On Whistle Street, which runs parallel to Town Line Road but is clear on the other side of the village, the new Fuller Brush man was bitten one morning shortly after the war by old Mr. Boyd, whose nephew still has a farm over near Livingstone. Old Mr. Boyd was crazy, but he stayed close to home until the day he died. He was the same one who used to steal huge peony blossoms from his neighbors' yards in broad daylight and eat them on the spot, hunched down like an ancient peasant over the pink and magenta cabbages of near-starvation.

Kicking in the weeds across the road, Chris hits an old tail pipe with his foot. It's a better excuse than he could have asked for. He picks it up, holds it to his eye, sights back at the Darcy boys casually, scanning the oceans for sight of a sail, as if he's come off over here on his own quite by accident, meaning no insubordination. But Allen and Tony are staring at nothing, and they don't look over at him. Chris takes the pipe from his eye, lowers it along his leg, and drops it carefully back into the weeds. He starts a casual amble back across the road, to arrive a few yards from them. The rust of the pipe rings his eye. He doesn't know that, and neither of the Darcy boys mentions it.

The way Allen leads misses the hidden pipe by a good bit, and Chris is sorry about that. If they could have found it he could have showed them how to see the hole in your hand, pipe to one eye, palm over the other. A clean hole right through your hand.

Up ahead is Jacob's hedge. Beyond the hedge is the visible front porch and the half-hidden back yard and garden. Boys don't pay any attention to the house itself. What can be seen at Jacob's is outside. It happens for them when Jacob comes out: Allen has seen it, back and front.

Many days, Jacob leaves his Bridge Road house and goes to town, where these boys have seen him their whole lives, his eyes cast down to this side and that side, back over one thin shoulder with a snarl of cursing, at the ugliness of his pursuers (who are not there, no one ever follows Jacob, not the children, not the dogs, no one), at the way they'll all suffer when the world comes round again and Jacob Wilcox has his rightful power restored: Then! He boasts of it, sometimes he laughs, Lucifer naming God's true hypocrisy in the void, wild with despair and hate. But not a word emerges from the steady bitter flow: it is syllables and sounds of pure curse, but impersonal because there are no words, no namings. In the store, Amos Brown knows what Jacob's come for, and he adds up the bill on a scrap of brown paper, just as he would for anybody else. Muttering steadily, moving from leg to leg in impotent pause, Jacob flicks his eyes back and forth, sharp, watching the column of figures grow as the pile of food dwindles, the column resolving into a total just as the awkward bacon, cornmeal, coffee, eggs, have resolved into a solidly packed brown paper sack. Jacob has walked the creaking floor of the three-aisle store to bring these things to the counter himself. His legs move him around like a crazy man, and the speech without words continues its furious harangue from his face, so that anybody who didn't know would swear he was damning Amos and store alike to some particularized hell. But Jacob's hands are as casual as anyone's here. He chooses his packages of food and sets each one with complete assurance and respect before Amos. If there are customers ahead of him (rare, more than a customer at a time except around noon), he waits, milling and muttering. When he's finished and Amos adds up the list and circles the total, Jacob's voice is still going, meaningless, outraged and vengeful, as his long white gentleman's hand writes a calm check in a smooth cursive, and places it in the waiting, habitual palm of Mr. Amos Brown, Proprietor. It's the same in the post office, Jacob's fluent speech always a scant edge away from choking collapse under the always cresting sound of unbearable outrage, while his elegant fingers calmly turn the tiny combination lock on the Wilcox mailbox and lift the fliers and rare envelopes carefully from the tiny square vault, or count change from his wallet into the hand of Nobel Aldrich, Postmaster, and receive in exchange stamps in a neat small folder.

So boys come to the nests behind the hedges to watch for Jacob coming out his front door. Maybe years ago one or two crept close to an open window and discovered how silent it was inside, somehow more silent when Jacob was in there than when he'd gone out. Or maybe they deduced that silence from the way he comes out that quaint old door: A thin and fussy old gentleman with long white hair combed smoothly back from his narrow forehead, he pulls open the inside door, pushes open the screen door. He stands between the doors and fusses in the deep pocket of his good wool trousers; the unchosen keys dangle and jingle and the chain glints as Jacob carefully locks his front door, stooping ever so slightly to see where to fit the key. He turns around, and is still a vaguely peering, vaguely blinking old gentleman, thin, solemn, and a little doubtful. He lets the screen door close.

His lips move the least bit. Reminding himself. He steps forward on the deep porch.

His forehead and eyebrows lower. He shakes his head slowly.

The keys are still in his hand, and he always discovers them just before he reaches the top step. Keys! Offensive burdens, a crude joke. He pulls them up for a good look. The sneer begins on his thin-lipped mouth as he whispers to the keys, the chain taut between his hand and his trousers. He is silent for the smallest moment there at the edge of his front porch. Then, slowly, he seems to understand. He was mistaken. Only keys. Only his own keys. He raises his head. Not the keys, but something. Something else.

He drops the keys back into the pocket of his trousers; speaking a mournful hatred, he takes the first step down, the second and third, and his voice begins to rise. It is a deep voice, too deep and too sure for the slightness of his chest and shoulders. That voice is Orator, Evangelist, it is the Curse of Tongues and it descends upon him, and the boys love it like they've never loved anything. What it does to them makes them wish they were alone, but when Jacob gets to the walk in front of his steps and begins for real, when his head begins to jerk and his spit webs the corners of his mouth and he raises his fist for the first time and shouts the first time, they are frozen, they are damned and alone beyond the delight they've sought, beyond, beyond, they are out there with Jacob.

Then Jacob walks away.

He walks into the village, raving, to Amos Brown's store, to the post office. Then he comes back. Most boys who have seen him come out the front door have stayed at least once, or come back at least once, to watch him return, but it's not the same. They can hear him coming up the rise, and when he gets to his house he goes around back for a while, and the shouting dies out slowly there, in the old rocker, in the march he does beside his garden, in his putting down and taking up his bag of groceries before he finally goes in the back door, into absolute and sudden silence, as if he were a candle blown out quickly in a dark room.

The boys never mock him, and if sometimes one or another, fascinated, tries to follow Jacob's model, tries out an unworded shouting and that wildness of arms and that unheeding pace, he tries it alone, far from his own house and far from his friends, and he never speaks of the trial or its failure, or of how he never wants to try it again. Jacob touches them deeply, these ordinary town boys and farm boys, but they know what Jacob does and Jacob is all unaware; the mad display that is a tantalizing revelation to the boys is hidden to Jacob, who is so simply unable to bear the ordinary touches of life, who believes himself merely hurrying along and back to the sanctuary of this garden.

The boys come according to their own boredom, and so sometimes they see Jacob come out of his silent house by the back door, see him turning his damp laundry in the sun, or storkstepping through his garden to choose a tomato or to thin out the carrots. Allen has seen that, Jacob in the back in his long bare feet; Allen once saw Jacob come out and stroke the leaves of the blueberry bush and then settle peacefully into the rocker and sleep. That was the time Allen dared come alone into the shade of the privet trees, back in the fall. The leaves of the bush were red then, the reddest leaves Allen had ever seen. He watched for a long time that day. He watched old Jacob sleeping in his chair until he too was drowsy in the sun, without noticing just when or how quickly the sun had left Jacob and the fiery bush in shadow to come around behind the hedge and toast him. Now Allen can tell after only a few minutes behind the hedge whether Jacob is asleep inside or not, whether it's worth sitting there in the grass waiting or not, so sometimes he leaves almost as soon as everyone gets settled.

Today Allen leads the way along the hedge. A quick billow of the sheets on the maple surprises all three boys; then, quicker than that, all three imagine for a second that Jacob is in the rocker. But it's only his clothes, and they watch the front again.

In the long silence under the *shush* of the wind in the hedge trees and under the amazingly long cardinal songs, Tony forgets what he is watching for and takes himself for a glorious victory ride past the houses of all the children he knows, his bicycle faster than any car in town, the streamers floating back the whole length of the bike and snapping in the breeze. In front of Amos Brown's store a queen in a blue robe waits for him, and gives him four bags of miniature candy bars as a prize.

Chris holds up his forefingers before his eyes, pointing the fingers at one another, and stares past them at Jacob's shaded front door; the phantom hot dog appears floating between his blunt fingertips, just as the comic page said it would.

Allen seals his lips and blows his cheek out taut. It helps.

In the parlor inside Jacob's sleep, simple things dissolve into

14

their proper shapes: a gnarled umbrella comes round right as it is opened and he sees with relief and pride that it was nothing but the lamp with the green shade after all. He should have known, of course, but it's all right now.

The woman with the overnight case comes up the rise from the river, and by now she has been in the beautiful breeze of early afternoon for long enough that it's lifting her, too. Her stylish dress dances blue and white around her calves and rises away from her shoulders as the bodice fills front and back with a puff of the wind. Her hair still lies neatly, a city shape, but she feels the air beneath it next to her scalp. Forty years ago on a day like this, in the house up ahead where Jacob is sleeping, her mother would have washed this hair and made her sit out back by the garden to dry it in the sun. She comes up past the first hedge. It has grown fantastically high in her long absence from this road, a road grown so short that she is surprised that the house appears so suddenly, but in this sweet, sunny washday air there can be no hesitation: she goes right up the short walk, right up the four broad front steps of the deep front porch, right into the flickering shade, and knocks on Jacob's front door.

The boys watch her become still. They watch her set down her blue overnight bag and take hold of the screen door handle to pull it open. It's locked, latched on the inside with a hook; they know this as surely as they know that their mothers are home in a cloud of laundry smell in their kitchens.

CHAPTER 2

So here comes Rachel around back, nothing daunted by the locked screen door, for she knows this place like her own, since it was her own all those childhood years she remembers with efficient bitterness, and it's still her own now that she's come back to dispose of it, one way or another. The key to that front door (but there is no key to a hooked-shut screen door) has been drowsing for thirty years under the tangled necklaces and dowdy earrings in her oldest jewelry box, where maybe it yawned and stretched (as Rachel did, recognizing months after her husband's death that she had stopped grieving and was free now to do as she chose) and made a tiny tapping sound once or twice as it woke, and that is why she found it so easily, without even remembering that she had such a key in her keeping. Now that old key is on a new key ring, separate from the one that holds the keys to her life in the city three hundred miles west, and it's a key she means to be rid of, along with the house and the hedge full of breathless boys. She hasn't actually seen them, and if one of them sneezed she'd be startled, but it's just what she expects of this unpleasant little place—spying and gossip and the narrowness of mind and experience that had excluded the Wilcoxes, mother, son, and daughter, from the moment they appeared, friendless and unrelated to any living person here, over forty years ago. And Rachel regrets some things in her life: having left her mother alone to be ignored in solitude the years she herself grew sociable and confident in boarding school (and when she came home on holidays she found her mother increasingly isolated, increasingly uncertain) and then college (and when she came home, finally, that Christmas of her senior year she found Jacob there again, summoned by someone from wherever he'd been traveling that year, maybe Greece, Jacob home and their mother half-paralyzed by a massive stroke); she regrets having left Jacob (himself never certain, though always able, adult, genial) to endure their mother's age and infirmity, the paralysis of will and body that must have moved Jacob from the mild eccentricity of his aimless traveling adulthood to the concentrated reclusiveness and, yes, passive madness in which he now lives; she regrets having submitted with only impatience to her late husband's twenty-year insistence that Jacob (the brother-in-law he never met, knew only through Rachel's worry and rare reminiscence) be left to live as he chose (when she was more certain with every Christmas card that Jacob was not choosing but failing, dropping off the always narrow ledge of quiet oddity and beginning a spiral toward exactly this disturbed state, this insanity). Yes, Rachel has had her sincere regrets, but leaving this town is not one of them.

So Rachel has come back to see to Jacob, and she has not seen him since that distant Christmas of their mother's crippling. She has written him countless letters of invitation, advice, query, and in response has received, each year, a Christmas card and a birthday card, each containing a small check, each at once infuriating and charming her (as he charmed those years of her childhood when he was the often-absent center of her mother's life and of her own fantasies of the larger world), charming her in spite of her mature, active, efficient understanding of the world. Rachel came to this efficiency out of a three-year chaos of passionate marriage and infidelity and divorce, money spent madly in a life that seemed one of poverty, a Bohemian excitement that collapsed into bourgeois panic at the sudden violent death of three of her friends. The others, who had graduated as Rachel had from polite schools that taught them thought and encouraged ideals, withdrew into the quiet respectability from which they had come. But Rachel had come from this house in this town: return was unthinkable, however utterly she believed that wild life to have disappeared. Rachel withdrew instead into marriage with Richard Cavanaugh, the lawyer friend of a friend's father, and into the calm, distant, efficient coolness of his house just outside the city. She has been content enough these twenty years, living always as if she were fifteen years her own senior, relieved to be childless, to have had a husband moderate in all things, to have been able to share or ignore the opinions and pastimes of that husband and his moderate, careful world, which by now seems to her a good, safe world in a good, safe, prosperous time. And the occasional passion of her dreams, waking or sleeping, the occasional deep impatience with certainty, the wish to be utterly involved in something huge and loud, these things she has nearly succeeded in pretending into oblivion.

And she has come here now to see about Jacob. When no Christmas card arrived from Jacob last year, Richard was ill and the order of her life disturbed, and she thought perhaps the card had come and been overlooked, lost. But then in May, two months after Richard's death, her birthday also went by without Jacob's usual card. She wrote then to Emmons, the only doctor in the town, who had occasionally, years ago, let her know of her mother's setbacks. The doctor's letter described Jacob as certainly eccentric, possibly schizophrenic but perhaps not, only odd, and Rachel had thrown the letter angrily into the wastebasket in her bedroom, because the man seemed a fool. "Your brother," he wrote, "seems quite able to care for himself and his affairs despite his condition." So Rachel has conferred in the city, and she has read the recommended books, and she is here to save her brother from his madness and his life of lonely exclusion, seclusion, reclusion on the edge of this scarcely noticeable little village. So here she comes around back, here comes Rachel around back to get in.

The boys have mistaken her overnight bag for a sample case.

They think she is a saleslady in for a big surprise. Jacob will come out and shout at her. Jacob will spring out the back door and dance around her with the white spit flying out the corners of his mouth. Jacob will come out grinning and shake his old peter at her. Jacob will shoot her dead out the kitchen door with a big black blunderbuss musket. Cans of food will come whizzing out the upstairs window. She'll scream and try to run away, she'll say *oh please help,* she'll cover her face with her hands, she'll faint dead away, she'll fall down dead in the old rocker with her hair hanging back and her boobies almost showing. Of course they forget to breathe, and sit there with their mouths hanging open to the gentle drying breeze.

But Jacob is deep asleep in the old red Morris chair in the parlor, and Rachel sails on through his crazy garden as if it were as familiar as the front porch, as if this accidental but well-weeded garden of zinnias and poppies and tangled nasturtiums were her mother's bosomy beds of phlox and solemn little pansies. After all her preparation she understands from the garden only that she was right in the first place: Jacob is probably crazy but certainly harmless. And since she knows, firmly, that Jacob has not always been crazy (all her friends at college were in love with Jacob in his white flannel trousers and his shirts open at the neck when he came to visit her and took her to dinner), she means to do something about that. True, true—she had not expected these carnival colors, this menacing, tidy, outsized plantation back here. She had, perhaps, vaguely assumed a riot, but a riot of neglect. The first thing that must be done, however, is not some gaping analysis of Jacob's wildly thriving poppy garden but the confronting of Jacob himself. She had thought it would come at the front door: "Jacob," she would say. "It's Rachel. Let me in." And he would let her in.

But then she stood on the swept front porch with the curved handle of the locked screen door in her fingers' grasp, and there was no sound, no moving curtain, no shy brother hiding just inside for her to speak to in her matter-of-fact announcing voice. So she has come around back, and she keeps her pace steady and brisk. She doesn't pause even for Jacob's jubilee wash but passes right by the bush that's nearly covered with his undershorts. She pushes open the back door without so much as a warning tap, and steps right into the kitchen of her childhood.

Where nothing at all has changed in the years Rachel thought she was living her life, and that stops her on the rag rug just inside the door. For a ticking second, it is 3:20 in the afternoon and she has come straight home from fifth grade into the silence of one of Mother's naps. The kitchen is at peace. A white coffee mug and one of the red-rimmed white bread-and-butter plates have been set to dry on a tea towel beside the sink. The cupboards are closed. The yellow and white squares of the floor are clean and tranquil. A smell of laundry soap so vague Rachel cannot recognize that it is a smell at all fills her chest with the soft pressure of a sob. At the windows over the sink the yellow checked curtains drift out and fall back in the steady breeze, and the three white chairs are tucked up close under the white painted, enamel-topped table.

"Why—" Rachel whispers, "why—!" But she can't find words to express her astonishment at the order, the cleanliness, the continuity of this pleasant and undistinguished kitchen. This is her own childhood's kitchen from the early happy times of food smelled and eaten with childhood's simple greed and pleasure, times of a mother well and hopeful, the kitchen that was warm in winter and bright in spring. For a moment this window, wall, table, floor, this air, pretend that none of that early, lost comfort has died, could ever die, pretend that this is home and she can return, has returned, and in a moment, before the curtains have been moved past their fullness again, something will welcome her here. In that moment Rachel is bereft, but before any more than a dancing leaf shadow of that unmemoried loss can close over her heart, she finds outrage, Outrage! She drops her overnight case to the floor with a hard thump (for this place deserves no silence from her, no whispering care), and she sets her hands on her hips to say, "Why, there's nothing wrong with that man!"

And, "Jacob!" she calls down the hallway; she just knows he's in there on the long sofa, snoring gently; she can hear him snoring in there! "Jacob!"

In the hedge, the boys hear through the open windows that

scolding call hit the walls and ceilings that have been stone silent their whole lives and longer. Chris looks at Allen for a sign, but Allen just stares for a moment, disgusted and heartsick. Already he knows, a boy of eight, what the town will need weeks to discover: Jacob is lost to them all now, stolen by this woman. Allen gets up slowly, making no pretense of stealth, and walks away toward the road, his shoulders hunched like his father's at the end of a frustrating day. Chris follows him obediently. They reach the road and Allen stops, in plain sight of the house; he stands still in the road, staring at the bridge, to wait for Tony. Tony, who sits more enthralled than ever, waiting to see the woman come back out.

Jacob Jacob: the sound comes tumbling around the edge of Jacob's dream like little wooden ark animals, flat-sided and barely familiar, but it doesn't bother his sleep. He's been hearing *Jacob Jacob* awake and asleep for more than thirty years. Mother's not here at all, not drooping her head and needing him, not helpless and demanding in her paralysis upstairs; she's dead this long time. So he gently puts the colored animal shapes of sound in a parade around the outside, like animal crackers on the side of a birthday cake, and he goes on sleeping as simply as his trousers go on drying out back in the sunshine.

At the doorway of the darkened parlor, Rachel sees him closer and quicker than she'd figured on: the anciently thinned man with prophet's hair and sleeping face so quiet it's nearly unseeable, his body perfectly straight in the big chair, his legs thin and straight and perfectly parallel, and on each broad wooden arm of the chair a white-sleeved thin man's arm ending in an elegant hand whose fingers lie perfectly composed against the smoothed dark wood. This man is so unlike anyone she has ever seen that she is suddenly aware that she has intruded into the very heart of a stranger's house while her host lay sleeping, that she has come in unexpected, uninvited, mortally unprepared, and she moves back down the hall to the kitchen, away from the shocking and enduring frailty of that sleeping man, with her heart as wild with fear and guilt as Jacob's is when he steps off the front porch and starts for town. She grabs up her blue case and goes back out to the garden and closes the door behind her, quietly.

In time, and gently, Jacob wakes into the neatly patterned silence of his house. He remembers, gently and in time, that his wash is dancing dry out back. In the kitchen he takes a long pause to plan vaguely: perhaps later he will have some tea. He fills the teakettle with fresh cold water and sets it to heat before he goes out to finger his sheets and undervests. There is a woman standing at the edge of his yard, just where the flowers stop and the clipped grass begins.

Sometimes, on long summer evenings thick with moths and bats, Jacob comes out his door and there is a man standing just there. After a bit Jacob always remembers that it is Mr. Parsons, and it is all right. Sometimes they talk quietly about the garden or about bees or weather, and Mr. Parsons doesn't upset things. Jacob has grown used to his visits, even though he knows they are not quite what they might be.

Sometimes when Jacob goes to town he sees women along the way, but he is always so frightened and hurried that they pass by, like scudding clouds, and if he turns his head to look again they've changed to something else; he is never certain, perhaps it was only that hydrant in the first place, that shadow, or that shrub. The women he thinks might have been there seem often to be carrying things or leading things—oh, he supposes, probably little wagons or leashed dogs. Or bundles of things. Groceries. They all jerk past so quickly and change color and shape and substance: perhaps they weren't there at all, and in the nap he takes after he comes back home they all change gently again and melt off, gone and gone.

Another sometimes nudges at Jacob standing on the low door-step with a woman in his yard. Some kind of woman, very gentle, very pale in the darkness, a smell of something weedy and sweet. There is music to it, but it doesn't come close and he can't see it just now. He wonders, at this distance, whether it might have something to do with something he saw once in a theater. Or read, long ago. At least this woman in the yard stays still, there by the poppies. She holds something in her hands in front of her in a way that reminds him of autumn and resignation.

22

Upright and awake, Jacob appears anew to Rachel, less strange but still anew, barely familiar. She is not ashamed or frightened by him now, only shy. Still, she has planned only the one speech, thinking no other could be needed, and it still seems to her the way to begin.

"Jacob?"

He doesn't stir. His hair is lifted from around his neck by the drying wind, and his trousers rock the chair just the least bit.

"Jacob. It's Rachel."

Of course it is. He should have known. The eyes, that way of holding what is clearly a small suitcase, that odd little stance with one knee a little bent and forward—of course, and Rachel has grown up to be a woman, a fine-looking woman. And she has come home. Jacob smiles. All the poppies and nasturtiums give three cheers, the zinnias shake their pom-poms like celebrators in a dense crowd, as Jacob steps out across his yard to welcome little Rachel home.

"Rachel! Welcome, welcome!" he says, and his voice is as strong as a young, young man's, the same voice, exactly the same, and it calls up in Rachel the old pride of the little sister recognized by the grown man who haunts her home. She gives him her hands, and he takes her case from her and holds her other hand and kisses her cheek, courtly and warm, and she lets him lead her to the rocker by the back door.

But there on the chair, the seven socks! The trousers! The undervests! And the nightshirt! Jacob is shocked. Even here in the back, where some things can mix and there is so little danger, even back here, what is he to do, with Rachel to set down and a chair covered in clothing? He stops and stares and begins to swing her hand in his fret. He swings it high and low, staring furiously at the laden chair, the chair that is not a chair and is the only chair. As his other arm picks up the rhythm and the blue overnight case begins to swing, Rachel comes back to herself and touches his arm, stops it, takes her hand from his, and then her bag. Jacob takes his hands to his pockets, and Rachel presses his arm. "It's all right, Jacob," she says.

He just keeps glaring at the chair.

"Is this the clothes basket, Jacob?"

23

He jerks his head with such a start that she knows he had forgotten her already, but Rachel doesn't mind. The day has returned and is hers once more, for Jacob is mad after all, and there is a need for her after all. The house and garden make a new kind of sense that she knows she'll understand when there's time, but now Jacob is glaring at her, aghast and appalled, as she steps over and picks up the basket.

Does she mean to sit in the laundry basket? Since the chair is filled with clothing, the basket must be made to serve?

Rachel pairs the first two socks and drops them into the basket. In his relief, Jacob laughs, and the wind carries the jubilation up through his dancing sheets and off toward town.

CHAPTER 3

*I*n town the cold suppers are coming out, potato salads, sliced bread, cherry tomatoes, cold chicken, and the children begin to move toward home. The men stand by their garages and back sheds a minute or two and light cigarettes, listen to the pings of their cooling mowers.

"There you are," Rachel says, folding the shirt neatly into the basket.

Jacob admires the tidy pile. Into the air comes a thin whistle. He looks up from the basket, and Rachel's new, familiar face catches him for the length of a smile, but she is not whistling, so he looks beyond her, vaguely, looking for the noise.

In town, Rose Deery stands beside her kitchen sink with a breaded pork chop in her hand and feels a long firm contraction possess her back and belly. She holds the chop away from her and stares down at her round plaid smock. The pressure passes away, and she is careful not to glance toward the back door, where her young husband is reeling in the dry bedspread and throw rug.

"Tea!" Jacob cries. He looks quickly back at Rachel, delighted. "We'll have some tea now," he is proud to say.

"That would be lovely," says Rachel, who hasn't drunk tea in twenty years. "Let me help."

But Jacob smiles and unfolds his hand toward the empty green rocker. "You just rest," he says. "No, no—why! You just rest. Rachel," he says, and even though she is watching and listening carefully, analytically, efficiently, she is touched by the pure fondness of his voice on her name.

"All right, then," she says, and sits in the rocker, puts her purse down on the grass.

Jacob watches contentedly.

She smiles up at him. "There," she says. "Now I'm all ready for my tea."

Which makes him remember, gladly, to go into the kitchen where the kettle sings.

In town, Amos Brown stands at the open door of his store, idly open twenty minutes past his closing time. His generosity is rewarded by the hurried approach of Ellen Parsons, the minister's wife. She waves urgently as soon as she sees him standing there: she'd forgotten she was completely out of sugar, and Jim has come home from calling out at a farm with two quarts of late strawberries. Watching her come, Amos wonders again whether she is more like a sparrow or a little girl, she is always so solemn.

Jacob brings out a small folding table, then a kitchen chair, then a plate of plain cookies; finally he balances his way through the door with a tray heavy with tea things, and sets it all carefully before Rachel.

"Shall I pour?" she suggests, and he allows it, sitting quiet and tall opposite her with his napkin on his knee. Rachel pours, passes his cup, sips at her own. She says, quietly, "I have been away for a long time, Jacob."

He nods, that first smile returning. "And now here you are, come home again," he agrees.

"I think, perhaps, I should have come before," she says. "I'm sorry now I didn't come when Mother died."

He chooses a cookie, the smile lingering, but he seems not to hear.

"It must have been very hard for you, alone here then,"

Rachel insists quietly, forgetting that she had meant to speak to him of the years before that, the fifteen years that passed between their mother's stroke and her death, the years Jacob spent caring for her, and Rachel spent allowing her world and some part of herself to consider both mother and brother already dead.

He tastes his cookie.

"Was it?" She waits. "Jacob, was it very hard for you when Mother died?" He sips his tea. "Do you miss her, Jacob? Our mother?"

He sets his teacup down thoughtfully, wipes his fingers on his napkin. He leans forward, privately but calmly. "Our mother died," he explains gently. "She was very ill. She was very ill, and then . . . why, she was very ill, you know. And elderly. Nearly eighty. And then she died. It was very sad."

In town, Dinah Aldrich clears the supper table as her mother draws water in the dishpan. This time Dinah truly forgets without intending to, and she piles the unscraped plates all atilt, the chicken bones and the forks still lying between. She is dreaming, wondering whether Anne Boleyn was ever really a girl like herself to grow up to fascinate great kings. Her mother sees the dreaminess, the elegant lifting of wrists over work poorly done, but even she is mild this evening, and says only, "If you'd do it right the first time—." Dinah scarcely sighs, she is so far gone into the world of her day's reading, and she slowly unpiles, scrapes, sorts, restacks in the kitchen, where dusk is almost beginning. Mary Aldrich lets her sentence go unfinished, feeling instead a troubled admiration of her daughter's beauty before she stiffens a little, back into confidence in the need to train her well.

"Well," Rachel says, trying for briskness but falling short, into something that sounds like completion. "This was very refreshing. And I'll clear away—I insist."

He looks up, startled. "Must you go?" he asks.

Rachel sits back down quickly and reaches across the cluttered tray to touch her brother's knee. "Oh, no, Jacob—no, I'm not going yet. Why, don't you know?" and her voice is the voice almost of a woman speaking to a baby, "I won't leave you again, Jacob."

His frown fades. "Of course," he says, as gentle as she. "Of course. I had forgotten, just for the moment," he apologizes, patting the back of her hand with his fingertips. "Little Rachel, home again."

And Rachel is helpless for the moment before his misunderstanding. She nods.

"And have you been well, Rachel?" he asks.

She feels the tremble of a giggle deep in her throat, behind the silly acquiescent grin she wears, and distracts herself from it by rising again and clearing the tea things from the table back onto the tray. "Yes, very well, thank you." She lifts the tray and carries it to the back door, which still after all these years her body remembers will have left itself just enough ajar that she can bump it open with a motion of her foot and elbow. The unthinking memory of her body, the way this house has remembered her motions and responds, makes her breath catch suddenly. Jacob sits as she left him, straight and mild, his hair beginning to glow as the light in the sky fades and the shadows begin to rise.

In town, Timer Darcy reads the newspaper on the top step of his front porch; the words and numbers slide past his understanding as soon as he has read them, but tonight, with the breezy voices of boys calling game chants in the yards, with the thick, slow clacking of dishes being dried and put away in his own kitchen and the kitchens all around, he lets the paper go. In a few minutes he will put it down and walk around back to check the tomatoes.

Rachel dries her hands on the striped hand towel. She tries to square herself to go out and try again at explaining to Jacob her wish for him to leave this house and come with her. But Rachel is tired. The arrangements of the past weeks, yesterday's travel, today's surprises (and the wind, though Rachel has been in the city so long that she has forgotten how such a wind cajoles the very skin to glad acceptance of pillows and sheets), all have come settling on Rachel here in the unforgotten kitchen. She goes back out to Jacob, who is still there in the straight chair, and stands beside his chair, but she says, "I'm afraid I'm very tired, Jacob."

He looks up slowly, remembers her again. "Why, you *must* be tired," he says. "I'll take your bag up for you. To your room," he says, pleased, for he has prepared it without telling her, while she waited for the tea.

She follows him into the kitchen and down the dark hall to the foot of the stairs. As he steps neatly aside to let her go ahead of him up the stairs, poor Rachel, who cannot know how silent this house must be for Jacob to remain in it, how his need for a haven requires that the memories and the sounds of words that rouse those memories remain still, poor Rachel speaks. She remembers the somehow smooth whiskery touch of his cheek, and she desires, in her weariness and in the home of her childhood and in the uncertainty they combine to create, she desires the feel of that cheek on her lips and nose, so she pauses on the first step and turns back to touch his arm. "I'm glad I've come," she says, and means to lean and kiss his cheek, goodnight.

But Jacob lurches back, her bag clunks the wall and then the floor, and Jacob's face of terror and confusion is lighted by his wide-flying hair as he bolts away, down the hall for the kitchen, and he stumbles against the wall in looking back wildly, as if she pursued him, before he is gone, out the back door, which slaps shut like a thunderclap.

Poor Rachel! It is only her words, circling and circling in the air, the noise of them, their power to raise up the memories that all this unchangedness, this sameness of the house, keeps quiet, that have done this violence, but she cannot know that. She stands frozen and watching and knows deep fear: Jacob is mad through and through. The gentle tea party, the garden—all, all mad beyond her bearing. Shaking, she bends for her case, keeping watch for the return of that awful face, and then runs up the stairs for her own old room, and locks the old familiar bolt on the inside before she stops and presses her cold hands to her face.

"Oh," she whispers. But no more. After a full minute she forces herself to move carefully in the dark to where the lamp used always to be. And the lamp is there; the light of it shows her the bedroom of her memory, and the bed turned down. Clearly, clearly, Jacob did that for her while she sat in her mistaken comfort in the garden.

She is tired. Much too tired, tonight. Tomorrow, she will see about Jacob. She undresses for bed, and lies listening, although she is pretending to be imagining how pleased Jacob will be with her own tidy house, and the spacious bedroom she has prepared for him there.

CHAPTER 4

n the morning, Jacob waits for Rachel, alert and calm, between the table and the stove. He has heard her moving around upstairs all this time, while he set her place at the table, set the coffee to perking, set the Pyrex bowl of eggs to poaching, set the silver toast butler just to the right of the glass of orange juice on the white, white table. He's ready to go down to the store, with his checkbook ready in his pocket and his hair neatly brushed. Most days that Jacob goes in to Amos's store he goes much later, after his morning nap. But today Rachel is here, as she should be. Rachel has come home. Of course she has, which is right, and it will be all right. He puts away from his mind his near memory of Rachel speaking in the hallway. Instead, when he hears her at the head of the stairs, he is quick and tidy, toast on the rack, eggs uncovered and sliding to the plate, coffee steaming glory into the small blue coffeepot and lid clinked on, all! She turns down the hall; he sees her face and it smiles. She raises her hand as if to accept the whole kitchen, which he gives to her. Little Rachel! Home again! Of course she is!

"Why, Jacob," she begins.

Again! Jacob turns; his way is blocked by the door, and behind him she keeps on, other words out in the good air of the breakfast kitchen, though he hurries, hurries, clumsy with panic. *Why Jacob Why Jacob* on and on forever now in the good air, until at last the door swings open and Jacob is out.

The bees are preparing to swarm. The scouts have been at it all morning, and Jim Parsons can only imagine the dither those days of rain must have caused inside the hive. Now he wonders, crouched before his single beehive, whether they will go today, these eager emigrants, or if the scouts are just making up for lost time and the actual departure is still days off, and the clumping workers around the entry hole are just taking the air after their long confinement. It is possible, of course, that they won't swarm at all this year. If the new queen hatched during the rain, and went searching for the old queen and found her, and if they fought and murder was done, well then, 'twas done, and they'd all stay. And be too crowded, for Jim Parsons won't expand the hive, won't build a second box and send off for another queen in a buzzing wooden case and do the dividing himself. He's hardly a beekeeper at all: He has read the books on bee behavior, he provides the wooden box, and he keeps the grass mowed around it. But they keep their honey and must take care of themselves, for he provides only enough to keep them nearby, and wants nothing more than that from them.

Another scout hurries in: Jim Parsons imagines the dance he cannot see her doing, vaudeville in miniature across the face of the comb, an obsessed jig for an audience of golden feather shapes that seem to ignore her. Jim often feels this to be the case, that he alone realizes the astoundingly articulate displays of these bees, and he wonders sometimes if God ever feels that way. He can imagine God quite clearly as gigantic, too enormous to identify and further obscured by a device not unlike his own beekeeper's veil, peering closely but holding His breath for fear of disturbing us. The possibility is deeply pleasing to young parson Parsons; he is just old enough, at last, that he doesn't try to explain this idea in a sermon, but he feels no shame in it, either, no pride or heresy.

The first scout must still be gyrating when the second and third fly down to join her. Jim Parsons' heart leaps at the idea of them, a trio, triplets in perfect unison, more alike than three birch trees bending to the same wind. This is it, then. They have found a new site, they have soared far and shot back to bring the word, to draw the map in the air inside the hive with their bodies. He kneels to be more stable, for now he will wait. This year, this year he will watch the whole emigration and he will see the queen when she comes out. His veil flutters before his eyes but he doesn't notice. The three bees dance and dance, tilting, bending, and as he waits, hardly breathing, it seems that the whole wooden box grows still for an instant before it gives a silent shudder, and the first half-dozen workers emerge onto the stage.

They fly off, are replaced on the tiny ledge immediately, and the replacements take off; in less than moments the air all around the hive, high and low, is full of bees, as busily stalled and determined as laid-over travelers in a bus station. They swoop back again and again, and the scouts keep dancing their jig of description and destination, trying to get the whole show moving. Even the scouts aren't leaving, though, eager as they are. Nobody's going anywhere until She comes out. Every last one of them ignores the plump man kneeling in their midst. Bees after bees come steadily out the entrance of the old green hive, and if Jim had a little distance on it he'd see the shape of it, the funneling outward and growing raggedness of this mass evacuation.

All his vision is on the entrance, waiting for the queen. All his senses are trying to join with his sight to make him capable of recognizing her. Then, before he is really ready, what looks like a mistake clogs up the hole, a panic maybe, a pileup in the narrow space, but he's only playing at believing that. It is the court, the immediate handmaidens, assisting their only mistress and mother of them all in her departure. Pop! She's out, stunned and throbbing there on the landing stage, and the ladies leave her and join their soaring sisters.

Twice the size of any honeybee he has ever seen, she is still a mildly disappointing fact to the preacher. Large she is, certainly, but he had wished upon her a resplendence she does not have. She is only very large, though slender enough now to fly, no doubt; all the royal jelly she has fed on, all the grooming those ladies-in-waiting have lavished on her, all the power she exercises even now—none of that shows on her downy back, her unscarred wings. She is only, after all, the egg layer. Queen is just a word. Thinking this, Jim Parsons has failed his concentrating senses, and he hears, past the truly astounding racket of those thousands of bees, a rising chant of furious voice. He looks to the sound and sees only his own beige Pontiac, for he is kneeling and had forgotten his own yard's geography.

Even without seeing he recognizes that it is only Jacob Wilcox raging past, and so Jim turns back and he is in time—she flies! The scattered anxious travelers in the air leap at the scent of her. She's up, slowly, circling, consulting with her dancing advisers, who are the first to join her. And yes! She acquiesces and nods vaguely, majestically, to her palace, her throne, the dominion that has provided for so many for so long, and then away! Parsons is up and racing after her without thought, and her loyal subjects rally around his head to be at her side in this daring abdication. Past the garage he runs and out over the wide picnic lawn of the church, with his head in the bees.

Jacob shouts so loud up River Street that Allen, lying in the dim living room watching a movie about a boy who can't talk and his father who is some kind of cowboy, has no wish to go to the window and watch him flail by. It's too early, the wrong time of day for that stuff, and besides, it isn't real anymore, not like it was before yesterday. In the kitchen his mother shrieks open the legs of the ironing board. The television volume dips as she plugs in the iron.

It's early for Jacob, who won't remember until his hands find the bag of sugar on Amos's dark shelves that he has come so early for more of everything. Disturbed beyond his usual, spun deeper into fearful hurry than he's been in years, Jacob is almost running by the time he gets to the store, and there have been no shapes of any kind along his way today. He has traveled safe in the silence his shouting makes for him, the halo of throbbing noise that is his protection when he must leave the garden and the house.

Julia Cullinan waits in her big gray car at the town's stop sign while Jacob crosses. He's left his cuffs unlinked and they flap out and slide back as he throws his arms high, one fist and then the other; even in her state of weariness and joy, she notices and will remember that Jacob Wilcox is out on the street in black felt bedroom slippers that pop against his heels as he stork-steps along at his amazing pace.

So Jacob reaches the store in record time, just as Amos has poured himself the first cup of coffee behind the counter, and Jacob piles so much on the counter that Amos has trouble fitting it all into one bag. What a noise, Jacob alone in the store so early, fast around and around, coffee, bacon, bread, butter, eggs, coolers slamming shut everywhere at once, and the shouting itself louder and faster than usual, filling Amos's ears until they ring with a kind of deafness, too. He packs and adds, shows the list to Jacob, and Jacob signs and puts down the pen so fast it skates off the counter and falls at Amos's feet. That is so peculiar a thing both to the balding storekeeper and to Jacob, wild as he is, that there falls behind it an instant of actual silence in the little store, the barest tick of a pause in Jacob's harangue of betrayal and hurry.

And then he's off again, louder than before, grappling the overloaded bag into both arms and high-stepping out the door, out of sight, though Amos hears him farther off than usual. It's so early. The store is empty. His coffee is cooler. Anybody but Jacob, and Amos would surmise company, a second mouth to feed. But it's Jacob: Hurricane? Earthquake? Plague? Amos shakes his head, smooths his hand along the counter, puts Jacob's check into the cigar box underneath. But a little worry stays with him. It will make him brisk with the earliest shoppers, as if he had more necessary preparations to attend to elsewhere.

As Mary Aldrich goes through her living room with three freshly ironed shirts on hangers in each hand, the flash of light off a turning car's windshield glances in and blinds her for an instant, and though she knows it's important, almost knows what it means, she keeps going, takes those six shirts on up the stairs and settles them into her husband's closet. She's in her son's room pulling empty hangers from his closet (for the ironing basket is still full, though she's been at it since breakfast, mending and pressing and sorting and stowing the last two loads of yesterday's excess) when she hears the doorbell.

"Dinah!" she calls out into the hallway. "Get that, would you?"

Dinah, who is fourteen and just about out of patience with the incessant and demeaning requirements of life among her family, takes a quick deep breath and throws her book to the floor, sits up from the couch and, grudgingly, grudgingly, stands and walks the three steps to the front door, muttering, "Stinking old broads blibber blibber." The bell rings again. She opens the door, her jaw and arm muscles so tightly clenched in furious control that a bit of muscle in her thigh responds, fluttering mad and gentle.

"Hi," she says, leaving the door open for Old Broad Cullinan, who's so lazy she drove over from two doors down.

Julia Cullinan, who not only was once fourteen herself (though never as leggy and dark as this Dinah), but has lived through being the mother of a daughter who was once fourteen herself (again, shorter and fairer than elegant, slouchy Dinah, but no less sullen, at that age), and has, moreover, more important things on her mind this brilliant forenoon than the manners of Mary's younger child (whom she has also known at more charming ages, since her birth in fact, since before her birth in fact), Julia steps in, says, "Good morning, Dinah—your mother home?"

"Ma!" Dinah picks her book up tenderly, and reclines her long body tenderly back onto the couch. She finds her place but, magnanimously courteous, doesn't begin to read again until she hears her mother on the stairs. Julia sets her purse familiarly on the piano as Dinah stares, patient and condescending, at the ceiling.

"It's just me, Mary," Julia calls toward the stairway. She raises both hands to the top of her head and adjusts the heavy hairpins that hold her braid wrapped almost two full turns around her head. Julia's hair is only a darker gold than it was

36

twenty-one years ago, when her Rosie was born and she decided never to cut it again, and if mild Julia has a vanity it is this glossy coil of hair that has only improved with time. The braid secured again, and with it her certainty that changes in her life are always natural and for the best, she drops her hands to brush at invisible wrinkles in the front of her dress, and almost shakes her head in a tiny scolding of herself at how ample that front is, her heaviness seeming almost a penalty for the youth of her hair.

Mary hurries down, now that she knows it's Julia, and stops at the foot of the stairs to see first, before the particular news, whether everything is all right, though she has guessed that already from Julia's voice. Still—such a risky thing childbearing always is, so natural and unpredictable—she'll want the words themselves before she's really certain. And looking, she sees that Julia, kind friend of a lifetime, has forgotten any fears she may have had in her new delight, and has put on the next layer of calm beauty: Julia looks no older than she has the past few years, but still she is changed from the woman she was two days ago. There it is: Mary sees it. Julia is become a grandmother, moved on again well ahead of Mary into what comes next. And Mary is glad, of course (all unknown to herself she is scowling, but still she is glad, the scowl is only part of the searching for certainty that no disaster has befallen Rosie), to see the relief and excitement of Julia's face, but well behind her gladness is something very like envy. An envy grown tired of its own existence but unable to ignore that Julia is a substantial, comforting, golden grandmother, and Mary is not. That when this moment comes tardily for Mary she will find herself unchanged by it, still too blunt in body and speech, too sharp in face, to be anything as inefficient and whimsical as comfortable; too angry, somewhere older and deeper even than her friendship with Julia—a friendship begun on this very street as soon as both could walk—too angry to accept, as Julia does so simply, this or any other way time would push her from where she has decided to be into some other place of someone else's making.

"A boy!" Julia says, hardly seeing Mary's scowl, it is so common a face for her to wear. "Eight pounds seven ounces at seven thirty-five this morning!"

"A boy!" Mary congratulates, and her smile, tardy but strong now, everything sharp transformed in its broad generosity, takes her face, and the hangers jingle in her hand.

Dinah sighs. She pulls her book closer to her face and rolls her eyes.

"Coffee?" Mary says. "I've just made a new pot—and tell me all about it." She curves her arm briefly, as if in embrace, though her friend is half the room away and they are not women who embrace easily. Julia bows her head slightly, as if receiving that sturdy arm around her shoulders, and the women pass by the long-suffering Dinah and into the kitchen. Dinah curls up farther into the corner of the couch and fixes the two throw pillows so she can listen with both ears.

"Well," Julia begins, and Dinah wishes her mother'd stop walking and clanking things, "we got the call just about midnight—Dan was already asleep and I was just about to drift off, but I knew right away that it had to be Arnie."

"Always at night," Mary scolds.

"I know—even when they get born in the daytime! I don't think any baby ever was born the whole way in daylight. Well, so Arnie said they'd already talked to the doctor, and her pains were about ten minutes apart so they were going on over, and he said, Arnie said, 'So there's no big rush but Rosie said to call you anyway,' and I tell you, Mary, that boy's voice was just quivering with excitement."

The women laugh, and Dinah shifts, stretches a leg out quickly and curls it back, lays her hand gently on the muscle that still flutters just above her knee.

"So I got up and made us some coffee and got Dan up. I figured probably an hour or so till she was all checked in and prepped and all that, so we just took our time and went over about one thirty. Thank you—no, no, just milk, just a little milk, thanks."

Their spoons clink through the noise of Mary's chair moving.

"Well, so Dr. Emmons was there, and he said she was about three centimeters and doing fine, and when I went in she seemed fine—pretty excited, of course, and she told me how she'd done eight loads of wash—imagine that! Where she found eight loads of wash in that tiny little house I don't know, but she said she'd just been *full* of energy, and she'd done all that wash and had Arnie taking the last load down for her when he got home, and she was breading some pork chops when she got the first contraction."

"And you always know that first one, don't you? You wonder and wonder—'Is that a pain? Is that a pain?'—and then the first one comes and you just know."

Julia laughs, Mary laughs; they stir their coffee, delighted with everything.

"So did you stay with her the whole time?"

"Oh, I was back and forth for a while—you know, Dan doesn't talk much and poor Arnie—I think he's seen too many movies—he was pacing around like it was a crisis, so I went out every little while to keep him posted, and Jean Clark was on duty, so when she came in or Dr. Emmons came in, I'd step out and let Arnie know how it was going. Then around five she was having good hard contractions about three minutes apart, so they took her over to the labor room, and we three just waited it out."

"I remember with Brian I thought I was dying—I mean, I really didn't have any idea what it would be like—."

"Why, of course not—you listen to all the stories, you can't help it, but until you've actually been through it—! Well, they gave her something for pain around two thirty, so she was pretty groggy, but she seemed to be fairly comfortable. Jean told me later that she was about five centimeters when they moved her, and then she didn't make much progress for about an hour, but just about seven she rang and said she felt like pushing—oh, they gave her one of those cervical blocks right after they took her over. So she said she felt like pushing, and Jean said the doctor had just checked her at quarter of, so she doubted it was time, but she just took a look to be on the safe side. Rosie said she didn't *think* Jean believed her, but then she looked and said, 'Why, Rosie, you're crowning! Hold on a minute and we'll get you on the table!' "

Dinah, half drowsy with waiting for them to move on back to their own deliveries, especially to the story of her own birth, comes wide awake after five full seconds of silence, wide awake into a kind of fear, though she can't even imagine the way weeping has fallen so suddenly over Julia's face, the way the tears have suddenly created themselves and made the face helpless and ashamed. Dinah lies frozen on the couch, still with dread at the silence, waiting as if for a sudden sound in the night, unbreathing.

"There, now," her mother says out in the kitchen, and Dinah begins to tremble.

Julia's voice has become the voice of some small girl, a crushed voice, but she struggles and forces words through it in sobs, and Dinah would press her hands to her ears, flat barriers, if she didn't fear that flattened buzzing deafness as much as this terrible speaking of mothers.

"Oh, oh, I don't know what's wrong with me!"

"There, there—there, now, it's all right," Mary says. There is a faint rhythmic tinkling, a hand patting a hand on the kitchen table between two cups of coffee with their spoons in their saucers.

Julia blows her nose, but her sobbing goes on uncontrolled. "It's just so *hard!*"

"I know, I know."

For a moment there is only Julia's weeping, weeping, weeping, and then, loud, explosive, horrifying, "Oh, Mary, she's just *gone,* gone off all alone, and there's nothing I can do for her anymore—I'll just *meddle!*"

The last of the words: torn ragged as Julia's voice of speech gives up at last and an old old voice of sorrow draws, strong and clear, its own vigorous wail from deep in her body.

A chair grinds, quickly now, and Dinah is grateful beyond her age to hear it. She turns her own face into the dusty old back of the couch, and pretends that the peppery smell of old times and long evenings is the smell of her mother's deep shoulder. Through the three open windows of the living room at once

40

come the cursing shouts of crazy old Jacob Wilcox, in and then gone far off, while Dinah stops listening even to herself.

Farther up River Street this mild afternoon, Susan Darcy slides the iron up the front of Allen's one plaid shirt and wiggles the prow of it between the buttons. She has laid down newspapers to save the sheets from dirtying themselves as she irons their lengths and breadths, and beyond the newspapers, in the kitchen doorway, Allen himself sits, waiting for his shirt. He holds a small glass bowl on his knees. In the bowl is a teaspoon of alum, for him to dip his finger into and touch onto the canker sore in his cheek. Susan ignores his impatient, reluctant half groans: he has complained too much to deserve release from the cure, and he has demanded the right to administer it himself. All his mother can do for him now is to iron his shirt as slowly as possible, so that Tony, who drifts between the front porch and the kitchen doorway, won't suspect how long it is taking for Allen to be brave.

"It'll burn, right?" Allen asks, after Tony has drifted away again.

"Like fire," Susan nods, running the iron over the first sleeve, "but only for a while, and then it'll start to heal." He has already tasted it, bitter and dry. She turns the shirt to the second sleeve. "You might as well get it over with. I'm almost done here, and then you can go on out."

Allen scowls at the bowl, sips air over the sore. "Okay," he says, but he doesn't move.

Tony is back, leaning behind his brother, looking over Allen's bare shoulder at the ominous powder. "If I get a canker sore," he says, and Susan smiles before she can stop herself, at his advising, comforting tone, "I'm just going to let it grow until it wears out."

"They don't wear out," Allen growls.

"Don't they wear out, Mom?" Tony asks in surprise.

"Takes a long time sometimes, Tone—and it's pretty sore along the way. Might as well be brave like Allen and take care of it quick as a wink."

41

Tony grins. He and his mother wink at each other across the newspaper, over Allen's head. They always wink when she says "quick as a wink." Allen holds his breath and faster than anything scoops with his fingertip and presses the alum to the gray-centered sore.

All alone, Rachel, at the back door looking out, Rachel who meant to eat with grace her brother's kind gift of breakfast, though for years she has ignored breakfast: Rachel has been, habitually, asleep at this hour, and now she is preternaturally awake, with the hot breakfast insisting unpleasantly behind her, and Jacob gone off where? Does he have a place, she wonders, he runs to, hides in, when he is afraid? That face that seemed truly mad in the darkness of the hallway last night was the same face that came upon him again here in the morning kitchen, and Rachel can see, now, that what seemed mad was a madness of fear. So Jacob is afraid, apparently of her inside the house, terribly afraid, and he has gone to hide wherever he hides when he's afraid. Rachel cannot imagine his gentle dignity whimpering or crouching, nor can she really believe that he has a hidden lair or secret grove of trees; still, Jacob certainly ran away, and he certainly was afraid, and so he must have gone somewhere because he was afraid.

Rachel is not at all sure that this is right.

She'll go back through the kitchen a dozen times to watch for him out the back door because she's not really sure at all that he has a place to escape to.

While she waits to see when and where Jacob will return, she drinks a little of the excellent dark coffee: gallant and rich, it steams into her cup, and she is drawn to the back door: such foreign, worthy coffee should be drunk out in the breeze that nudges the old green rocker. But Rachel is shy of the chair, the garden, alone here. She drinks standing in the doorway instead. And while Jacob is gone she neither seeks nor happens upon his sleeping room, though last night, in her fear, she wondered where he had laid his long, thin body down, or if he had at all, and didn't stand somewhere down here, still and pale, shaking and shaking his glowing white hair. And now that she has seen that terror strike him into wild flight again in daylight, she can call it fear, though she chooses to recognize his fear and deny her own. Still, the respect that keeps her from peeking about in any but the most public rooms of what she feels to be Jacob's house today remembers her fear. And though she wants the telephone so she can call the hotel in Livingstone and have them send her two suitcases on, her search is quick: she opens no closed doors; she leaves the desk closed; she will wait and ask Jacob.

Out the back door, Jacob's garden waves and nods, a sociable gathering of friends and neighbors, mannerly in their greetings before things get started. Out the front door there is Bridge Road, a small bit close by, then the hedge, then the rest of the road from just before the dip, where it disappears and then shows again before the bridge. And there is the bridge with its zebra-striped posts on either side of either end, a low little bit of bridge that in rainy periods barely clears the water. Rachel has always found it difficult to remember the water itself, the willows hide it so completely. Beyond the willows, here and there, a patch of some village roof, blue or red or gray, shows between maple and willow leaves. And off to the right, away from the road and away from the river, lies the most contented meadow in the county, ungrazed for many years, uncut for a few: the closest of the fifteen Wilcox acres. In the sun, there, wild flowers turn and admire one another. Out back, the flowers are clearly Jacob's: even if Rachel found them pretty, which she doesn't, she'd be as circumspect about them as she is about Jacob's desk. Maybe, if she had found back there instead her mother's old flowers, the coral rose and the Mr. Lincoln rose, the tall sweet snapdragons, even the dense weedy marigolds with French nicknames, maybe she'd have cut a bunch (as her mother never allowed her to do, mild disallowing but steady) and taken them in and found one of the clumsy old white vases in a cupboard under the sink. But those poppies would drop their petals almost at once, and the zinnias are impossible. In the wide field, the lacy weed flowers sun themselves. She goes out to the meadow, scissors in her hand.

She has only daisies, with lace and chicory and cosmos still to go, when she hears Jacob coming up the rise from the bridge, shouting anger and warning. She runs with the daisies tattering in her hand to drive off whoever it is that must be tormenting him. The high grass whips at her skirt; she is furious that anyone could devil him so, that they should make that gentle aging man shout and curse so futilely, so piteously.

He has passed the house by the time Rachel reaches the empty road and shakes her scissored fist and shouts, "Stop it!" before she has seen that there is no one. The one shout leaves her hoarse for the rest of the day. Rachel looks up and down the emptiness of Bridge Road four times before she can believe that no one at all was making Jacob shout so. She tears off the few petals that are left on her flowers and tastes, with her disappointment and embarrassment, the coppery flavor of her mouth that has come from her sudden anger and her run through the high grass.

Jacob is marching back and forth between the tomatoes and the nasturtiums, his arms aching from the weight of the groceries, his cursing already in its decrescendo now that he's home, already back in the garden.

"Jacob, would you like some lunch?"

He looks up from his weeding and smiles. On the blue plate lie the four triangles of white sandwich, pointing outward, as they both remember. In her other hand is the narrow, tall glass of cold tea, whose lemon is centered on the blue blue plate.

"They are here, of course, they are here. The tree. . . ." He forgets for a moment, but she waits, steady at his side, stepping when he does, stopping when he does. "Yes," he nods, "the tree *grew,* and then there was too little *light* for roses." He nods sadly and puts his arm around his sister's shoulders.

"It's all right now, though?" She has already seen, just a few steps ahead, the majestic old rosebushes safe and flourishing beside a long shed she doesn't remember. She doesn't mean to be false with him, but he doesn't notice. Rachel believes she has never been sadder, could never be sadder.

"Come and see!" he says, and his sudden eager joy brings her immense shame.

Inside the shed the light of late afternoon disappears; it is not dark but only pale, as if the brightness outside were a part of the breeze, which is also absent here. From low rough rafters hang dried and drying flowers, thousands and thousands, years and years of gentled colors, antique perfumes as weightless as memory.

Jacob whispers, "All the roses are on the left. They dry very well, but I like—I like the dear old cornflowers best. There—"

He points along the other wall. The cornflower stems have been braided and the flowers hang in loops and wreaths; against the rough wood of the wall their deep blues and dusty pinks and lavenders are as hushed and comforting as a fine old carpet. Rachel nods, near tears.

The sun and its wind keep on in secret through this night too, as if the earth were only a thin barrier between day and night. Jacob dusts in the parlor, sweeps through all the downstairs rooms, runs the special cloth over each dark step of the stairs; in the silence of Rachel's secretly dreaming sleep (though he has nearly forgotten her again, and is silent from his own need and habit) he scours out the sink and tub, running the least and soundless trickle of water. Back in the kitchen he cleans the floor. He bends from his narrow waist and wipes the cupboard doors clean. It is nothing to Jacob to work so silently in the darkest hours, though he is growing weary now in the first small dawn. In the empty hours, the safe and silent hours, Jacob keeps his mother's house, and then, perhaps, he sleeps again. But this whole day Rachel has been about the house, and he has had no day sleep; deep in the house the sleep is waiting. He switches off the kitchen light and from the dark hall closet, in the dark and in habitual silence, he takes the long-handled sweeper. It makes as little sound as the quiet breathing of a dear sleeping friend: over and over the carpet of the long hall and the night parlor Jacob rolls the sweeper. There was no sleep for Jacob today, only the small silence of his drying shed, and now as he rolls the sweeper over and over the invisible carpets his dreams try to rise: it is dark, he is weary, the sweeper rolls and rolls: the dreams try to rise. But there is Jacob at the end of the handle, his long gentle hands, his sweet narrow shoulders, his soft shirt and his soft mouth, and Jacob glides with such slenderness he is like his dream's dream in the dark of his home, and at last, the sweeper tucked back in its closet, the dust smoothed from the frame of the mirror in the parlor, Jacob glides into his deep worn chair, and sleeps.

CHAPTER 5

*S*o it is that after night has faded off again, Rachel rises and finds Jacob asleep there in the parlor, and quietly lets herself out the back door and walks down Bridge Road and between the leaning willows to the village, where she uses the telephone in the booth in front of the one store, and she comes back over the bridge and up out of the dip, thinking about that odd politeness of the storekeeper, who tried not to ask and not to admit that he doesn't know who she is, and of how she supposes the people in town will remember and recognize her. She's smiling a small bitter smile when she comes back around to an empty garden, and goes inside to find Jacob as he was when she left, and when she first arrived, deep asleep in the old Morris chair.

There in the living room, which is cool and dark after the brisk bright warmth of her walk, the old red couch stretches, maroon in the dimness, its back draped with the quilt of velvets their grandmother left hiding in a bureau drawer in another house long ago, hiding to be discovered and claimed (not bequeathed, though she spent long hours of her years as a mother piecing it, too gentle a wrapper for assigning to one or another of the four sons and their vague wives), there in the midday dimness of triple-layered parlor-curtained windows stretches the couch. It can hold a napping woman through a long midday. Jacob sleeps upright and dreaming in the deep red chair, and off beside him stretches the couch. And Rachel stands in the doorway, nearly nearly beguiled. She holds a brown paper grocery bag with meat and bread in it for a dinner she has planned, and in her hair there is still the lift of the bright wind that walked her back from town. Already, in only two days, she has learned enough of Jacob's house silence, which is not so different after all from the silence she learned from their mother, that she could walk back up the hall to the kitchen and put things away without waking him. She could do that, and then walk back here, and into the parlor, and without any sound that might wake him she could lay herself down on the long low couch. She is almost beguiled, the house is so filled with sleep.

Once, Rachel fell in love. She was young at the time, and newly married, and the man was young and a stranger. For months she was overwhelmed, aimless, energized, helpless. Standing here in the parlor doorway she neither remembers nor forgets those aching and hopeless weeks and weeks; the air and light of this room are filled with the same passive yearning that those weeks of love held. But Rachel is no longer that young. She is here again, but not for rest. She is here, she knows now, to convince Jacob to leave, mad though he clearly is. If she submitted to the nap that calls her, her mother's nap, her brother's nap, she would be lost. She cannot leave Jacob again; his simple affection and his joy in her presence are too large a trust to betray. But she knows, already, that she must guard against this house, these habits, against, even, the relief she felt when she crossed the bridge coming back from town. And so Rachel goes back down the hall and quietly prepares a light lunch for herself before, quietly, she goes back up the stairs to her room, and writes letters: to her lawyer, to a real estate agency in the city, and to a doctor she knows who advised her as best he could about what to expect from her brother.

And so it is that Jacob wakes in the late afternoon to the impossibility of dinner laid for the two of them in the dining

48

room, where no dinner has been laid in many years, and to the impossibility of a huge bunch of his cornflowers in a vase on the table, and to the terrifying actuality of a woman humming in the kitchen.

And so it is that Rachel has driven Jacob from his home three times in only forty-eight hours. He would have given her anything she asked him for. Even now, in his shaking exile in the garden, he is angerless. His fear slides off quickly, now that he is here and the house an alien place behind him.

She follows him out, empty-handed, afraid that he's off again down the road with his terrible shouting. But Jacob has come only as far as the first zinnias. He is quite calm by the time she comes to stand with him, calm and slowly caressing the round blossoms that nod and quiver on their tall furry stems beneath his weightless fingers. It has been a long two days for Rachel, who came so well intentioned and so certain and is still without her luggage. She has divorced once and been recently widowed, but for years she was married, domestic; and now calm bitter sentences rise in her mind: *Is something troubling you? I'm terribly sorry—I had no idea you felt that way about roast pork. Perhaps we could discuss this after dinner, which is on the table. Must you leave so soon?*

But this is Jacob. She must learn how to manage this, if they are to live together; in her house dinner is eaten every night in the dining room. She breathes in through her mouth and out through her nose to relax her throat, so she can say, coaxing and kind, "What is it, Jacob?"

Above her in the dusk he inclines his face to her, and that same first smile of fond recognition spreads over his thin face, his slender man-in-the-moon face here in the darkening garden.

"Zinnias, Rachel," he says, and the merest edge of sorrow slides in under his deep voice. "Zinnias," as if she had forgotten so familiar a flower, and such a shame it was if she had, zinnias with their little crowns of stars.

And so it is that when Jim Parsons comes around back, Jacob is standing in the same spot in the dusk, finishing off a plate of roast pork stuffed with apples and raisins, rice with fresh parsley, and peas in a cream sauce. Through the window and the open back door the young minister sees a pretty woman with graying dark hair fussing tight-lipped around the kitchen. Jim had meant to come and be quiet in Jacob's garden for a while, perhaps to tell him about the disappointment of the queen, but now he watches the woman for less than ten seconds. Without greeting Jacob, who never seems to notice him in particular for many minutes after he arrives, Jim Parsons says, without object or curiosity or even disappointment, for his need is not great tonight, he came out of idleness and the smoothness of the night, "Well, goodnight," and goes back around front, down the road and back across the bridge, home.

In this dusky Friday evening, the fact of a stranger in town is known and unspoken all down the deep porches of River Street and across the stingy front steps of Whistle Street, and all back and forth the three false avenues, Mechanic and Church and Spare. Up on Pearl Street on Friday evenings, Alice Reese washes her sister's hair. Then they rest awhile. Then Elsie Reese washes Alice's hair. Tonight, because it is summer and because they too can feel how something is odd, far off from River Street and far into age as they are, they sit on the small back porch to comb out their long, thin white hair.

"I don't suppose," Alice says, "that you'd remember how Mother used to weep out here when the days grew this long, right under our window."

"Sometimes I remember," Elsie says, "how Mother used to weep out here on summer nights, but I don't suppose you'd know whether I dreamt such a thing without it being true."

They are both stone deaf, and they face their chairs, in delicacy, away from one another as their old dry fingers work their silver-backed combs over their pink scalps. "But I know one thing," Elsie goes on, and she stops combing to rock once and nod decidedly.

"That man certainly *did* eat her peonies," says Alice, setting the record straight.

They're braided and robed and tucked in their lavender-scented beds two full hours before the women on River Street call the last of the children in.

CHAPTER 6

*I*n the night the five-day wind drops. Toward dawn the trees here and there along River Street shake a little, settling back after the long airing out. Small breezes, idling unnoticed all week, dash out and run off, and in the pauses between their little escapades the heat begins to gather itself for the long march through August. Just past dawn babies begin to wake up; all alone in the precarious privacy of their cribs, the older ones work on subtle pronunciations, wizards mocking their assistants. Then the women wake, the youngest mothers last; at some houses boys are outside before they're fully awake, comfortable in the last waves of sleep and the softened shorts they've worn all night. The men wake up, habituated; the little girls wake up; the older boys rise. Last of all, the nearly grown girls are courted by sunlight through insufficient curtains, but they resist and resist, saving themselves for one last dream, until their mothers, surprised but helpless before their own flying impatience that they recognize, halfway up the stairs, as a kind of hatred, a sort of energized loathing that includes the approaching swelter of heat as well as their lazy, lazy daughters, until the mothers come upstairs and knock sarcastically on the boudoir doors.

Ten o'clock on a Saturday morning in the first week of August in a town with no sidewalks. Mary Aldrich is making pickles against her will, stuffing up the kitchen with vinegar and steam, slamming drawers, trying to find the tongs, as the jars rattle in the boiling water. If Nobel walked in now with airplane tickets instead of a peck of his little warty cucumbers, she'd turn the tickets down and go out for the cucumbers herself; it's a kind of inertia for her, this home work, this ironing and sweeping and preserving. Most of the time it's easy for her, and it's the heat, probably, that has set her off so uneven this morning, tightening her temper as the humidity tightens the curl in her hair until the gray at her temples shows like puffs of smoke against the darkness of the rest of her hair. But there's the tongs, hiding back in the odds-and-ends drawer with the potato masher, and she's got clean dish towels laid on the counter for the hot jars.

Dinah appears in one kitchen doorway just as Nobel appears in the other with the big tin basin of washed cucumbers.

"Are you making *pickles?*" Dinah says.

"Just set them in the sink," Mary says over her shoulder.

Dinah shifts her weight to the other leg. "There's no place to fix *break*fast," she says.

"Get some clothes on," Nobel says, pushing his glasses up his nose from where they've slipped, it's that hot already.

Mary hears the edge of a grin in his voice, and she looks sharply at him. What he finds so amusing about Dinah's whining is beyond her, but Dinah hasn't heard it; she hears only that nobody's listening to her.

"But I'm *hun*gry," she says, and folds her long arms over the small breasts that are indeed showing through her thin nightgown. "I'm starving, and you guys got the whole kitchen taken up with *pick*les!"

Mary sets the hot jars in a double row along the towel-covered counter; each jar makes a small dull thump as she releases it from the tongs. "Breakfast is no longer being served," she says, fishing for lids and jar rubbers in the bottom of the big pot. "You heard your father."

Dinah is on the very verge of a huff and a flounce when she sees that he's just waiting for her to try it. She holds herself still, and hopes she looks as pitiful as she feels, as thin and defenseless and hungry. And unjustly ignored.

Nobel nods briefly and looks away. "Get dressed," he says to her, and then, the grin back in his voice, to Mary, "Better cut some of that chard today, too, before it bolts."

He turns to leave the kitchen and return to his garden, and there is an unconscious confidence in the way he moves his shoulders that stirs in his wife something very like pity, and makes her want to touch his back.

Dinah inhales loudly, makes a little kissing sound of her petulance, but she hasn't waited long enough: she doesn't get to say even the first word. Both parents snap to face her full, and they both say, "Get dressed!" She turns and runs back through the dining room, and they've taken her so completely aback, startled her so, that she's all the way back up in her own little bedroom looking at her dresser before she stops stepping lively. She takes a deep breath and soothes her hands down her ribs to her narrow, high hips. "Honestly!" she says. She wishes for a telephone. "Honestly! Like it was some kind of crime to want breakfast!" She yanks open her top drawer for underpants, and something hard rolls inside the drawer. She smiles, suddenly delighted.

Maybelline Jet Black Eyeliner. Unopened.

The kids embarrass Amos, that's the truth. The little boys with their skinny bare backs and their hair always growing out, they'll steal from the glass tub of fireballs on the counter, and look Amos straight in the eye. He'd like to be the kind of storekeeper who pretended he didn't see, but it doesn't work like that. After a while they're walking out with a flashlight or a paring knife from the rack in the middle aisle, and then their mothers come trotting them in to give it back and apologize. The high school boys—they don't come in anymore with dark rings under their noses from wiping at the snot with grubby wrists, but they still look him straight in the eye, that same look, as they set the quart of beer on the counter. By the next day they've forgotten the insult of Amos's knowing just how old they aren't, but Amos hasn't, and so he lets them get away with horsing around by the soda cooler until somebody knocks over the flimsy stand of pretzels and potato chips.

The girls, though, they're the mystery. Little girls come in, a note from their mother and a cool two or three dollars slipped neatly into one pocket, no nonsense of any kind. They're so concentrating, Amos has to treat them more carefully and politely than the crankiest of their mothers, and God help the world if he's out of something in the note, because the only thing worse than crying is the way they keep themselves from it. But one week, there they are like that, and it isn't like they grow up. It's like they disappear and a whole new batch moves in, the worst. Every last one set on looking like she's either dead or has a high fever, wearing clothes that don't fit in every possible way, too tight, too loose, too high, and never warm enough or cool enough to do the right job for the right weather—they just start appearing like that, and they buy one orange soda for three girls and sit on the soda cooler, so they have to keep hopping off for other people, and they stay and stay, and use his phone in the back in relays, and then, just as suddenly, they're gone. Just gone. And then a couple, three years later, they've turned into women, and they don't seem connected at all to who they were when they were sitting there with high-heeled shoes half dangling off their skinny feet. A mystery, and embarrassing to boot, so when the kids come in, especially the girls that age, and there aren't any grownups to occupy him, Amos stands uneasily behind the counter and looks out the window at River Street.

Dinah stands in the bathroom and watches unbreathing as black flows shiny and smooth as India ink in a line that is at last, on this fourth attempt, even and fat along the bases of her dark eyelashes. She stands, with the thin brush drying in her hand, with both eyes closed, waiting as long as she can bear it for the makeup to dry. Tall, brown, naked except for white cotton underpants with the waist folded down so they'll at least feel like the bikini panties her mother won't buy for her, Dinah stands with the black wand held just away from her right temple, and her left hand flat against her chest, breathing shallow and delicate, feeling the cool line on her eyelid disappear. Then slowly, as if waking in a perfumed palace bedroom to raise her innocent but knowing gaze to the face of her lover, Dinah opens her eyes and meets her new face in the mirror of the medicine chest over the sink.

Dinah.

She sees it, knows it: a beauty past any face she has ever seen, glamour come true and trembling to face her in the glass. Blind to the bright crimson spot on her right cheek where the heel of her hand pressed all through the four painstaking passes with the thick brush, blind to the trio of inflamed pimples at her hairline, Dinah has found the face of herself that she will love more than any face in the world for the next eight years, until her moment of broader passion, deeper helplessness, than she can now imagine. She knows so well what she sees there in the face with the suddenly subtle eyes that she doesn't smile. She hears Brian on the stairs; if there weren't that need to hurry, she might have come so far in only a clock's minute more that she would slip the wand back into its case, lay it respectfully aside, and with proper and confused reverence take her mother's cold cream and remove the magic darkness from her eyes.

Instead, she turns and grabs up the orange and white sundress that lies across the towel rack, ducks into it, and sails out past Brian in the hall, before he's even gotten his chance to pound on the door.

That is how she comes to be sitting, barefoot and in a dress that is almost childish, on the soda cooler at Amos's with Pam and Janet Tolli, all three girls with eyes dark rimmed, when Rachel Wilcox (Martin) Cavanaugh walks in to see if the Greyhound from Livingstone has dropped her suitcases off yet.

All over town in the early forenoon of this Saturday, with the wind gone and the heat settling in and the children scattered out for the day, the women who were girls here twenty years, twenty-five years ago—these women who can wash and bake and plant bulbs and mend zippers, who can crease and tear wrapping paper into perfect squares without ruler or scissors, who can peel apples and potatoes so thin and steady the parings fall like rich ribbon in coils around their wrists; these women who have grown close to middle age here in the town where they have lived their whole lives and somehow, by growing older where they were young, have had to grow older more deeply than if they had gone off somewhere to grow older, have had to submit more completely to time in order to displace their own girl-selves who threaten sometimes to reemerge and rob them; these women who have known things they first guessed at when they first slid their hands into pure white rayon Easter gloves at the Newberry's in Coville some snow-threatening day thirty years dead, and who stood only days ago like queens over their laundry and all it signified and knew for an exalted moment the true reach of their power—all over town on this first truly August Saturday afternoon these women nod in satisfaction of various kinds, and say or whisper or keep secret in their minds, "Rachel Wilcox!" And then they go on with their dust mops or trowels or dishrags, wondering a little distantly still what she's come back *here* for.

Even Mary Aldrich goes on poking dill heads into jars of steaming brine, the work before her, but more roughly than the work requires. She keeps at it because the name of this woman she has not seen in more than twenty years has been for twice that long an irritation that has hardly diminished with familiarity. She has her reasons, though she chooses to keep them out of conscious memory just now. Mary is not a woman to stand with sterilized jars cooling before her as some old scene of pain rises, but the scene is there, hidden, running its worn length whether Mary will stop to watch it or not.

Forty-two years ago the old Wilcox house smelled of lavender, lemon, a sweetness and a lightness utterly lacking in the smells of the de Marco house, where Mary lived with her father and sometimes his sister. The old Wilcox house smelled (even then, only six years old and motherless her whole life, Mary knew this, and held her father's hand roughly for it, fierce) of a pretty woman, and the house that was Mary's home and rightful place, that she would guard and keep sufficient, smelled of a man and his child alone. No announcement had been made (or ever was, or ever was retracted either) to explain why Joe de Marco had shaved that Saturday morning and helped Mary to put on her church dress, why he had made her stand until her ears rang while he worked his own comb through her rough hair and tied it, neat at last and unbecoming, with a pink ribbon. No explanations, but Mary knew by the smell of the house he led her to, by the icing (the same delicate pink as the foreign ribbon she could feel but no longer see) on the tiny cakes in that house, by the thin brightness of all the sounds (except the ones she made, and the ones her father made) of that house, Mary knew that her father meant to marry that house. Betray the rich, heavy, easy safety of home, make this vaguely laughing thin woman a mother to his own dark daughter. Who knew then, for the first time, that she was dark, and sturdy, and useful, and would never be like this woman her father wished (so pitiably, even Mary could see how he wouldn't do, any more than she herself would) to please. But Mary, fierce and miserable as she was, said *thank you very much* and then sat beside her father with a pink cake on a plate in her lap. The woman had lifted the cake with tongs from among the other cakes and had put it on the small plate and given the plate to Mary, who dared neither ask for a fork (there were no forks on the table in this parlor) nor pick the iced cake up with her fingers. She sat straight and polite, and furious with her mouth, which watered greedily. This betrayal, this paralysis, held her whole attention, and that was why Rachel, when she appeared, appeared all at once and without warning, like what happened when one of the big boys said *look over there* and when she looked he pulled her hair. Rachel appeared: a lovely thin child in a pale dress and white stockings, her eyes large and calmly curious, who shook hands with Mary's father (and Mary knew, staring, that her father was no stranger to this girl who was a stranger to Mary), a delicate little girl whose light hair was held shining and straight by the original of the pink ribbon in Mary's heavy hair.

Even if Mary would give the memory her direct attention, she wouldn't be able to recall what was said back and forth, by the woman, the child, her father, herself, but the memory has run its length now, as she snaps shut the bails of the dozen glass canning jars, sealing the garlic and dill and vinegar inside. She moves more smoothly in the wake of her refused recollection, just as she walked more smoothly home with her father that day, down Bridge Road and home, after she had stubbornly stayed by him, sullen in the face of all that Wilcox politeness. After she had refused to follow Rachel away from the parlor, refused to leave her father with all that daintiness, insisted with her sturdy, stubborn presence that she and he were not and could not be joined to that scentedness. And won. Joe de Marco didn't marry that house, or any house; he stayed where he belonged, and even when Mary has looked at his life squarely, she can see no harm in it, no lingering unhappiness or dissatisfaction. He's been dead ten years now. He gave his daughter away at her wedding, held his grandson, held his granddaughter. And did not see or chose not to notice that even as an infant, even with the darkness of the deMarco hair, his granddaughter had about her an air like a memory of that particular thinness, that delicateness. Which Mary also does not see, refuses to recognize, but it is part of what worries her in Dinah's beauty this summer.

This afternoon, in kitchens and yards here and there in town and out on the farms, women are keeping their distance from remembering, a distance already so large and old for even the youngest of them that the memory is paler than a memory of a dream forgotten before waking, a memory that has been kept secret even from their dreaming selves. It is nothing, it is a thing that doesn't exist, never has, never could.

Rachel Wilcox is nothing to them, though they have placed her with a firmness and satisfaction that is like a diagnosis. They go on with their work; here and there one scolds a child for slouching, tells a child sharply to stop that endless humming. They go on with their work, and from now on all these women will be surprised almost honestly if someone, some man or some woman who didn't grow up here, needs Rachel Wilcox explained.

The village itself has grown even smaller than Rachel remembers it, and what is now Brown's Groceries was, she thinks,

Kelvin's Dry Goods when she was a child, the lesser (she knew even then) of the two groceries, the one her mother did not go to. Brown's is the last business left, the Emporium (where her mother did go, with Rachel at her side, formal and obedient in a way that she knew at first by intuition and then by experience no other child in this town accompanied a mother) gone without a trace, the old drugstore boarded up and wearing the remains of "Valley Lunch" painted across the window of the door. But Brown's Groceries remains, in spirit, Kelvin's, where earlier village girls and boys used to stand around in easy familiarity, and Rachel had avoided passing whenever possible and had passed, when she could not avoid it, as if deaf and blind, feeling them watching her. Even after she had been a term at boarding school and found it a world where she moved naturally, learned that her clothes and manners were not outlandish in the world, and had made two friends who listened with awe as she told of life in this tiny town as if it were a remote exotic village where the natives were barely civilized—even then, when the gang at Kelvin's watched her (and of course they were even more curious then, now that she'd been away, "Boarding school!" their mothers said, more or less astonished to be expected to believe in such things in the real modern world, more or less disbelieving, what it must cost in times like these, or was Mrs. Wilcox rich as well as a widow, her widowhood still and always in doubt in a town like this, in times like these), she knew she was not unique in the thrilling way girls in books sometimes were. She knew that here she was alien, awkward, ill fitted, and they were at home. And although she had really never wanted to stand around Kelvin's, partly because she couldn't even imagine what they might all be doing when they didn't have her to watch, and partly because what she did see them doing (pushing, sharing sodas, making faces) seemed pointless, she would have liked—what?

Walking carefully across the dirt parking area and up the one step to that old porch, Rachel still wonders, because that old stiffness between her shoulder blades descended on her as soon as she saw the three teenaged girls entering the store forty paces ahead of her, descended as unchanged as if it had hovered in this air for thirty-four years waiting for her. But Rachel isn't fourteen anymore. She ices a smile across her face and goes into the dark-floored, low-ceilinged, stale little store.

The three girls sit on the soda cooler, behind her as she speaks to Brown. She assumes this is Brown; there can't be business enough to employ a clerk.

"Excuse me," Rachel says pleasantly, although she already has his full and grateful attention and, she can feel, the full attention of the three girls. "About what time does the Greyhound bus from Livingstone come in today?"

"About eleven thirty, eleven thirty-five," Amos apologizes, since it is now a quarter till twelve. "Any time now." He'd like to offer her a seat, point out a comfortable bench near the door or something. Himself, when he wants to sit and there're kids hanging around so he can't go in the back, he perches awhile on the edge of the floor of the display window, but he could hardly offer her that.

"Thank you," she says, and half turns from him.

"Nice day," he says, eager to keep her. "You going into Coville? If you don't mind my asking," he hurries.

"Actually, no. I'm just waiting for my bags to come from Livingstone."

"Ah," he nods. "Came on without them, huh?"

"Yes," she says, to end it; she can feel those eyes on her, and an adolescent desire for revenge against this talkative man and those three girls rises in her.

Janet and Pam *are* staring, but they've no idea that Rachel could know they exist; they cannot fathom that a woman like her, purse and stockings and dress and hair just like someone in a magazine, ever lived in this town (which even they know to be tiny and backward, though they know it from magazines and not experience—*they* would believe she came from Livingstone, the biggest town any of them has seen, though they've known people who've been to Boston and New York, and they know there is a Paris and a Rome), much less ever cared what their mothers thought of her. If they knew her name it would mean nothing to them; her story hasn't yet been pulled out, and probably won't be until long after she's left again. What they know is that before them stands a woman who can actually do the things with clothes and hair and makeup that they struggle for, and because she has done them, they can measure their own failures.

And since they have never cared at all about what they could learn even surreptitiously from any other adult woman they have ever seen (their mothers laboring to show them kitchen skills, clothing skills, hygiene; their teachers laboring to convince them of habits and facts) until just this moment (as they study from the back the way her hair holds itself still but supple, the way the bodice of her dress sits neatly but not tight at her waist), and since they are still at an age when they believe in their own invisibility, they keep staring.

Dinah alone looks off out the window, bitter and ashamed in this woman's presence, and the swift longing that makes her shoulders curve in more sharply than ever is a longing for the day to start over, for the Maybelline Jet Black Eyeliner to catch on a pair of socks, for herself to have come down to the store in her shorts and blouse, with her face clean as a kid's.

"Well," Amos offers uneasily. "Should be here any minute."

"Yes," she says, clearly irritated, and turns away from Amos and the window.

And she almost laughs aloud when she turns to face the girls she has felt judging and snubbing her: *How much I have forgotten I had learned!* she thinks. For a sparkling, soothing second she sees herself separate from the facts and truths of her long life far from this musty little store. The faces of the girls reveal to her her smooth, elegant hair and dress, reveal her to herself as the fascinating stranger she has always, she guesses, wished to be, and she is delighted. She pauses, smiles, reaches into her white summer purse. "Would you girls excuse me?" she says. "I'd like a soft drink."

Dinah's the first one down, but not before Rachel sees her full face, and takes, still generous, the small shock of the girl's elegance. *De Marco,* Rachel thinks, Rachel who had forgotten to remember a soul in this town by name besides Jacob. *Mary de Marco,* and she is surprised that the girl looks so familiar, that the face of dark Mary de Marco must have been so firmly embedded in her memory. But by then the other two are standing aside from the soda cooler, and Dinah has gone, off across the hot dirt of the parking lot in her long bare feet.

Saturdays Amos Brown takes the week's receipts to the night deposit of the bank in Livingstone, and every Saturday he means to act like the single man he is, but most Saturdays he drops the envelope in the slot, gets his hair cut at Louie Centra's, and decides, between supper alone in Connor's Diner and supper alone back over the store, that he'd probably better head on back. Today, because of taking Mrs. Cavanaugh home, he's a good hour behind himself. He runs into a crowd at Louie's, and by the time he's done there and steps out into the rich heat of late afternoon in a bigger town than he's used to anymore, he doesn't feel like a man alone, like the widower he's been for seven years, or even like a bachelor with the length of a summer Saturday night before him and money in his pocket. He feels like a husband on holiday. Rachel has done that for him, with her perfume maybe, with that smooth prettiness that ought to be shocking in a woman his own age. That's what Amos thinks as he walks big as life into the diner and takes his time over the mimeographed menu.

She warmed up some after she got her cold drink, so when her bags came it was easy to offer her a lift out to her brother's place with them. "I close at noon anyway," he told her, which was true, "and I could give you a lift with those bags."

"It's not far," she said, "just out to my brother's house on Bridge Road. And I would appreciate it."

And he had hurried through the connections that came clear in his mind then, when he realized who she was—Jacob's big shopping a few days ago, her showing up so suddenly but buying like a native, not a traveler. "I go right out Bridge Road," he had said, which wasn't exactly always the true case, but no reason it couldn't be.

She ended up talking most of the way out to the house. "I've come back to see for myself how Jacob is," she said, and he hadn't said a word before she seemed to make up her mind to finish saying the whole thing. "Jacob has lived alone too long," she said. "He needs someone to bring him—oh, back to reality, I suppose you'd say. He hasn't been well, really, since our mother died. And I think he's failed some this past year or so."

And Amos had agreed, with due respect and as few clear words as possible, but wasn't it time? And by the time he'd carried her suitcases (top quality, all leather, he could tell) into the front hall, he was so sure she'd do just what needed doing that he'd said to her, "Good luck, Mrs. Cavanaugh," and shook her hand. She shook hands strong, too, stronger than he'd have guessed when she first came into the store, but that sturdy grip and her kind face made him feel triumphant, as if Jacob was already taken care of. And the fact that she never said just what she meant to do about him doesn't bother Amos at all. Why, Amos feels as he cuts his thin ham steak and pierces the tasteless pineapple chunks, why, Amos feels as if the town belongs to him at last; after fifteen years of living there and running his store, that town belongs to him and he's about to see it saved by some event of quiet heroism, some shake-up it's been needing. And she's a handsome woman.

Triumph, that's what makes Amos walk down the street in Livingstone in the first dusk of Saturday night with his hands in his pockets. Triumph, and he could no more say over what than he could fly, for Jacob never hurt a soul, he didn't even upset anybody with all his flailing except maybe the Reese sisters, and even they only sniffed in a put-out way when Jacob went high-stepping around them in the road. Still, there Amos is, feeling like a free man at last, strolling through the door of the Livingstone Hotel and Bar just like he was putting one over on his dead wife Ginny, rest her soul.

CHAPTER 7

*A*ll around in the mock coolness of the first dark the peepers are keeping perfect time, the cicadas are keeping perfect time in counterpoint, the stars are beating with the frogs, and far-off truck and car motors rise and fall with the crickets. This orderly nightfall delights and calms Jacob Wilcox, and he rocks in the old green chair in the garden, rocks to the regular throb of the world. The crunching footsteps along the road even match the whisper of his rocking on the grass, and when the footsteps turn in and come to a stop, they stop just as Rachel, behind him in the lighted house, closes a cupboard door. Jacob smiles at it, grateful and at peace.

Jacob sees after a moment from the way the round little man stands at the edge of the grass with his hands in his pockets, his arms bowed slightly out like the handles of a sugar bowl, that Mr. Parsons has come talking about his bees. Bees are fitting for this night, and Jacob lets the pastor's quiet words float out and drift in the air of the garden for quite a time before he begins to pay close enough notice to hear what they say. They are good clean words, with no more heat to them than smoke rings, twirling slowly in the dark, the biggest ones slowly vanishing out over the tomatoes. "They led me," Jacob hears, and "like fur, like feathers," and without a clear sound to see it by, Jacob understands: the swarm suddenly massing downward and coming to cluster in perfection, a golden feathered orb suspending itself, inevitable and living, from the eaves of a young blue spruce. And Jacob tastes in the quiet levity of the circling words a regret, but so sweet in the deep rolling quiet that it carries no more sharpness than the rough smell of zinnias.

Today, all day, the Reverend Parsons has been required and has fulfilled, and has had a steady need for this recitation of the flight he followed. He ran after the swirling bees until dinnertime and doubt made him give it up. Then he pretended for hours that the swarm might hang there in contented hiatus for his return. The young parson has carried his loss of the swarm and of its mystery here to Jacob, where he can always tell out an entire thing without interruption. Already, he can feel again the coins in his left pocket and his keys in his right, and he can tell that his memory of that swarm is saved and safe; the telling has done its work. He wonders, as he always does out here, whether Jacob has actually heard him, or has only kept silent and let him go on. And he decides, idly now, that this is how wise men have probably always worked, this is why so many cultures and times revere madness.

Jacob feels the words dissolving in the darkness, becoming invisible and formless again, and he remembers sliced bread floating on a park pond in a city as some rain began, and how the ducks floated off to the middle of the water, how the women in dark capes floated off away, with children docile between them. The smell of marmalade, the steam off a cup of tea. Jacob's eyes are closed in the dark. "You saw it," he says, gently, affirming. "Yes. You saw it."

And then Jacob is silent for so long that Mr. Parsons remembers the presence of the woman in the house—the sister, he believes he's been told—and he takes himself away without farewell. He no longer pretends to himself that his visits are pastoral; he knows that the gentle madman scarcely recognizes him; he cannot imagine (and doesn't try) explaining himself to this sister in the house. Still, Jacob's silence itself is a gift, and this rare speech of Jacob's is a blessing he carries off, half guilty, half humbly grateful. Vaguely, he promises himself that he'll do better by the old man the next time.

He carries Jacob's words down across the bridge, up the street to his house where his wife, Ellen, sits in the kitchen writing a letter, and he sees her through the open window. If he had stayed, surrendered out in Jacob's garden to the gentle rocking of night, just about now he'd hear Jacob beginning to hum as Rachel turns off the lamp in the parlor and goes on up to bed. Instead, he stands in the dark and sees his wife's bare shoulder, her forearm on the dark table, the miraculous way the pen scarcely moves in her hand, and the childishness of her pauses. She takes a sip of water from the glass that stands on a folded napkin on the table beside her, and her lips shine. For just that moment, Jim would like to call softly to her, and have her come to the window and smile gravely.

From two porches up River Street, he hears Sandy Clark calling for her oldest, "Monty! Monty!" In a moment the boy seems to answer from some shadow by the driveway. The screen door closes quietly, then yawns sharply and slaps shut. Everybody's in but Jim; the last boy out tonight is Jim. And then, sliding his hands back into his pockets, he goes in, too.

An hour passes, and another.

Susan Darcy startles awake to a loud groan from Tony's sleep.

Mary Aldrich, stunned by a dream of her dead father's grin and the shaving cream left under his ears, lies awake now.

Elsie Reese lies dreamless under a thin cover of sleep, almost aware of her own sleep, her own dreamlessness. Julia Cullinan floats in the middle layers of sleep, unaware and unaware. Out past the bridge, Rachel sleeps deeper than dreams.

Jacob, who dozed for a while in his chair, is awake now. He sits and rocks a while longer, feeling the hum in his chest, before he picks his way through the starlit garden to the door of the shed. He goes in, pride and peace growing louder: with a kind of gratitude, as if the vision he suddenly sees here in the dark were already accomplished, he feels the space in the drying shed open and arrange itself to receive a chair and table, a quilt-covered mattress, the round-topped trunk: he can almost touch the dark shapes of his perfect, solitary, silent home.

When Jacob goes to town in the day, he is a shouting madman, but there are nights like these when Jacob goes walking, nights when all has come round astonishing and right: Jacob sings, he walks with his singing, and the singing of Jacob on these nights is pure song. There may have been lyrics once, when these tunes first came floating up through Jacob and over his throat to stretch out this way in the dark; now there are no words, and there could be no words that could follow these melodies: deep-voiced, his raging surrendered to the sure proofs of good and solace in the world, his song trails out endlessly in the warm night, rises to the open windows of River Street, or Town Line Road, or Spare Avenue, wherever he walks, and he walks where he will, sometimes up beyond the town on the roads to Living-stone or Coville, past farms and open fields. Sleepers hear, and their dreams grow golden and sandy: the babies relax their curled bodies and nearly know how spacious the world might be; the men remember; the women remember; and every lonely person asleep in that voice is comforted as if by love remem-bered in love. Jacob walks with his singing, and the song stays quiet as shadow in the bedrooms as he passes, until it fades off like forgotten joy.

But some nights, and this is such a night, his singing lifts through the dark to a woman awake. Tonight Susan is awake, and Mary, and young Ellen Parsons, who has been crying alone in the dark because she wants a baby so very much. She hears Jacob from far off, and she knows that she has never heard this singing before in her waking life. She rises in the wide smooth-ness of the song. At the window she holds her arms cradled before her as if to hold what she hears, the promise of comfort and pleasure she hears, as if offering to be blessed by the slow-moving song. Jacob passes; Ellen looks out into the dark away from the road where he walks.

Mary Aldrich lies awake beside her husband, listening. As Jacob comes along he takes the song and flips it up high and sweet, from the strong depth into falsetto, and he sings his own harmony and echo beneath the full trees of the wide summer road. Mary lies still and feels how it lingers just above the trees, high and light and slow as stars. She feels how it comes sifting down through the dark leaves, how it lies like sugar along the roadside after he has gone on. But she lies still. She has had her times of standing at the window, and she has had her time of being borne out into the night on that song. For tonight, as for many years now, she lies still. After the song melts and the silence fills again with the sounds of her house, the sounds she doesn't hear, she moves her hand, and quietly touches one finger to Nobel's sleeping back. He doesn't wake, and Mary is glad of it, for she has what she wished for, the feel of his warm skin breathing beneath the soft knit of his white T-shirt. Before Jacob comes back through the village, back down River Street from wherever he has walked with his singing, Mary will be asleep again.

But Susan Darcy stands in the upstairs hall outside the room where her sons sleep, next to the room where her husband sleeps beside the place where she was sleeping only minutes ago. She stands there in the hall in her pale summer nightgown and Jacob's song moves her, silent through her sleeping house. With her hair down and comforting her neck in the warm night, Susan leaves her house and walks out into the darkness of the road that is River Street. Jacob has already gone on, but his song lingers, and Susan moves in it, almost as high and slow as Jacob's falsetto. She walks barefoot down the sugary dirt beside the road, toward the river. She goes a ways, and there at a place that is level and long-grassed, a place that is no particular place but only how far she has come when the first certainty thrills through her, Susan lifts her thin nightdress over her head, and she lies down on the grass of the roadside with her gown a pool of light beside the light of her skin. She waits there in the dark. All around her is the darkness, and beyond her are the silver willows of the river's banks.

Drifting up toward the surface of sleep, Nobel Aldrich feels his wife's warm calf against his calf, Dan Cullinan feels his wife's warm breath on his shoulder, Arnie Deery hears the gentle creaking of the crib as his wife settles their baby back into sleep. Jim Parsons stays deep in his sleep, and Timer Darcy, huddled over as if he were chilled, clings to the bottommost depths of sleep.

It may be hours before Jacob comes back through town, down and over the bridge for home.

It may be that when he comes he walks past without seeing Susan lying there.

But if Jacob returns and happens upon her, and sometimes this is how it comes about, his singing will grow so quiet and strong that she will not be able to hear whether it is high or low. She will lie waiting in the dark grass, and she will open herself with her own fingertips, an offering of such delicacy and gentle poise that Jacob will know it as part of the mystery of his own sweet joy, as part of the darkness itself. Tall Jacob will kneel at the roadside, his song like a breath on her skin, his hair more silver than the willows beyond. He will kneel before her, and within his song he will cover her until she believes that she and he are part of the song, part of something far more beautiful and helpless than her life. He will be taken by the woman, and the woman will be taken by him, all in the slow and wordless dark of the roadside. It is for this that Susan has come gliding out in the mildness of the August night, for this dream of passion, as free and unthinking as if she had never lain in the grass before, as if no woman had lain in this grass before.

PART II

CHAPTER 8

*A*larms sound on both sides of River Street. Brown radios the size and shape of toasters are turned on to verify the weather: muggy, hot, continued hot and humid. Simple breathing seems hardly worth the trouble. Timing is off, even in washing and shaving, measuring coffee, turning eggs. Drawers stick and have to be banged shut.

"Hi, Daddy," Tony says, smiling through his sleepiness as calmly as if he weren't pinching himself to keep from peeing.

"Go pee," Timer says, "and then change your clothes." He goes on to the head of the stairs. Over the tinkling sound of Tony in the bathroom, he barks, "And shut the bathroom door!"

In the kitchen, Susan stands by the stove sipping her coffee. That means his'll be tepid by now. He had half meant to skip the coffee this morning anyway, skip everything but some juice and a long drink of water, but he goes to the table now. He pulls his chair out and props first one foot and then the other on the seat to tie his shoes, and then he sits down. She's in nothing but her nightgown, as bad as the kids, and she's pulled her hair back with a rubber band without even combing it. Timer runs his hand along his smooth jaw, scratches behind his ear; he feels fastidious in the sullen air, and he glares at a bit of dried something stuck to the table at Allen's place. Susan sets a plate in front of him, jangles his silverware beside it. He doesn't need to look down to know there're two eggs and two slices of buttered toast on the plate, but he looks anyway. It's better than looking up, this morning, where he knows she's as vague-faced as Tony, just as ready with that same smile that doesn't mean anything. She brings his coffee, and sits down herself, brushing crumbs automatically away before she sets her half-empty cup on the table.

Timer looks at the coffee. "No juice?" he asks, politely.

"Oh," she says, and begins to get up.

"Never mind," he says. She settles back down, and he extracts his fork from the tangle of silverware beside his plate. He pokes the yolk of an egg. It crumbles like a worn eraser. He puts the fork down, picks up a slice of the toast, looks at how it bends, limp, soaked with margarine that sat out all night melting into the plate. He puts the toast down, chooses his spoon, stirs sugar into the coffee. Sips. Even the eggs are hotter than the coffee. Even the table is hotter. He leaves the spoon in the cup and pushes his chair back from the table.

She pulls a piece of her hair back behind her ear and looks up. "Too hot, huh?" she says, as if to comfort him.

He doesn't answer, tucks his shirt in more smoothly, goes to the counter for his lunch box. "I told Tony to get some clean clothes on," he says, barely keeping the threat out of his voice.

But Susan is reaching for the toast he left on his plate and doesn't say a thing.

"He's had the same damn clothes on for three days," Timer says.

Susan shrugs. "Okay," she says, and when he looks her full in the face from across the kitchen she's chewing. She smiles right at him, her cheek bulged out, like it was all a sweet life. He stalks out the back door and lets the screen dangle open behind him; he knows it serves her right, even if he's not precise about why. For a good forty paces his fury is so complete that he's purely satisfied in it, a kind of happy, really, and almost blue as it begins to fade off.

74

*

One last alarm spurts, long after the others are forgotten for the day: Rachel's small black-cased travel alarm, the only clock in the old Wilcox place. Rachel is already awake, lying on her back with her hands behind her head. *Yes,* she agrees with the alarm. *Today.*

The noise of the alarm confuses Jacob utterly for a full clock minute. He stands in the kitchen with the sponge in his hand and stares at the cleanser he has sprinkled into the sink. It is dissolving with a sharp smell, but he doesn't notice. Jacob has been cleaning his mother's house in absolute forgetfulness since a while before dawn. But dawn was blank today, sunless and heavy, and Jacob hadn't noticed when it came. He's just been going on as he has a thousand times before, task by task and room by room, knowing without thought or plan that by and by a breeze will come and lift him floating off to his morning sleep, as sure and gentle and indulgent as a father in evening clothes who carries his drowsing boy from the parlor to his bedroom after the guests have gone. And then this miniature noise jingles into the silence of the house and takes Jacob by surprise. Like a premonition, the certainty of loss and sorrow enters his hands and feet and courses swift and leaden to his heart. For the first time in many years Jacob utters a sound in the house, and the sound is a sob, a single gulping sob like the last of many from the throat of an exhausted and betrayed child. But then there is the sound of footsteps overhead. He remembers Rachel; his hand remembers the sponge; he hurries with the sink, to finish and be done and wait for her in the garden, where she takes pleasure, he remembers it all now, in drinking coffee with him in the gentle mornings.

But by the time Rachel has dressed for town (a habit she is almost conscious of refusing to omit, here in the country, here under the heat, here in the peculiarly charming lassitude of Jacob's life), and come down and out through the house that seems in the steady heated dimness of this morning more and more filled with objects she does not remember, objects she will have to dispose of soon in some way, Jacob is nearly asleep in his chair out back. Thunder rumbles far off. The air is so heavy that even the excellent coffee is distasteful. Rachel stands beside the table for a moment and watches Jacob to see if he will notice, and then she takes a chance, carries the coffee and cup back inside, all untasted. When she gets back outside, her mind already full of the things they need from the store and the need to get there and back before the rain comes, and the need to check at the post office and the need to telephone the real estate agency in Livingstone, Jacob isn't there. She listens for a moment. But Jacob isn't to be seen or heard. She glances over the madness of his flowers, the zinnias' gaudiness burnished in the glower of the coming storm; half guilty, she hurries off toward town in her high-heeled shoes and with her umbrella neat at her side.

One of the Neadom children was waiting this morning at eight when Amos came downstairs and unlocked the store door. By the time the little girl had carried away her two quarts of breakfast milk there were two more uncombed children there, one for a loaf of bread and the other, odd and amusing to Amos's imagination of how these early errands begin, for toothpicks and toilet paper. Then Julia Cullinan hurried in for cupcake papers, and that, Amos knew, was the end of his morning's business. Nobody else will think of anything to need until around ten-thirty, when one of the men from the crew working out on Route 71 will come in for seven coffees to go and a box of plain doughnuts. Then the trickle of shoppers will begin and grow until it peaks between one and two. So between about nine and ten, Amos cleans and restocks. He's on his knees in the middle aisle shifting two-pound boxes of sugar when Rachel comes in. He hurries to his feet.

"Mrs. Cavanaugh!" he says, dusting off his knees, surprised at his own panic. "Good morning!"

"Good morning," she says, but her smile agrees with him that the morning is anything but good.

Amos manages a smile although she isn't stopping to visit. He pulls his handkerchief from his pocket and dabs at the sweat on the sides of his face. "Warm," he apologizes.

"I know—it's just terrible, isn't it," she agrees, glancing out the front door. "It's a little cooler out at the house. Maybe the rain will help."

Amos chuckles, and feels foolish for it. He wishes he were up front behind the counter. "Hope so," he says. "You let me know if you need help with anything."

She turns from the shelf of spices and gives him an odd look before she seems to remember something, and she smiles. "Well, I need a roasting chicken, if you have one," she says. Amos can't get over how fast she changes from really distant to this charming smile. He nods gratefully. "Coming right up," he says, and goes in relief behind the meat case to the old sink, washes his hands. Over the noise of the water he says, "About four, five pounds?"

"Fine," she calls back, and the tones of their voices over the sound of the running water are so casual and domestic that it twists Amos's heart.

But when he comes out with her chicken wrapped plump and cold in white paper, she is very much the pleasant shopper. "By the way," she says, putting a can of cranberry sauce on the counter, "that dark-haired girl who was in here the day my suitcases came—she looked so familiar to me. What's her name?"

"That would be Dinah Aldrich," he says.

"Aldrich?" she wonders, almost elaborately. "I don't remember the name. Oh!" she almost laughs. "Of course—but what is her mother's name?"

"Maiden name, you mean? Huh. Well, I really can't say that I know—Mary's her mother, and her father's Nobel Aldrich, the postmaster."

A full week has passed since Jacob last shouted his way up River Street and back with his overloaded sack of groceries. Julia, hurrying into Amos's store the second time this morning (for confectioner's sugar, though she can hardly believe she didn't check for it before she started the cupcakes, any more than she can believe she didn't check for cupcake papers at the same time), recognizes at the same instant Rachel's actual presence and the week's lack of Jacob. It pulls her up short.

"Well," Amos says, and Julia feels a blush rising, certain he's about to tease her for this second trip. "Mrs. Cullinan, do you know Mrs. Cavanaugh?"

She nods, her smile automatically kind. "Of course—Rachel!"

"Julia," Rachel replies, and offers her hand. "It's been a long time. You still look wonderful."

Julia laughs. "Wonderful? Well, not bad for my age maybe, but—oh, well!" She wonders at herself: she'd been going to say *not bad for a grandmother,* and then she hadn't. "So—well, are you back for a visit?"

"A working visit, yes," Rachel says.

"Well, welcome back, then. We should see some of you soon—catch you up on all the latest excitement!" Julia jokes, scarcely trying to imagine this stylish woman in her kitchen. "And your family?"

Rachel shakes her head the least bit. "Jacob's all there is now, and you know Jacob."

"Oh—I'm so sorry," Julia says.

Amos hurries into what might have become a pause. "Now, you'd know—we were just wondering what Mrs. Aldrich's maiden name was."

"Why, Rachel! Mary de Marco—I *know* you knew her," Julia says, and her tone is mock scolding, friendly, pleasant, but in her eyes is a flash of suspicion, almost a memory of some old rumor of Rachel's fast life in the city, years and years ago, though time has passed more completely for Julia than for Rachel. The look passes from her face and almost from her mind before she sorts it out to see that she was shamefully capable, for an instant, of fearing that that old ragged gossip was true, and that Rachel would be after Nobel now.

"Mary de Marco," Rachel agrees. "Of course! And her daughter is *very* like her. I saw her in here on Saturday, and I couldn't get over how familiar she looked, but I couldn't quite place the face." Rachel sounds as if she's explaining her poor memory, but she's not a woman to miss a suspicion in another woman's eye. It pleases her vanity, but she has no desire to increase it. "But Aldrich—?" she asks.

"Yes, Nobel Aldrich—but of course, you'd gone off to college, I guess, before he came to town. He's the postmaster now.

They bought the Goddard place three years ago, and Mary's got it all so nice—you remember how artistic she always was with colors and all that." Julia is so completely reassured by Rachel's ignorance of Nobel that she allows herself to overlook how little they all knew one another after grade school, how little they knew even then, but thunder breaks the heavy silence outside. "Oh! Here comes that rain now—I'd better get moving!"

"I guess I'd better, too," Rachel says. "I'm so glad I saw you, Julia. And thank you again, Mr. Brown."

Amos nods, easy again, and almost sure her thanks are sincere and friendly. "Glad you remembered your umbrella," he says.

"Why, Rachel, you're not walking, are you? No, no—heavens, an umbrella's not going to be any help in this!" Julia insists, and it's true. A wall of rain suddenly drops beyond the porch of the store, and the thunder is enormous. "I've got my car right up close out front, just let me get my sugar and I'll drive you home."

The last time Rachel saw Julia was the day that Julia married Dan Cullinan, and that wedding scandalized the whole town for a full year before it happened. Dan was Rachel's age, four years younger than Julia; he and Julia had known each other forever, but when Dan started visiting at the Stones' every Friday night with his hair combed wet, more than a few people got upset. Julia Stone was a pretty girl, of course, or would have been if she weren't so heavy, and the Stones were good people, but it wasn't seemly for a boy still in school to be courting a young woman who worked and boarded during the week over in Livingstone. As the months wore on, Julia grew thinner and Dan kept growing taller, but still when they went walking they looked enough like a woman and a boy to make people uncomfortable. Dan was quiet and earnest; people expected he'd do important things, and a number of girls his own age (and their mothers) were deeply offended that he so clearly preferred Julia Stone, who was sort of old, after all. People said, of course, that the Orchards was what attracted him, and that still waters run deep. Even Rachel's mother, who seldom had attention to spare from her single-minded maintenance of calm, once asked Rachel if it was true that the Cullinan boy was mixed up with some town woman. By their wedding day, the week after Dan's graduation, people had seemed resigned to it, but Rachel felt a sympathy greater than their slight friendship warranted as she watched Julia, slender by then but still looking more like a goddess than a nymph with her full breasts and her calm face, exchange solemn vows with Dan, whose Adam's apple pointed in his skinny neck and who still looked, at eighteen, as if his mother had scrubbed him well and dressed him for Sunday school. Thirty years, but Rachel would have known Julia Stone anywhere.

And it occurs to Rachel on the drive home, which is slow and chatty, that the Orchards borders the Wilcox acres, and that, perhaps, selling to the Orchards would be easier and, somehow, friendlier than selling to strangers. The idea pleases her, and her pleasure surprises her: she had forgotten, besides her new curiosity about Mary de Marco, that there were people in this town she wanted to be kind to.

On the other side of town, toward Coville, Timer Darcy stands in the doorway of the office of Stone Orchards and watches the rain. The two high school boys come stomping and laughing in from the mailing room behind him. The smell of their warm wet hair reaches Timer along with their laughter, and he thinks of Allen as a baby, freshly bathed and handed to him, and he falls suddenly in love with Susan again.

Up on Pearl Street, Alice Reese lies on the silver-blue bedspread of her neatly made bed in the front bedroom. Elsie lies on the yellow chenille bedspread of her neatly made bed in the old sun-room downstairs. Elsie doesn't climb stairs well anymore. Alice knows that Elsie can't come upstairs. Elsie knows for a fact that Alice won't come down the stairs until exactly noon. The sisters lie apart and see the rain on the windows. They are trying to remember the sound of it. After a while Alice remembers something else even farther away, and she passes her hands flat down her front, from shoulder to midthigh, and back up again. Then she passes on to sleep. Elsie doesn't sleep today at all. She just keeps having that feeling she woke up with, that something is gathering into so heavy a pile that it will begin to topple and fall any time now. It isn't the weather, either, because the rain hasn't changed anything. So Elsie lies on her back and watches her window ripple. "I do wonder what she does up there," Elsie says aloud, "two hours every morning."

The rain goes lazy after the first torrent and falls all afternoon in great plopping calmness that keeps the leaves spinning but lets the ground drink at leisure. Julia takes the plate of frosted cupcakes from the cupboard over the counter and sets them on the kitchen table. She turns the two cups on their saucers so each handle is to the right. It's a lonely moment in the gloomed light of her kitchen, and she is waiting in that moment purely without hope, though she knows that Mary is just now standing on her front steps readying her umbrella for the few steps to Julia's front porch, and she knows that when Mary comes in there will be comfort and the light will change. Still, something in the sound of slow rain outside and the delicacy of the thin china and the paleness of the silver spoons makes Julia very sad and reluctant. She smooths her hands over her abdomen, and waits.

Dinah watches her mother cross the wet road. Although there is no sunlight, the yellow of the umbrella glows down on the head of Dinah's mother, like the glow of a buttercup under a chin. Years from now Dinah will feel this vision of her mother as a moment of tenderness that crosses over their misunderstandings, but at this actual moment she only records the likeness to buttercups, and notices with distaste how the yellow light stains the gray in her mother's hair. Dinah watches in her displeasure from the green metal chair on the front porch, watches over her open book until her mother disappears into the Cullinans' house, for their afternoon coffee, a tradition of years and years. Then Dinah goes inside.

She leaves her book facedown on the dining room table, unhooks the cellar door, and goes down. Under a wide shelf that holds coffee cans and baby food jars filled with screws and nails

81

and small parts of other things, stands a pile of magazines. The first ten or so are *Popular Mechanics* and *Home Repairs,* but the last ten are not. They are magazines without covers, so Dinah couldn't name them, and inside are pictures of naked women and of women wearing filmy nightgowns or lacy underwear. Even the jokes and cartoons have naked women in them. The pages of these magazines are stiff and buckled from years of sitting on the damp basement floor. They have been here since long before the Aldriches bought this house. Dinah turns the pages deliberately, ignoring most of the pictures, but in each magazine there is one certain picture, a full-page color painting of a woman. When Dinah finds this particular picture she folds the magazine open there and puts it aside, and begins paging through the next magazine. When all ten are found, she arranges the magazines so that there are two rows of these pictures, and by the light of the bulb over the makeshift workbench she studies them solemnly.

The pictures have captions, but Dinah knows that these are not really cartoons and doesn't bother herself with trying to decipher the jokes. The women are flawless. They are smooth, pink and gold and white, their hair and faces the essence of cleanliness and purity. They wear little or nothing. Some of them talk on telephones, some arch or recline on beds or on sofas as voluptuous and as glamorous as the women themselves.

Dinah looks for a long time.

When she closes the magazines and replaces them, she makes sure they are in the order she found them in, and she lifts the equally aged *Popular Mechanics* back to the top of the stack. She cannot imagine how this pile of magazines came to be here, and she has not yet gone so far as to wonder, although she is always careful about replacing them. When everything is as she found it, she goes back up the stairs, turns out the light with the switch by the door, and hooks the door shut.

Then she goes upstairs to the bathroom and washes her hands; the slick and nearly damp pages have left a film of discomfort on her skin. Then she goes into her bedroom and shuts the door. She undresses slowly in the moody near-dark. When all of her clothes, her shirt and shorts and underpants, lie in a pile beside her, she goes to her bed and practices the poses she remembers from the magazines. She has no mirror, nor does she want one. A few times she sees a certain gleam off her calf or along the plane of her thigh or instep that pleases her, but mostly she is trying to feel the way those pictures looked.

In the office at Stone Orchards, Dan Cullinan stares just over Rachel's shoulder and waits for her to get to her point. *I've got a business proposition,* she said; so now, having nodded, he waits for her to make it.

"I've come back," she begins, "to see about Jacob." Then she stares for a long silence at the puddle forming around the tip of her furled umbrella. "As you must know, he's declined rather sharply in the past two years." She glances, wondering if she should have said "as you must know," but Dan's face is as smooth as his amazingly bald head. "I'm no doctor, but it seems to me that he shouldn't be living alone anymore."

Rachel talks on about the options she has considered, the people she has consulted, the state of the house as she found it upon her arrival a week ago, but Dan is only slightly listening, just enough so he won't miss the real question when she gets to it. Instead, he's trying to track down the last time, not long ago, when someone spoke to him about Jacob. As he tries to narrow it down, he's also remembering the morning after his grandson was born, when Jacob went by the window at such a clip just as he was dropping off to sleep, and thinking that he doesn't recall having seen or heard Jacob since then, a long time for Jacob not to make his rounds, and how odd it had been, back at the hospital, to recognize in the face of that newborn grandson the face of his own brother, what, eleven years or more since he's seen him.

"So what I'd like to do is sell the house and the land, and I thought that since the Orchards abuts the property along the north, you might like the chance to make an offer before I put it on the market."

Dan hears the statement just as he's certain it was Timer Darcy, and that Timer had been disturbed about the language his kids were picking up from somewhere. Dan had laughed, said if those kids could figure out what Jacob was saying they had pretty keen ears.

Dan nods calmly, as if Rachel's suggestion were perfectly rational; and if he had felt, when she first appeared, any discomfort because she hadn't recognized him, had clearly been expecting to see the Dan Cullinan he'd been thirty years ago instead of the heavier, bald man he'd become, the grandfather, if he'd felt the least twinge of regret that he hadn't had a chance to prepare in any way for the visit of this classmate from so long ago who is still so well turned out, that regret vanishes as if he'd dropped it into a box and shut the lid. "And what price did you think the land should bring?" he asks. He doesn't even try to resist the transformation that has occurred in his mind with Rachel's question. She has ceased to be an attractive woman he knew long ago who has begun to show a laudable responsibility to her difficult brother, and she has become instead a sly, shrewd, unwomanly figure who must be outguessed and outmaneuvered, despite the fact that the Orchards doesn't need and likely wouldn't use another fifteen acres of fallow land.

Julia offers Mary the coffeepot again. "I just wish I knew what it was that's so sad about it," she says. "There's no earthly reason for me to feel so blue about Rachel Wilcox coming back. She has every right."

Mary stirs her second cup of coffee. "Why is she here, though—I know. Seems like whatever needs to be looked into, she could have sent somebody."

Julia nods, but reluctantly. Mary has been more than ready to see Rachel Wilcox as an unpleasantness, but Mary didn't ride in the car with her. Didn't hear that oddly casual report of all those years, how she almost seemed as young and vulnerable as Rosie when she rushed past the whole story of her husband's illness, as if to prove it hadn't mattered. And it's not just that, that Rachel's younger and richer and more fashionable than Julia and Mary but already alone, a widow, childless. It's something else, more complicated, sadder. "It just makes you wonder," she compromises.

84

"All those years—she didn't seem too terribly concerned about him all those years she had something else to keep her occupied in the city," Mary says.

"She looks young."

"Yes. We'd look young, too, if we'd had somebody to do our housework and worry about the money and wash and set our hair every week for us. We should try it, Julia—the life of leisure!"

But Julia won't be joshed out of her blueness. "Maybe she blames us," she says, feeling her way along.

"For what, for heaven's sake?" Mary protests.

"Oh, for her mother, or her brother."

"Feathers," Mary says firmly. "We've taken better care of him than she has, and she knows it. Where does she think his tomato plants come from, and who does she think checks on him when he seems to be sick, who got the doctor for him that time he fell? Not her, that's for sure."

"That's true," Julia says. She touches her hair, as if counting the hairpins. "But there's something . . . just upsetting, I guess. I wonder what she's going to do about him."

"Maybe she's just come to have a look and then she'll go back where she belongs," Mary says.

"Maybe," Julia says.

"Or maybe," Mary says slyly, "maybe she's looking for another husband!"

The idea is so outrageous and it leaps so suddenly into the air over the kitchen table that it drives from Julia's throat a quick, harsh bark of laughter, which is half shame at being caught in the suspicion she had in the store. She pops her hand to her lips to catch it back, but too late, and Mary grins. For an instant, no more, the two friends meet each other's eyes in full shocked and delighted agreement before they give way to a fit of sharp, exhausting laughter at everything they've always thought, in private, of Rachel Wilcox and her peculiar old mother, who showed up in town one December in their childhood with her beautiful adolescent son and her beautiful little daughter and never in all their lives a hint of a husband. Julia and Mary cover their cheeks as they laugh through tightened throats at all the things no woman had ever hinted at all the years they were growing up, all the years when Rachel's mother was a pretty woman alone out there across the bridge, all the years when nobody married her; and their daughters, if they could hear, would be astounded that these good women could create such nasal laughing, such a wiping of the eyes as they finally subside into a last low pair of sniggers, before they sigh and are quiet again.

Dan doesn't say yes and he doesn't say no. He says, as he meant to at the beginning, before he even knew what her proposal was about, "Well, Rachel, I'll consider it."

She doesn't move to go. Dan moves his penholder an inch to the side, but he doesn't take the pen out. He nods firmly. "I will consider it."

Rachel smiles calmly, as if she believes he has something more to say.

The rain has lightened on the metal roof of the Orchards office. It is hardly enough to listen to in the thick silence of Rachel not moving and Dan not speaking. Dan runs his hand helplessly over the top of his head.

He sighs. He can't help it; the air is so heavy that breathing is an effort. But Rachel's smile brightens the least degree, an invitation he can feel, an opportunity grasped. "I will let you know," Dan says wearily, feeling defeat like a sodden weight in his gut, "in a day or two."

Rachel moves briskly now, makes her umbrella neat in her hand. "Shall I stop back?" She laughs a short, light, apologetic sound. "I'd call, but there doesn't seem to be a telephone at the house."

"I'll drop you a note," Dan says. He is angry and doesn't quite know why or with whom, but he knows he is still sitting; he knows he's not walking her to the damned door, that's for damned sure. No matter what price she offers to take for her worthless land.

Timer Darcy appears in the office doorway. They both turn to look at him as if they had half expected his interruption. He carries a clipboard stuffed with dog-eared order forms through which he is searching as he slowly enters the room. His head comes up sharply at their silence. He looks hard at Rachel, his eyes very blue in his sun-darkened face, then quickly over to Dan, who is scowling.

"Sorry, Dan—didn't know you were busy," Timer says. He lowers the clipboard, but there is no apology in his voice. "I can come back. I was just trying to figure out the timing for the October shipments."

"Really," Rachel says, rising, "I think we've covered every-thing—for now, at least. Please go right ahead." She smiles briefly at Timer, who is neither familiar nor interesting to her, and then she turns to extend her hand to Dan. "And thanks for your time, Dan—I do appreciate your seeing me, whatever you decide."

Dan, cornered by Timer's presence, stands and shakes her hand one quick stroke. "No trouble," he says evenly.

Timer steps aside to let her pass.

"It's been lovely seeing you again, after all this time," she says, turning her head with a last smile just at the door. "And I'll be hearing from you in a day or two."

Dan gapes for an instant at the audacity in her voice, what anybody'd take for flirtation, and then he nods, reaches toward Timer for the clipboard. "Yes," he says, either to Rachel or to the untidy pile of orders.

Then she is quite gone, and Dan has to pull his mind strongly to the dates and numbers on the papers to keep from feeling how baldly Timer is waiting for some comment about her, some explanation. Some boast.

Mary looks toward home as she opens her umbrella and takes the last step from Julia's porch. She's refreshed, after that long, hard laughter, just what she needed to get rid of the urgent feeling, almost of danger, that has kept cropping up since she realized that Rachel Wilcox had decided to come back to town for more than a weekend. She and Julia have talked now of sewing and suppers and Rosie's little boy, and Mary feels re-turned to the solidity of her real and present life. She looks toward home, but she is thinking about Graham Daniel Deery as a name, awfully long for such a little boy as Rosie's. She looks toward home, and sees Dinah.

The girl is standing on the porch, leaning out over the railing, which she holds with both hands near her sides, like hope. Her head is up; she is arched out almost into the rain, looking away from her mother toward the bridge end of town. What Mary sees is the taut line of the slender body yearning out of the porch dusk, and the purity of it strikes her as suddenly and completely as a forgotten scent. She stops for a full second, her hand still at the top latch of the umbrella, before she turns her head to see what Dinah is watching.

And sees a dark blue umbrella tilted slightly back above a swaying blue skirt and high-heeled shoes that can only be Rachel Wilcox on her way back home from somewhere she has been up River Street, well past Mary's house and Julia's. Nobody out that way except newcomers, the Blandell tribe, and the Orchards. Mary tries to feel suspicion lunge through her, or at least satisfaction—she and Julia were right, you can't trust that woman, no telling what she's up to. But Mary feels instead the dread she had thought the laughter and accusations had erased.

Her hand slides down the umbrella shaft slowly as she looks again, keenly, toward Dinah. Who slouches now, hip against the railing, biting at the skin around her thumbnail.

Mary is not quite even with the corner of the house when Dinah turns her head, so slowly that her glance falls behind her mother, and follows behind her until Mary stands beside the front door and sets the open umbrella down to dry.

"Leave that thumb alone," Mary says evenly. "It'll get infected."

Dinah takes her hand down from her mouth and looks with a martyr's face just past her mother's ear.

Mary shifts her jaw but keeps her voice level. "Use a bookmark. You'll break the spine if you leave the book laying like that."

She turns and goes into the dim house; as she steps into the kitchen and reaches for her apron, loss hovers over her upraised wrist for a long sad instant. She cannot remember the last time Dinah touched her. She shifts her jaw again, takes the apron briskly from its hook and snaps on the light. She pulls a cupboard door open with conviction, but it is the plate and bowl cupboard, and the blank dishes mock her. She slams the door shut and wipes her dry hands on her apron.

"Dinah," she calls, irritation in her voice at last. "Go down cellar and bring up some potatoes."

Dinah's sigh extends all the way from the porch through the dining room and into the kitchen.

"Now!" Mary snaps, and turns on the water hard.

Before he draws the bath, Dan fills the four-gallon bucket with hot water and sets it on the bathmat. Then he strips as the tub fills, and in the tub he washes slowly and steadily, soaping and rinsing from his head down, section by section. While the water drains from the tub he stands and pours the water from the bucket slowly over his head. Then he steps heavily out of the tub and dries himself from his head down, section by section, thoroughly.

In the bedroom he turns the fan to high and gets into bed beside Julia with a sigh. The light is already off, and for a few minutes he feels nothing but the relief of finally being cool and clean.

"I ran into Rachel Wilcox at the store today," Julia says into the darkness.

Hunh, Dan thinks.

"I gave her a lift back out to her house. It was raining."

"Rained hard," Dan says automatically.

Julia stirs under the sheet. "I guess she's come to take care of her brother," she says. "She seems worried about him."

Dan makes a sound just louder than a sigh. He's glad Julia's not a suspicious woman, but sometimes she's a little too innocent.

"Her husband died just a year ago, she told me. He was a lawyer." She lowers her voice. "Heart attack."

In the pause Dan waits. There is something in Julia's voice, some sorrowing, hinting tone, as if she's waiting for him to say something, to make some kind of offering.

"Sixty-two years old," she says, finally.

"Young," Dan agrees.

The fan roars in the window.

Julia sighs deeply. "I imagine it won't be easy for her, taking on her brother. She never had children."

Stone Orchards belongs to Julia, on paper, a legal fact that Dan is always aware of and has never mentioned. Nor has Julia, to his knowledge, which is accurate, though he cannot know that certainly. He waits.

"But of course," Julia continues, and he hears that sad urging in her voice again, "I suppose she has friends there, who can help her. After all these years. And good doctors and all. Maybe it would be good for him. Of course, they'll have to sell out here."

In the past twenty years Julia has never even asked in a general way how the business was going. Dan lies rigid with bewilderment; he feels sweat beginning to slick his armpits. Damn this town and its secret ways. He never noticed and can't remember: Was Rachel Wilcox some special friend of Julia's in school or something? What is it her voice is asking him to do?

"You know I saw him the other day crossing River Street in his bedroom slippers," she says.

"The man's crazy, Julia," Dan argues. *What the hell is going on,* he thinks.

"Oh but, Dan, he was always so fastidious," Julia says.

"Fastidious," Dan says bitterly.

Now Julia turns in bed, apologetic, a little surprised. "I just meant he seemed to be getting worse lately, you know. That's all. So maybe it *is* good that his sister's come back to look out for him."

I see, Dan thinks. And, *Why didn't you just say so.* He turns, too, away from his wife; he has nothing to say. She can talk all night if she wants to.

"I do wonder why he hasn't come into town since she got back, though," Julia says, more lightly.

"I imagine," Dan says after a heavy pause, "that she's taking care of all that."

Julia yawns. "It was odd seeing her, though. After all these years."

Dan waits. Then, "Goodnight," he says formally.

"Goodnight, Dan," she says, and he tightens his jaw, too angry to sleep now, at the lightness of her voice, the absence of either gratitude or apology. *She doesn't know a damn thing about those orchards,* he thinks. *And she wants another fifteen acres and a house for what?*

But tomorrow, in a fury still, he will write Rachel a note and offer her a fair price for the land; the note will say, however, unequivocally, that Stone Orchards does not want to buy the house. And Rachel will reply, as formally and unequivocally, that the house must be bought with the land. She is sure he will understand; she must dispose of the whole lot at once.

And Julia, when Dan reports this fact to her in his cool business voice, which she cannot remember his ever turning on her before, is astonished and cannot immediately resist the lurch of jealous suspicion that shakes her from her heart outward. By the next day, however, with the facility that has made her the easiest of wives, the least offensive of neighbors, the most delightful of daughters, she has transformed it all into solid outrage and resentment that Rachel Wilcox could deal so coldly with Dan, with the Orchards, with the town, and probably with her brother; only to Mary does she reveal anything else, the merest edge of her surprise and fear, but it is enough.

CHAPTER 9

*S*usan goes to the back door to call the boys in. She can hear rustling at the back of the dark yard, where she thinks they may be hiding or searching for night crawlers or lightning bugs. Earlier there was a game out front, in the Aldriches' side yard, but River Street is almost quiet now.

"Allen! Tony!" She waits. The rustling stops, starts again, no faster than before. She leans, patient and quietly amused, in the doorway. The screen door is a warm bitter smell in front of her. "Tony, Allen, time to come in now!" It seems long ago that her own mother used to call *Thomas, Susan, William* in long and longer syllables off a front porch.

Back where their yard joins the Deerys', a shape bigger than a boy moves, stops, and lumbers out from between the dusty lilacs: a cow, so surprising Susan cannot name it for several seconds. Casual, loose-jointed, it ambles down the middle of the yard a ways as Susan watches, grinning delight at its oddity and the excitement about to begin. The boys will love it! Then the cow stops, looks back over its shoulder, half turns, and heads more certainly for the garden.

Susan turns, too, but reluctantly, though her voice is appropriately urgent when she speaks into the house, through the kitchen and down the front hall to where Timer sits with the newspaper on the front steps. "Timer? There's a cow in our back yard!"

"A what?" he shouts, but he's up and halfway to the kitchen before he drops the paper. He pushes past her to stop in the open door and look. "Where did that come from?" he demands.

"I don't know," she apologizes, keeping her smile down. "I was just calling the boys—"

"Hey!" they hear. It is Nobel Aldrich out front. "Hey! Get out of there!"

Timer hurries back through the house, leaving Susan holding the screen open. The cow has its head down, but Susan can't quite make out whether it's eating anything or not. Then Timer is back, trailing voices from the front, and he pushes past her, down the steps and onto the grass. "Get out of there," he shouts at the cow. "Go on! Get!"

The cow raises its head to look calmly at Timer.

"There's another one in Aldrich's front yard," he says to Susan. "Go on!" he says to the cow, who still looks at him, patiently. He waves his arms at it. "Go on! Get out of my garden!"

From behind them, out on River Street, they hear more voices, Mary, Brian, the Stokes children, people laughing and shouting at the other cow, screen doors yawning and slapping. Allen comes running barefoot through the house. "Daddy! There's two *cows* out front, come on! Hey, Daddy?" He stops beside Susan. "Where's Daddy? There's this cow over by the Aldriches' porch and you should see Mr. Aldrich, Mommy!" She points. Timer is walking cautiously down the side of the yard to get between the cow and the lilacs. "Wow!" Allen says reverently. "Another one!" He turns and runs back to the front porch, shouting, "We got another one! Hey, there's another one in our back yard!"

Susan sees another shape coming through the lilacs. "Timer?" she says, too softly for him to hear, but then she sees that it's Arnie Deery. His voice comes oddly clear across the yard, despite the growing noise from the crowd out front.

"Got a visitor, Timer?" he says pleasantly.

Timer stands with his hands on his hips, watching the cow, who stands calmly just beside the garden, looking past the house toward River Street. "You know anything about cows?" Timer asks.

"They give milk," Arnie says.

"Right," Timer says. "How do I get it out of here without making it smash through the cucumbers?"

Arnie crosses his arms. "I don't know—it got here through my garden."

Timer looks over at him for the first time. "No kidding," he says sympathetically.

"Right through the tomatoes. Scared Rosie half to death."

"Where'd they *come* from?"

"They?" Arnie says.

"Two more out front."

Arnie snorts, then laughs ruefully. "Two more? Is that all, you think?"

"Susan?" A woman's voice from the front door. Susan steps back into the kitchen.

"Mary!" she says, surprised, and then not surprised, because a crisis like cows would bring Mary Aldrich into her house, of course, and it would take such a crisis, just because of Susan doesn't quite know what but accepts as age, the more than ten years between them. "What's going on out front?"

Mary comes down the hall, laughs. "A stampede, you'd think from the noise of it. You've got one out back?" Half shyly, Susan notices how wide and generous Mary's mouth is when she smiles that way.

"Yeah—Timer and Arnie are trying to figure out how to get it to go on out front, I think—so they can join the party, probably."

"Might as well—everybody else is there. I called Jack Haines, though, and he should be here soon."

"Oh, Haines—they're his cows?"

Mary laughs, the two women standing at the back door, watching Arnie and Timer swishing long lilac switches behind the cow, who ignores them. "Well, that was my guess, since they're closest. I spoke to his mother, though, and she didn't sound surprised."

Timer touches the cow's haunch gingerly with his switch, and the cow jumps a little, surprised.

"Why, *hit* her!" Mary calls. Susan is as startled as the men, and the cow makes to turn back toward the Deerys'. Arnie whips at the cow's broad face. "Lord!" Mary laughs, more quietly, to Susan alone, but without acknowledging the surprising loudness of her shout to the men. "Helpless, aren't they?"

But the cow has wheeled away from the men and trots briskly past the house and off toward the street, with Timer and Arnie behind her. The women hurry through the house and out onto the front porch.

In the street, Nobel Aldrich stands in his shirtsleeves, holding one heifer by a length of clothesline and directing the capture of the other with sober gestures of his free arm. The captured cow stands quietly, and Nobel seems to have nearly forgotten her. The other cow, Susan sees in the second she has before her own cow comes bursting out of the dark between houses and changes everything around, is trying steadily to escape from the shifting ring of men and boys that is closing in on her. She walks a few steps, then turns and bolts two or three strides and subsides when the men shout at her. The men laugh when she turns away from them. *Monkey in the middle,* Susan thinks.

But then, *"Look* out!" Timer shouts. Out comes the third cow. The ring breaks and scatters as Nobel's caught cow suddenly lurches and kicks out, pulls the short rope through Nobel's careless fingers and is free.

"Get her!" Nobel shouts, one arm still raised. "Grab that rope!"

By the time Jack Haines arrives half an hour later, even Jim Parsons is there, drawn up River Street by the carnival noise. Everybody on River Street and no small number from the avenues have come out to watch the three heifers standing restlessly between increasingly halfhearted attempts to escape from the circle of men. When Jack Haines pulls up with his big truck the boys cheer, the women move up onto their porches and call their children from the crowd. It's after ten, now, they say, enough of this foolishness. But the boys hang back, loiter on the broad roadside to watch Jack Haines with his rope halter and his berry pail of grain lead the first cow up the cleated wooden ramp and into the dark, resounding truck. To their immense disappointment, the other two follow.

"They look worn out, don't they?" Mary says, but Susan hears her from a porch away, where Mary now stands, as is more usual and appropriate, on Julia's front porch, not Susan's. There's a certain relief to having her at a distance, Susan realizes, but not without a real swoop of disappointment.

And then it's over. The children go in, the adults drift back to their own porches, the truck pulls away. Susan tells her boys to wash their feet before they get into bed, and then she goes back out to sit on the porch and wait for Timer. Like everyone else, Susan feels calmed and satisfied; they have all had an adventure. She slips off her shoes as she sits back in the rocker, in the comfortable light breeze, in the quiet of Timer and Arnie and Nobel still standing at the foot of Aldrich's steps, talking. After a few minutes, the men laugh quietly. Nobel grasps Arnie's shoulder briefly; Susan guesses they have been talking about Arnie's new baby, in that half joking, half competing way fathers have. Then they say goodnights, their voices fuller; Nobel goes up his steps and in, Timer and Arnie come slowly along in the dark. Now they are talking work, she can tell, and she thinks, without rancor, because of the depth of her satisfied feeling, that she may as well go on up to bed: Timer won't be coming to sit with her on the porch tonight, it looks like, and the mosquitoes are beginning to come up from the river.

Timer shakes his head. "No, I didn't even know about it."

"About fifteen acres, I think," Arnie says. "And the house. She won't let the land go without the house."

Timer looks off toward the river. "Seems like there's already enough unworked acreage in the Orchards."

Arnie straightens up, shakes his head more decidedly. "Funny he wouldn't want it more than that, though. It's a good house, isn't it?"

Timer shifts, glances at the house, and Susan feels him see her. "Well, maybe he's leaving it for somebody who needs it more. His business, I guess. Or maybe she wants too much."

"I guess Rosie's mother's a little put out he made an offer at all."

Timer laughs, brittle and warning, reaches out to slap Arnie's shoulder. "Women!" he says. "Who knows what they think? Anyway, she'll be taking him off pretty soon whether she sells or not, right?"

Even through the dark Susan knows the falsely rueful face Arnie puts on because he has understood that she is there and listening. "Yeah, I guess so," he says. "Not likely she's going to stay here."

"Not likely," Timer agrees.

"Well, it'll keep him off the streets," Arnie says, chuckling. "Street'll be safe as a tomb—no lunatics and no cattle."

Still, Susan waits until Timer walks by the house with Arnie, into the back yard to see him off through the lilacs, and probably to say more she will not hear, does not really care to hear, before she goes in for the night, her easy comfort, her pleasure in the cows, wrenched away.

And tonight, very late and again very early, Susan will wake into the silence of River Street.

Ellen Parsons has come to Amos's store for a tablet of unlined linen-weave notepaper, which is on the rack with the school supplies near the meat counter. The walk up was hot this bright morning, so she's lingering in the dimness of the cool store, reading the verses on the greeting cards. She's only twenty-six, but long ago she accepted that she was not a person who chatted easily, and she gave up trying. She does her duties formally: the visiting, the women's sewing society, choir. In the five years she's been the minister's wife here, people have gradually stopped expecting her to pass the time of day, and now after just "Hello," Amos goes on with his inventory at the counter as if he were alone.

Susan Darcy comes in; Amos has the door propped open, so the first Ellen knows of her entrance is his voice: "Susan," he says cheerfully.

"Morning, Amos—hot out there today."

"Mmm," he says, the sound of papers folded aside. "Good day for lemonade in the shade."

Susan laughs. "Why? You got lemons on sale?"

Ellen stays where she is, uncertain as always when she is away from home without Jim. Susan, with that easiness about her that is almost carelessness, is a particularly difficult case for Ellen. Ellen knows, knew from the time Jim took this church, that the minister's wife is expected to pass judgments, or seem to pass or hold them, or at least to hold opinions that Ellen herself has no solid sense of. So how is she to act with Susan Darcy, who has two children but still wears her hair in a teen-ager's ponytail tied with a scarf? Who lounges against the counter talking to Amos Brown? Susan comes to church in spurts but never to Dorcas Society, and Ellen has never seen her carry a purse or wear a hat. Should Mrs. Parsons approach and speak, seeming perhaps to be interrupting intentionally what might appear to be a flirtation (for Ellen knows how the other women chat with Amos, never with a hip half hiked onto the counter)? Silently leave her money and take her tablet, seeming eager to avoid either Susan herself or the flirtation, whether or not the flirtation exists? Or remain unobtrusive, here behind the card rack, and seem to be spying? Anyone coming in would make Ellen worry in some of these ways, but with Susan—Ellen quietly (but not silently) replaces the *Congratula-tions, Graduate* card in the rack, takes up a *Belated Birthday Wishes* with a pitcher of yellow chrysanthemums on it, and pretends she has felt no thrusting dip of something like lust as a vision of Susan Darcy smiling a casual intimacy to Amos Brown in the masculine brown light of the apartment upstairs, which Ellen has never seen, passes across her imagination.

"Matter of fact," Amos says, and both of them laugh. "So how is everything? Timer?"

"Hot. He's fine. What's good for dinner?" Susan says.

"Let's see," Amos says. "Chicken?"

Susan doesn't say anything, but whatever she has done makes Amos chuckle.

"Well, how about cold cuts?" he offers.

"Better," she says. "You have any ham? I could have cold ham and some macaroni salad."

"Sorry, not until Thursday—sold the last of my ham to Mrs. Cavanaugh."

"Well!" Susan mocks a huff. "That woman *keeps* beating me to my supper—Friday she took the last roasting chicken, too."

"Have to look sharp to beat her, that's true."

"Not for long, though, I hear—she's put the place up for sale."

"For sale?"

"So I hear. Going to sell out and take her brother to the city."

"Taking Jacob to live with her in the city? *That's* brave."

"Live with her or put him away—who knows?"

"Oh, I don't think she'd do that. She seems to have his best interests in mind. But I didn't know she meant to sell out."

"Well," Susan laughs, "whatever she does, I won't have to race her to dinner anymore."

Amos laughs too, a little uneasy. "And meanwhile?" he says. "Some bologna, madam?"

"Bologna it is, sir!"

Susan comes by the card rack, following Amos back to the meat case. "Oh, hello, Ellen," she says in the most ordinary and unstartled voice. "I didn't know you were here."

The rain returns after lunch, the last rain this town will see for a week, though the thunder will keep grumbling. Mary Aldrich brings all her ferns out onto the porch for a good misting and sets them along the porch railing, one by one, carefully. *I hope Nobel took his umbrella,* she thinks, and looks over the Boston fern toward the post office, just as Rachel comes out the propped-open door, opens her umbrella, and walks up River Street toward Mary's house. This is the third time Mary has glimpsed her since her return, almost three weeks, in which Mary has deliberately found no opportunity for renewing their old acquaintance, elaborately avoiding even the chance for a casual recognition, a nod. Mary has preferred to consider Rachel temporary, which is accurate, and to assume that the whole flippity-flap over what she's going to do or not going to do with her brother or her house will fade off without effect. And if she does take her brother away—well, it had to happen sooner or later. Now Mary's first thought is *High heels!* in amused scorn, but then there is something in the near slouch of Rachel's shoulders that makes Mary catch her breath and step back. She stands deep in the shadow of the porch and watches Rachel come up the street, watches her shoulders move as she walks, watches the slightly turned wrist of the hand that holds the umbrella, watches (holding her breath, wishing she had already gone back inside) as Rachel comes even with the porch and her profile appears for an instant before she's gone by, hidden by the umbrella and unaware of Mary.

Mary stares for a moment at the rain dripping off the porch roof of the Neadoms' house and then forces herself to step forward and look after Rachel. Even her ankles, Mary believes, are the same, the strong tendon and the prominent, delicately pointed bones: Dinah's, exactly. Mary holds her practical self steady against a sweep of sweet memory and shame. But she lets herself go no further. She does not think, *Now everyone will see and know, now Nobel will be ashamed, now I will be revealed and cast away as a woman of the ditches.* She doesn't think, even, of her father's thwarted hope to make Rachel her sister by marriage, and that a song in the night fifteen years ago seems by the evidence of the flesh to have accomplished what he could not. Especially, she does not think of the song or of the night. She holds herself steady as the dripping rain.

Dinah comes out onto the porch, reading as she walks. Mary turns slowly, and watches the girl step, vaguely feeling for the chair.

"Look where you're going," Mary says.

"Mm." Dinah finds the chair and sits down without taking her eyes from her book.

The similarity is not so strong, maybe. *My hair,* Mary thinks in sudden fierceness. *And my eyes, my father's eyes.* As if the question lay between herself and Rachel.

Dinah looks up. "Huh?" she says.

Dan locks up the office and goes out onto the gravel.

" 'Night, Dan," Timer says, startling him.

" 'Night," he replies. He watches Timer walk off toward town, the springy walk of the high school athlete still faintly discernible despite the black lunch box of husband and father.

Dan likes his son-in-law, Arnie, but the boy sells insurance for a living. Timer would have been more like it, somehow.

Dan gets into his car, slides his own lunch box across the seat, and starts the excellent motor. He sits for a minute just listening to it, watching pointlessly the shimmer of heat off the roof of the office. "Might as well take a look," he says, and puts the car in reverse.

He heads away from town and home, along the west side of the orchard and then over across the south boundary, and then turns onto Town Line Road, which runs along the east edge, until Orchards land stops and Wilcox land begins. He turns down Bridge Road and slows only slightly, as he passes the privet stand and the realtor's "For Sale" sign that has appeared on the edge of the road, before he shifts down into second to cruise across the bridge and then up into the village and home. "Shame," he states, just before he turns the ignition off. Since nobody's there to ask, he doesn't have to refine his comment.

But after supper, after Julia has run over to see Rosie and the baby, he cleans up almost as if he were going calling, and he walks out that way again; by some kind of instinct he follows the unmarked cross-lot path to end up standing in the gloom of the hedge, watching Jacob sit straight and calm and alone as the cicadas begin and darkness spreads from shadows to fill the night.

Ellen is so pleased with her idea she can hardly resist waking Jim and telling him. The solution is so very simple! Mrs. Cavanaugh should be made to feel welcome here. And then no one from some city or something will be buying the property and moving in, and there will be no worry about what's to become of poor Mr. Wilcox, and the town would certainly be gaining a very worthwhile citizen. Jim should call on her, of course; Ellen will do her part as well. And then there will be no problem. And Ellen doesn't worry herself about why the idea of Jacob Wilcox swept suddenly out of town disturbed her so much that she's spent the whole evening trying to imagine some way to prevent it. She is so pleased with her plan, it seems so simple and inevitable a series of events, that she doesn't wake at all until morning, and doesn't hear the ringing silence of River Street, one more night in a row.

So the rumors flit out along River Street and up and down the avenues, even out among the farms. Women who have no particular old grudge still feel their sleep is too simple now, their homes too quiet, and when their small restlessness arises, the tale of the city sister selling out mad Jacob's house from under him gives them a person to blame, and they too look pointedly away from Rachel as they drive past her on her daily walks to and from the village. Rosie's friends, women too young yet to fear the effects of Rachel's city smoothness on their men, too young even to have heard Jacob's singing, please themselves with their loyalty to the Cullinans by icily nodding in response to Rachel's least and most ordinary civilities in the post office, in the store. In houses on Spare Avenue and over on Whistle Street, where the grownups take no care of what they say in front of the children, the rumors swell rank and idle in the heat until the little girls stare unabashed at Rachel walking and run giggling and flushed away when she smiles or nods; their brothers, deep and vicious in their own summer fantasies and violences, sneer almost openly at her clothes and body, and in a week, two weeks, it all begins to touch her. One night she wonders, looking at the little tray of bobby pins, if she really must do her hair every night. One morning she looks into the mirror and wonders if she really must do her face, just for the walk to the post office. She is aware now, every day, that this is the country deep in the summer, that her own mother, carefully elegant as she was, would disapprove, call ostentation, Rachel's hairspray and lacquered fingernails. Every day Rachel feels the temptation to submit, and every day she resists, sprays her perfume emphatically at the base of her throat just before she goes down the stairs.

CHAPTER 10

Three times now, since that first time, Dinah has been at Amos's or at the post office when Rachel comes in, and she watches for her all the time: to Dinah Rachel always appears as anonymous and romantic as something in an old book, and she is always half disappointed, half thrilled to see again that she is real and present. Dinah has mentioned her to no one. She lives in such a thick wrapping of boredom and imagination this summer that she has almost forgotten she can speak, hardly notices what she hears. Her mother says she is lazy and ill-tempered. Dinah sleeps late and then lounges languid through the day, impatient of interruption. Dinah hunches on the porch chair, staring, dreaming:

At twenty, Dinah Aldrich returns here, briefly but kindly, from her life as a great equestrienne in England. She passes an old woman outside the post office (an old woman delicate and silver), who stops and calls after her: "Aren't you Dinah? Yes, of course. I remember when you were hardly more than a girl, and already you had this beauty, this elegance." Dinah will pause, patience will be her gracious habit, and the woman will smile, ruefully but with a reasonable pride. "You don't remember me, do you? I'm Rachel Cavanaugh. I came back when you were still very young, of course you wouldn't remember. But I do—how you used to be, even then, the loveliest of all the girls, there in Brown's store, a dark pearl you were."

Or sooner even, at high school graduation, a gift left mysteriously for Dinah by the front door; sometimes it is an elaborate old necklace, or a wrought-gold bracelet, or a gown so classic and diaphanous that even folded it takes the breath away from Janet or Dinah's mother or the young man (who often has appeared from no known place to woo or claim Dinah Aldrich as his own) who stands beside her as she opens the glossy white box and folds back the wealth of tissue paper.

Sometimes it is simply a check in a heavy envelope, but always the note is there: "I hope you will not mind accepting this small gift of congratulations. From the first, you have reminded me of myself as a young woman, for you are full of hope and talent, though your beauty is greater than mine. Take this, then, and may it help you achieve all the great dreams I know you must have." And the signature, florid sometimes, sometimes angular and restrained: "Rachel Cavanaugh."

Sometimes it comes even sooner, a note on the same heavy, soft paper, but any day, soon, asking her to call at the old Wilcox house. Demurely, she goes, and Mrs. Cavanaugh explains: the son of a dear friend, arriving for some reason, needing young companions, Dinah clearly the only appropriate friend, would she mind; and then with such sensitivity offering a little help with matters of clothing, a slight assistance with makeup, if she twisted her hair so, and by then laughter between them, delight as Dinah's true beauty emerges, and at that moment, into the elegant dark old parlor brightened by the easy affection between the older woman and the innocent but dramatically beautiful girl, the young man steps. He is perfect, of course, and utterly under her spell; he hangs about at every opportunity for several years while Dinah and Rachel talk together and laugh, and while he is absent they plan the gowns, the dates, the wedding, and even after, Dinah comes often to Rachel to confide, ask advice. Then their first child is a daughter, brought to Rachel for blessing, and

Rachel, strong but deeply touched, holds the infant and lets the proud tears fall, grateful.

So Dinah is lazy and ill-tempered, she won't answer when spoken to, she's sloppy about her few chores, she spends too much time in her room (for the first time, however, and Mary notices it and is suspicious and confused, Dinah's room is spotless, Spartan, for instead of a message Rachel might come herself). She spends too much time admiring herself in the bathroom mirror (long baths, so hot they leave the tiny room wilting from the steam for hours after she finally forces herself out and into her room, where she lies drained and floating on the cool sheets), and won't even be polite to her own friends.

(Janet Tolli comes up and knocks on Dinah's door, which is always locked now, despite her mother's warnings about what if there were a fire, for heaven's sake, and Nobel's mild jokes about hidden treasure.

Who is it?

Janet. Let me in, Di.

Okay. Just a minute. Shorts pulled on, jersey pulled on.

Are you sick or something.

No.

Listen, I've got an idea.

Yeah.

No, listen. We need money for school clothes, right? And so we need a job, and I thought we could go around and ask if people need odd jobs done or something. Poor plump Janet's voice fading already.

Like what? We can't do anything.

We could—we could wash windows or trim grass or do housecleaning.

Nobody wants to pay us to do that stuff, Janet. Nobody around here is rich.

Well,

and Dinah hears it, desire, in stupid Janet's stupid mincing voice

Well, Mrs. Cavanaugh might need some help out there.

And Dinah can't help it, she looks Janet full in the face and takes in with a sudden nausea the helpless look in the girl's face.

Dinah whispers, *You're disgusting.*

Janet doesn't come back again, and even two years later, in high school in Livingstone, she pretends she hardly knows Dinah Aldrich, and always laughs loudest with her friends when Dinah comes down the hall or into the lunchroom.)

So after weeks of her mother's badgering her (about half-dirty drinking glasses in the cupboard, about the state of her hair, about her boyish clothes, for Dinah has given up dresses as well as eyeliner, keeping herself scrubbed and simple, about her attitude, manners, posture, library books, all and none of which Dinah hears), Dinah makes a change. After her late breakfast, she packs a lunch and goes to the riverbank, where she sits awhile, hidden from the road by the willows. She wades awhile on the round mossed pebbles of the riverbed, suns herself for awhile on an uncomfortable rock midstream, and settles at last, just in time, on a narrow stretch of cool moss, surrounded by shrubby weeds, flat on her back, distracted from her fantasies only by the water's low sound, the murmurings of the willows, and the attentions of myriad insects. It is almost like waking when she hears the sound of someone walking over the bridge. She pretends, deliciously, that it might be Mrs. Cavanaugh, or the son of the dear friend. Then, realistic and cautious, she opens her eyes and raises up on one elbow to see if she can see who it really is.

The high-heeled sling-back shoes and the wide border-print skirt can be nobody else, and Dinah hardly breathes.

By the time she goes to bed tonight her fantasies have undergone a change of time and scene, become Rachel injured crossing the bridge, saved by Dinah; Rachel shouting *Fire!* and Dinah racing like a thoroughbred for help; Rachel pausing on the bridge, then deciding, quick graceful removing of the fine shoes, Rachel calm and strong walking down the bank to discover Dinah. *I thought I might find you here. May I join you?*

The next day she is ready and waiting under the bridge by the time Tony Darcy is firmly wedged into the hedge, ten o'clock, no later. Boys don't come to watch for Jacob anymore, because Jacob is almost invisible now; they aren't even quite sure he used to come shouting through town the way they think they used to see him. But Tony comes here just at this time every day, and he doesn't tell even Allen, who fishes all the time now with Chris and doesn't ever want Tony to come along. He crouches farther back along the hedge, where he can see the woman when she comes out the back door.

She always wears a dress with a particular kind of pictures around the bottom of it. Tony's favorite, he supposes, is the blue skirt with the prancing horses all brown and black around the bottom, but there's another one (she's not wearing it today, today it's a yellow skirt with ballerinas around the bottom) he might like better if he could get a closer look at it: it seems to be scenes, like paintings of a story or something, a fairy tale or a Robin Hood kind of story, and the skirt is dark green.

Sometimes she stands there outside the door a minute with her head bent down and she lifts the hair up off her neck. Sometimes she takes a big straw hat from a nail by the door and ties it on her head with a scarf.

But always Tony can see her ankles and the delicate shoes she wears, and almost always he can smell her perfume.

Today, for the first time, he dares himself: he waits for a count of twenty after she has walked off down Bridge Road toward town, and then he stands up and pushes through the hedge to stand in the road and watch her ankles twinkle as she walks away. She doesn't know about him at all; he's an invisible boy, and she is a queen with enchanted candy hidden in her white purse.

But Dan beat both of them by more than an hour. It was Dan who stood in the damp of early morning and saw Jacob emerge from the door of the drying shed as graceful and absorbed as if he were floating, who saw Jacob approach the back door of the house and then stop and stand, unmoving, for a long, long moment, and then go and sit, as if waiting for someone, in the straight chair that sits beside the scarred table. It was Dan who watched and whose heart was oddly twisted with something we have no other word for than longing, unless it is love.

107

CHAPTER 11

*L*ike the first two, the third case comes into Amos's arms a little too fast and a little too hard, and he has to step back to catch his balance.

"Easy on that," he says to the kid in the back of the truck. But the kid has already swung around to grab the next mixed case of canned goods (all Amos's cases are mixed except the soups, and so all Amos's cases shift and lurch when he catches them) to hand down, and the truck's motor (no need to shut it off for such a quick stop, ten cases) is loud. Amos slides the third case hurriedly on top of the first two and tries to brace himself for the fourth. But the kid's in too much of a hurry: Amos catches the heavy end of the box and the light end catches him in the soft flesh between his shoulder and chest.

"Watch it!" he barks.

This time the kid hears, looks out of the truck's dark cavern, blinks. "Sorry, Pop," he says.

Amos blows out his breath and wipes his hands down his apron. The next three cases come into his arms as gentle as sleeping babies, embarrassingly easy, before the kid hits his rhythm again and starts dropping them hard and automatic.

Amos keeps up, and says nothing; he signs the slip the kid pulls out of his pocket, and turns deliberately away to miss having to return the kid's he-man wave out the cab window as he guns the big truck and drives off.

Which leaves Amos standing with his ten mixed cases piled up beside the silence of River Street at seven-thirty on Thursday morning in the promise of another day of real heat. He rubs just inside his shoulder bitterly. If he'd turn around, he'd see the fog as thick as cotton over the river's willows, and in just a few seconds he'd see Dinah Aldrich, as silent and graceful as a faun, slip out of a back yard and disappear into the mist, and he'd see the beauty and mystery of it, put the kid in the truck where he belongs, far off, not part of his world.

Instead, he rolls his left shirtsleeve down to loosen it, and pulls the open sleeve up almost to his shoulder so he can examine the inside of his arm for bruises.

A crow calls, taunting. Amos adjusts his sleeve busily, runs his hand over his head to smooth the thin hair that's so easily disturbed, and he winces with the movement. He lifts the first case and carries it inside, down the left aisle, past the chips and the soda machine, past the card rack and the meat case, into the back room. By the sixth trip he's puffing and sweaty. He drops the case, loud, in front of the shelves and without pausing goes back out for the next one.

"Pop," he sneers, kicking the last case into place in the dark back room. But by now he's so worn out his sneer sounds, even to him in this solitude, more like a plea than a sneer. It humbles him, his voice does, and he sits down on an uneven case of tomato and orange juice cans. In a few minutes, he has caught his breath, his muscles have stopped feeling shaky, he's ready to get on with the day's work, but it's a few minutes more before he submits to his own insistence that it's got to be done. He sighs and gets up, feels in his pocket under the apron for the copy of the order, and starts checking the cases against the typed list.

Rachel's coming down River Street as he goes up front to the counter, the week's inventory stowed properly in the back, and he has a vague feeling of being rightfully exposed. He hardly notices that her approach is nearly as forlorn as his own gait; he just goes and stands behind the counter, feeling ready and fit only to ring up the groceries of children and women who never spend ten dollars at a time, and no reason why they should, here. He can't remember the last time a grown man came in. He spreads the folded order sheet out on the counter, and smooths its wrinkles.

Rachel comes in and pauses. She exhales as if she's been holding her breath. "Well," she says, and reaches into the pocket of her skirt almost shyly.

Amos watches with an odd expectation, as if she might have a gift for him, but of course it is only a bit of paper that she pulls out, her little list. His gaze drops to the floor, and he sees why she looks so small: she's wearing cloth shoes, not her usual high heels. When he looks up, she's looking at her shoes too, as if she were as surprised at them as he is, interested.

"So what do we need this morning," he says gently.

Someone comes up to the open door, hurried steps on the wooden porch, and Amos looks over to see Julia, flushed as always and about to speak. But Julia stops in the doorway, blocking the low bar of sunlight that lies like a chalk line from the doorsill to Rachel's blue shoes. Julia makes a sound like a hiss as her teeth and then her lips close down over whatever she was about to say. She turns and hurries back toward her house.

Must have forgotten something, Amos thinks, as Rachel speaks, her voice suddenly clear and formal.

"I believe you expected to receive tins of cling peaches this morning?"

"Not on the shelf yet, but I can bring them out—how many did you want?"

"Two, please." She lifts her list high to consult it for the next item, her neck tense, but her voice stays cool. "And were you able to order more roasting chickens?"

He catches himself quickly, turns his eyes away from the bright red flush that has risen from her throat to the tops of her cheeks, leaving her forehead and eyes peculiarly visible. "Not until this afternoon," he says.

She nods stiffly. "The rest I believe I can find," she says. "I'll get those peaches," he says.

From the back room he can see her moving quietly from shelf to counter. The softness of her shoes, the stillness of her face, make her seem like a dream, or like someone he's watching secretly through glass. When she stops at the counter again, finished, he comes out, down the aisle toward her. He scowls a little at the dust that sparkles in the vacant block of bright sunshine that is the doorway.

"Another hot one," he says carefully as he begins to add up the prices.

"Yes," she says.

He looks at her now with the scowl he had for the shimmering dust motes. There's a tense smile on her face, and in the bright sunshine he can see the threads of gray in her dark hair and the fine lines around her eyes. She's looking just away from his eyes. In a flush of warmth and understanding, Amos recognizes in her pretty eyes that caught look the littlest girls get when they've been sent for a bottle of vanilla and he has no vanilla. He spreads his hand over the broad top of the can of peaches, and he pauses: there is nothing he can say to comfort her, but his voice is ready, low and sympathetic, he can feel it in his throat. So he hums a tuneless murmur as he nods, and then begins to write down the prices.

She inhales deeply, and Amos is touched again by the tremor of her breath, the softening of her face, even before she brightens her smile and meets his eyes. "You know, I think I need a few more things—some cleaning supplies."

He is delighted beyond reason, as if this were proof she could stick it out, clean house, and stay. "All righty," he says. "You name it!"

Together they bring more to the counter: a string mophead, wax remover, scouring powder, sponges, oil soap, ammonia. Lemon oil, steel wool, floor wax, chamois cloth. A stiff brush, oven cleaner. Silver polish. The whole front half of the store is sunny when they finish and come to stand opposite one another with the crowded counter between.

"There!" Rachel says.

111

Amos beams, nods, pulls a flat paper bag from under the counter and his pencil from beside the cash register, begins an orderly file of figures. As he marks down the prices, he stops now and then to pack things into a large bag. When it is full, the fresh celery and the string mop showing at the top, Rachel says, "I *have* overdone, haven't I?" and her voice is absolutely back to brisk normal.

But Amos sees the problem. How will she carry all of it home? And he won't close for hours and hours, though the thought of meeting her at her kitchen door swells warm.

On goes the column of figures, in go the bottles and boxes, and a total is reached, two bags full. She smiles and lays her checkbook on the counter between the two bags, bends her head and writes. A shadow passes through their sunlight: Rachel pauses, Amos turns, defensive, to see Dinah Aldrich going slowly, lingeringly, by.

"Well," Amos says in low approval, and then, calling, "Dinah?"

The girl stops just past the doorway, turns, comes back, the sun bright behind and around her.

"Huh?"

Amos, jovial, "Pardon me, but are you very late for an important date?"

The girl blushes and Amos is sorry. She shakes her head, stares at the floor. Amos goes on more quietly, more seriously. "We've got a little problem here I thought you might give us a hand—see, Mrs. Cavanaugh needs a little help getting her groceries home."

The girl stands stiller than ever in the sunlight. Rachel finishes writing her check and the sound of the paper tearing along the perforation is soft and definite in the quiet.

"If you had a few minutes and could carry one of the bags, I'd be very grateful," she says, her voice careful, almost neutral.

"Sure," Dinah says. "I can." She clears her throat and comes, barefoot, to the counter, her arms close to her sides.

"Well, there we are," Amos says to Rachel, glad to think that he's solved a problem for her.

Rachel doesn't actually lean toward him, but he feels it in her

112

voice. "Thank you," she says: very definitely, he thinks, a new tone of voice.

The girl picks up one of the bags almost violently and walks out into the sun with it in front of her. Rachel smiles, picks up the other and rests it on her hip. The pair of them are good to look at, walking away in the still-early sunshine. They're about the same height, which makes Amos think the girl's growing fast and Rachel isn't as tall as he'd thought, without her high-heeled shoes.

One step out of Amos's store and Dinah just knows her mother must be standing on their front porch; any second she'll yell something awful. Dinah can feel it. Her back prickles and heat rises from her shirtfront. She holds the bag tighter and shuts her eyes, but her feet keep on walking. The dirt is soft and dusty and already warm.

She opens her eyes. In front of her Mrs. Cavanaugh's skirt hangs and swings in perfect wide pleats. Dinah follows her, past the empty brown house, past the post office where her father never looks out, past Mrs. Phoebe's house, finally into and then around the bend toward the church and the Parsonses' house, and Dinah's mother fades out of the world. Mrs. Cavanaugh glances back over her shoulder and Dinah smiles weakly, as if she's been caught at something. But Mrs. Cavanaugh smiles, too. In a way.

Something in the bag is poking Dinah's forearm. She moves her arm up a little to get away from it, and something else in the bag shifts. The sound and feel of it sends a swift panic through Dinah's throat and arms, as if she'd almost dropped the bag, and she clutches it and almost lurches in something like vertigo. Mrs. Cavanaugh glances back again and Dinah just stares.

Then they are past the church, going down to the bridge. Very carefully, Dinah works her arms around the bag more comfortably. The dust changes to dirt here and then, soon, to a coarser dirt that becomes stones. If Dinah were alone, she'd move off the dirt here onto the pavement and save her feet, but she's following Mrs. Cavanaugh, who walks very precisely just off the pavement in blue cloth shoes that look like they came from a foreign country. Dinah loses herself in the shoes as they cross the bridge and start up the rise. Everything in the world is quiet and blue and textured. Even the sourish smell of the brown paper bag has a woven feel to it, crossed by the celery tops and the warm smell of river rocks in the sun. This side of the bridge, the stone is gravel sharp. Dinah moves into the short weeds without thinking. She has almost forgotten that Mrs. Cavanaugh has a face, she's been seeing her skirt and shoes so long. She's almost forgotten that they are going anywhere. The weeds brush her ankles and calves in a pleasant dry way, and she begins, almost unconsciously, to try to walk with the swing of Mrs. Cavanaugh's pleats.

When they enter the shadow of the house, Dinah looks up as alertly as if she had just startled awake. She remembers crazy old Jacob Wilcox with a chill, and looks down again, follows Mrs. Cavanaugh's blue heels until they stop.

Over the rustling of the paper bag and a rusty sound of old screen spring, Mrs. Cavanaugh says, "Well, here we are," and Dinah obediently enters the door that is held open for her. The kitchen floor is smooth and cold under her feet. "You can just set that there on the table, Dinah." The table is a small white rectangle, and it rings metallic as Dinah sets the bag on it. One corner has a black oval chip in it. Dinah tries to be thrilled that Mrs. Cavanaugh knows her name, but she is only surprised, as she is surprised at the kitchen. She takes a quick guilty look around: a kitchen. Smaller, cooler than her mother's, but with the same kind of towel hung as limply through a drawer handle, counters bare, a yellow-petaled daisy clock with its cord running at a wrinkled angle to the outlet. Mrs. Cavanaugh sets her bag beside Dinah's on the table.

"There!" she says, nudging Dinah's bag a little to make room. "Well. Thank you so much, Dinah. I certainly could never have carried all that alone."

Dinah nods, her hands helplessly empty and foolish now. *Of course, this would have been part of the servants' quarters* runs through her mind like a speech from a book.

"Now—well, let's see. Would you like a glass of lemonade? Are you thirsty?" Mrs. Cavanaugh opens the refrigerator.

"Oh, that's okay," Dinah says, uncertain which question she's answering.

Mrs. Cavanaugh shuts the refrigerator and turns to Dinah. "All right," she says seriously, as if they are about to have a talk.

Dinah looks down at the yellow and white squares of the floor. She swallows, desperately thirsty. "Just water would be fine," she says.

Mrs. Cavanaugh takes a glass from the cupboard over the sink and runs water for a few seconds. *Originally, of course, this would have been.* She fills the glass and hands it to Dinah.

The glass has yellow daisies on the side.

Dinah drinks half the water before she raises her eyes apologetically. But Mrs. Cavanaugh isn't looking at her. She's looking at the bags on the table.

"Dinah," she says slowly, "would you be interested in working with me for a few hours tomorrow? And Monday?"

Dinah shrugs, out of habit. "Sure," she says.

Mrs. Cavanaugh makes a half-laughing sound and flips her hand at the bags. "I've got a bit of cleaning lined up." She smiles at Dinah. "I could use the help if you've got some free time."

Dinah shrugs again, but only one shoulder, and she can't help it: she grins back. "Sure," she says. "I can."

"Maybe around one?"

"Okay."

Mrs. Cavanaugh looks back at the bags and shakes her head as if something in them were comical. Dinah looks past the bags into the dim hallway. *Of course, this area would originally have been.*

By the time she reaches the bridge again, the hallway has doubled in length and the glimpse of carpet has grown thick and richly glowing. She and Mrs. Cavanaugh will remove the priceless vases from their carven niches, bathe them gently in huge basins, and dry them with soft cloths, restoring their luster. They will polish brass andirons and great silver candelabra and aged mahogany panels: the house will glow, and the light from the fire in the massive marble-manteled fireplace will illuminate

Dinah's face. She will raise her eyes innocently from the delicate lace she is mending, and Mrs. Cavanaugh will be smiling. *Dinah,* she will say; and all the while Dinah searches through her bureau drawers and then through her brother's for a kerchief to wear tied over her hair tomorrow, all the afternoon while she sits sullen-faced on the porch, Dinah is trying to find the words Mrs. Cavanaugh will use to describe how beautiful Dinah is, how perfectly she fits in the midst of the reemerging splendor of the family home.

Nobel runs cold water at the kitchen sink, rinses his coffee cup, then fills it with water and drinks. Dinah reaches in front of him for the hot water faucet, to begin filling the dishpan.

"Big hurry?" he asks.

"Third Thursday," she complains, and her voice is just barely like Mary's. He hasn't noticed that before, along with all the other ways she's so suddenly turning into a physical woman this long summer.

"Where's Brian?" he asks.

"How should I know?" she says.

In spite of the sullen edge in her voice, he feels a sudden sympathy for her, that she has Brian instead of a sister, that she will have to stand here in the supper-heated kitchen and do the washing up, that her shoulders are still so thin.

"Third Thursday," he says, and she smiles at him suddenly, conspiratorial. Every third Thursday is Dorcas Society, the women's service group of the church, and they meet here summers, for reasons that seem to have been forgotten, sending Nobel and the children free into the summer evenings after the required greetings. "Guess I'll weed for a while," he says, "after they get going. How about you?"

She shrugs.

"Better get a wiggle on with those dishes," he says, pretending that he's not still in her way.

"Daddy!" she protests, but in fun too; still, it's true—her voice is more and more like Mary's, and there won't be many more chances for teasing fun, he knows. Already she's so distant, and he knows how completely he seems to have lost touch with Brian this past year or two. As if Brian had never been his son. And now Dinah will go off, too. He pats her shoulder more tenderly than he'd meant to and goes into the living room to tell Mary where he'll be. She's not there, but he hears her on the phone in the front hall, and waits.

"I sincerely doubt it, Ellen. As I understand it, she has a house in the city—" A long pause of listening. "That may well be true, but I don't believe that economic—" Another pause, shorter. "I have no idea, Ellen. Who knows what she's thinking? But I am absolutely sure that Rachel Wilcox has no intention of changing her mind about selling." A very short pause. "Ellen . . . that may be, but I suspect she has her own resources."

Nobel shifts, and after a pause Mary's voice has a heavily disapproving tone, one he remembers from when the children were very small. "Of course not. It's not a thing we discuss, his business decisions." Nobel can imagine skinny little Ellen Parsons sitting by her telephone, trying to find some way of backing out of whatever it is she has suggested that has brought that note into Mary's voice, and he grins, both in sympathy with the minister's little wife and in a kind of pride in his wife. But then Mary speaks again, rapidly but more quietly, and as Nobel listens he feels a sudden worry, connected somehow to the tenderness he felt for Dinah in the kitchen, a kind of fear of loss. "I would be more inclined to believe that she has decided that her life will be simpler if she has him in a home of some kind closer to where she is, so she can keep track of him. Not everyone is a saint, Ellen, and I'm actually surprised she's bothering to sell before she has him committed. I don't see that she's particularly interested in what becomes of any of us. Including her brother."

This seems harsh to Nobel: the woman who has come almost daily into the post office has not seemed to him unpleasant or particularly hard-boiled. Still, he wonders, and he steps into the hall to make sure Mary doesn't rush off to some last-minute adjustment of the guest towels or something before he gets a chance to ask her.

Her back is to him, and she bends over the telephone. "Of course that is up to you, Ellen, as the pastor's wife, but I doubt, I doubt very much that Rachel Wilcox has much interest in sewing, or in our fellowship." And then, "Of course I did. In a town like this everybody knew her." And then, with bitter humor, "I don't know that she had *any* friends, Ellen. I don't remember that the Wilcoxes were interested in having friends here. And I do not believe that she has any interest in staying here now." And then, "Yes, I do—goodbye." She hangs up the receiver and turns; he has not kept purposeful silence but she is startled nonetheless. Still, she smiles wryly, shakes her head. "That woman!" she says, but her eyes dart away from him suddenly and then back.

"Rachel Cavanaugh?"

"*And* Ellen Parsons—she's all atremble about trying to keep her from putting Jacob away."

Nobel nods, as if the effort would be reasonable. "He does seem to get along okay."

Her face goes blank for a beat. "None of my business," she says almost pleasantly. "I've got that bathroom to get done now," she says, and turns from him. He watches where she was for a few seconds, the worry going round and round. Then he goes on out back and walks by the garden, no interest in weeding left. Mary's rarely so intolerant, he thinks. And he wonders, *Business decisions, had to be about Julia and Dan. And somebody's said Dan made an offer on the Wilcox land and Mrs. Cavanaugh turned him down. And Dan's been distant the past week. Stiff.*

Wonder if that's what it's about. Handsome woman. No doubt about that. He looks down two back yards to the Cullinans'.

Dan is out there, free too, now that his wife is on her way to Nobel's house, and Dan stands, like Nobel, beside his garden. As Nobel watches his neighbor, Dan hawks and spits off to the side. Nobel grins. *No, Dan's no candidate for serious foolishness with Mrs. Cavanaugh. Something else, then, but no matter—old prejudices dying hard, probably.* Nobel turns back to his own vigorous cucumbers, and kneels to begin searching for the overgrown seedy ones that he might as well pick now before he starts in on retying the tomatoes. They might get rain, who knows.

*

Dinah slips around the side of the house under the bright chatter
of the nine women leaving her mother's front porch, and escapes having to let them speak to her again. She goes into the
kitchen and finds, as she hoped she would, the leftovers: two
chocolate-frosted cupcakes, a few cookies, and a small strawberry tart. She thinks it's strawberry, anyway, and is leaning
over to smell it to be sure when Nobel comes in the back door.

"Anything good?" he asks.

She grins and steps out of his way so he can see.

"Not bad," he says. "Where've you been?" He goes to the
sink and washes his hands. She can smell a faint bready scent,
and knows he's been drinking a beer with Mr. Cullinan or Arnie
Deery.

"Janet's," she lies, for she has been sitting, silent and dreaming, alone in the dark of the small playground behind the church.

But coming in tonight the smell of her own mother's kitchen
has made her wish for childishness again, and she pours herself
a glass of milk. Her mother should come out to the kitchen in
a minute and give permission, and Dinah's only fear is that Brian
will come in and narrow her choices before she's decided firmly
between the tart and the cupcake. Her father will take the
cookies, she knows, because they're those powdery almond
things that nobody else likes.

Dinah's mother is still on the front porch talking and talking
to somebody, though the voices of the rest of them are long
gone, and Dinah grows impatient. "Daddy?" she says.

"Don't ask me," he says. "She'll be in in a minute."

But she isn't, her voice and the other voice, Mrs. Parsons',
Dinah thinks, going back and forth for several minutes more,
before there is the sound of the front screen door yawning and
shutting. And then she's doing things in the living room, moving
chairs back and straightening things. Dinah's sure her milk is
getting warm and she gives her father a pleading look. He's
looking down the hall, frowning, although Dinah knows he was
in a good mood when he came in, and then he gets up from the
table and goes to the living room. Dinah sighs. "Forget this,"
she whispers to her milk.

119

"Dinah in?" she hears her mother ask.

"Yup, waiting for her dessert," he answers.

"Dinah?"

"Yes?"

"Go ahead, and then get to bed."

"Okay," she says, and chooses the tart: there is just a chance that her mother, who sounds so cross, won't eat the second cupcake and Dinah will discover it tomorrow in the bread box. The tart is strawberry, and Dinah eats it delicately, trying not to end up with more crust than filling or more filling than crust in any bite. She drinks her milk in one long pull after the tart is gone, and holds her glass aloft with a feeling of delight, which she suddenly remembers as stemming from her appointment with Mrs. Cavanaugh for tomorrow at one. Then she hears that her mother is talking to her father very quietly. Dinah sits very still, trying to hear the words, but then there is silence again.

"Dinah, are you finished?" her mother says.

"Yes."

"Rinse your glass and get to bed, then," her mother says.

Dinah runs water as briefly as possible into the glass and then listens again.

"Goodnight, Dinah," her father says, and he sounds amused.

Dinah goes down the hall and looks at them in the living room, her mother standing by the window with her arms crossed and her father relaxed in his chair. "Okay. Goodnight," she says.

"Where's Brian?" her mother asks, as if Dinah were in charge of him.

Dinah shrugs hugely. "I don't know."

Her mother grimaces, her father says, "Mary," and Dinah goes on upstairs before her mother can scold her for her tone of voice. She goes to her room, half believing that she'll go on in and imagine more about tomorrow, but she doesn't: she opens and shuts the door, and tiptoes back close enough to the top of the stairs to hear what they're talking about. Her mother's mad about something, that's for sure. With a shiver, Dinah almost hopes it is about her father drinking beer.

His chuckle comes up the stairs.

"Laugh," her mother says.

"Now, Mary, you know you've got this blown all out of proportion."

"She's a mischief-maker," she says.

"Ellen Parsons isn't capable of mischief."

"Oh, Nobel! She's a ninny, but she means well—I know that. I just *do* not understand why she won't listen to people who know what they're talking about."

He chuckles again.

"And you, too—*you* didn't know them before, either."

"Nope, I'm a newcomer, me and the minister's wife. What is it I don't know—she steal your boyfriend or something?"

"Nobel Aldrich—"

"Come on, Mary—let Ellen invite her. What's the worst thing that can happen?"

There is a pause.

"Nothing. I am sure that nothing at all can happen."

"Seriously, Mary. You say she's a mischief-maker, and I don't know what it is you think she's going to do."

"She has a heart of gold. Her motives are pure as the driven snow. She's Mary and Martha rolled into one, a blessing on us all."

"Mary."

"That does seem to be the opinion of the gentlemen in this town."

"What?"

"Amos Brown falls all over himself when she walks in, Dan Cullinan apparently finds her irresistible, and you seem to—"

"Dan Cullinan made an offer on her land. She turned it down. That's *all*. I don't see how that gives you—"

"So why does he keep surveying the land?"

"Surveying?"

"He seems to have to walk in that direction about once a day the past week. I assume the attraction is a survey."

"Well, maybe it is. Maybe he's decided to get a look at the house and see if it might be worth buying after all, if leaving it out of his offer is what made her turn it down."

"Maybe."

121

"Mary, Mary—he only made the offer in the first place because Julia and Rachel were friends and—"

"Dan told you that?"

"Well, he implied that it was for Julia that he—"

"Dan Cullinan is a liar."

"Mary!"

"Julia was more surprised than anyone. Dan didn't even tell her that Rachel had approached him."

Another pause.

"That would be their business, wouldn't it?" he says evenly.

"Yes, it would," she snaps back. "But I will tell you this, Nobel Aldrich: I will not have Rachel Wilcox in my house. And that is *my* business."

"Cavanaugh," he corrects.

"Pardon me," she says. "I had forgotten. Like her mother, she is a widow." There is a long pause, and then she speaks again, in a voice so nastily sweet that Dinah is shocked. "And does the good widow *Cavanaugh* receive a great deal of mail?"

He says something so low that Dinah knows it is a swear word, and at the same moment she hears her mother starting up the stairs, and she just has time to get back to her door before her mother is in the hall.

"Aren't you ready for bed yet?" she snaps.

"I was reading," Dinah says.

Her mother glares at her. "Well, *get* ready," she says.

"I was going to the bathroom," Dinah says.

Her mother tightens her jaw and walks stiffly past Dinah and into her own room and shuts the door.

CHAPTER 12

*S*usan can hear in the heaviness of his feet on the stairs how tired Timer is, and she wishes, in the kitchen that seems to her suddenly as cluttered as it will look to him, that there was something nice she could do for him. But it's seven-thirty in the morning and she subdues the wish with a shrug, and pours his coffee. At least it's hot this morning, the coffee; at least she's timed it right today. She turns the gas up under the frying pan and cracks the first egg into the already melted butter.

"Morning," she says over her shoulder.

"Mm," he says, pulls his chair out and sits heavily.

She cracks the second egg, pushes the toast down, turns to get his juice from the refrigerator. He's sitting with his arms on the table, half asleep, the way Allen does on school mornings in the winter. She pours the juice, holding the refrigerator door open with her knee, thinking vaguely not to disturb him with the sound of it chunking shut.

"God, Susan," he growls without moving, making her jump and chatter the lip of the juice jug against the rim of the glass. "Stand there with the door open!"

She steps back, lets the door shut, carries the full glass and the jug to the table. Juice splashes up as she sets the glass in front of him.

His eggs are overdone, the toast dry. He eats in silence and she stands by the sink with her arms crossed, staring steadily out the window. The only reason he's so tired is that he stayed up over at Arnie's until after midnight. And then woke her up all romantic when he got home. When he scrapes his chair back to get up, she reaches out and slams his full lunch box shut, flips the catch down.

He's tying his shoes with his foot on the chair. She listens to his tightened breath for a minute. "There's your lunch," she says, and goes out of the kitchen toward the stairs. Halfway up she hears him leave, the screen door slapping shut behind him. She pauses a second, then turns, hurries down, but it's too late: he's long gone now, and she'd meant to ask him for some money.

"Is Daddy *gone?*" Allen complains behind her.

He's standing in the kitchen doorway in his underpants looking as if he's ready to cry. Susan smiles wanly in answer.

"Is he gone *already?*" Allen whines, looking past her as if she were hiding Timer from him.

"Yes, Allen," Susan says, trying not to whine back. "He's gone."

Allen glares at her for a second and then goes back up the stairs, stomping his bare feet.

Two hours later, she's finished cleaning up the kitchen in a temper, had a bath, and dressed, and she feels better. Amos will let her have what she needs on the slip. She walks barefoot through the kitchen brushing her hair and looking for Allen. She stops in the doorway to the living room, where Tony is walking slowly around, singing softly a song he makes up as he goes and touching things, trailing his hand over the back of the chair, swooping the hand through the air and touching along the lampshade; he stops to kneel on the couch and then goes along its length on all fours. He turns his head to smile at her, and she smiles back, working her fingers through a snarl at the back of her neck. Then she goes on through and Tony goes on singing, undisturbed by her passage.

Allen sits humpbacked on the top step. Susan pauses just inside the screen door and watches him. She gives her hair one more tug with the brush and opens the door. His rounded back stiffens. The boards of the porch are warm and gritty underfoot. She takes a deep breath of the heavy morning as she sits down beside him; she tucks the brush into her lap and crosses her arms on her knees, so she's sitting just the way he is. Behind them Tony's song goes on and on.

"Hey," she says. "Why so glum, sugarplum?"

He shrugs.

She looks away from him, up River Street. "Beautiful day," she offers.

He pulls his feet to the back of the step, close under him.

"I'd think you and Chris would be out fishing on a day like this," she says.

He shrugs again.

"Chris can't go?"

"I don't know."

"Oh. You guys have a fight?"

"No," he says, resentful.

"You ought to go alone, Allen, if Chris won't—too hot to just hang around the house."

"No pole," he mutters, and she can hardly understand the words, he says them so crossly, almost into his folded arm.

She thinks a minute, trying to remember what became of his pole, the perfect red pole he bought with his birthday money back in April. Nothing comes to mind, so, "No pole?" she asks.

"Broke it," he says.

"Oh," she agrees. She takes the brush out of her lap and pulls hairs out of it, lets them float off in the little breeze. "I guess your dad knew that, huh?"

He shrugs.

"So why don't you go ahead and use his pole?"

"I couldn't ask," he complains, his voice harsh. And then, more sadly, "He was gone, already."

"Well," she says, "I don't think you need to." He sits very

125

still. "When I saw what a hot day it was going to be again, and cloudy, I just happened to say to him at breakfast that you and Chris would probably be going fishing. Then he said he thought you'd broken your pole. Then *I* said really, I didn't know that, what a shame. Then *he* said he supposed you could use his pole, if you wanted to go." She pauses, exhilarated. "And I said I'd tell you."

Allen is quiet for a long few seconds. He doesn't believe me, Susan thinks. "Really?" Allen asks.

"Sure. As long, he said, as you were really careful not to break *his* pole, and had it back exactly where it belongs, all packed up right, before he gets home. And he'll be home kind of early, probably. So you probably better get moving if you want to get some good fishing in."

"Really?" Allen insists.

"Really!" she says. She takes a couple of long strokes along her hair with the brush, and he gets up and stands beside her for a second. "Go on! Beat it!" she says, and taps his calf with the back of the brush. He goes, and she sits a few minutes more, listening to Tony's humming and feeling the smooth warmth of the steps under her bare feet.

Just before harvest at the orchard, this lull comes, three or four weeks when the fruit is safe on the trees, finished, and all that's left to do is wait, and clean up. Timer's first choice for a day like this, cloudy and hot with a breeze, would be fishing, sleeping on a bank all alone. But his second choice would be just what he's trying to do, clearing and cleaning the storage rooms. It's stupid work in a way, but pleasurable; the dim coolness of the apple-smelling rooms; quiet, drowsy work alone on a day when he wants to be alone and drowse. He piles the trash near the door until there's a good armful, and then carries it out and dumps it into the back of the pickup: that's enough fresh air and motion for him after the whole summer outside. The trouble is, every time he's gone out there this morning with his arms full of slats and trash, somebody's caught him, first to take a look at the green tractor's carburetor, then to settle which wagon it was Dan said needed mending, both things Dan ought to be there to do, but Dan's off again, wherever it is he takes off to these days. In fact, Timer knows as well as the rest of the guys that it's got something to do with Jacob Wilcox. Something like his sister, probably, but nothing gets said about it. So Timer does what has to be done when Dan takes off, but it irks him, and today it irks him more: he's tired and it's his own damn fault, Susan's all pissy about something these days, and all he wants to do, all he's asking of the world, is to be able to sweep the morning away in the dry, deep smell of last year's fruit in the storage room. So when he's settled the business about the wagon and he comes back into the sweet silence, he decides to eat now, hours before lunch.

He takes his lunch pail down from the rafter where he stowed it when he came in, and he's pleased to find that Susan's packed him a piece of last night's lemon cake, even if she was in a bad mood. He eats quickly, almost self-consciously in the silence, and then stretches out on the stack of burlap bags. He can't help it, and there's no rush today. And no boss to tell him otherwise. If he sleeps in here for an hour, even, the world won't come to an end.

Dan stands well within the town-side privet hedge and watches Jacob walk among his plants, brushing the palm of his left hand over their uneven tops. A few minutes more and yes, there he goes, approaching the back door of the house as if he were unaware of it; the door opens almost of its own will and Jacob glides inside. How one man, whom Dan has seen for years now as the source of steady, intense, and pointless noise, can generate such calm silence is the forward curiosity in Dan's mind this torpid morning: that, and whether Jacob actually lives in the shed from which Dan has seen him, twice now, emerge fairly early in the morning, and if he does live in there, whether that's been true for a long time or just since the sister's arrival, and if just since then, whose idea it was. But behind all that curiosity Dan wonders, really, whether he's just as crazy as Jacob, sneaking out here to spy every little while, a thing he never meant to do but doesn't seem to be able to stop. That first time, when he watched Jacob moving in the dusk with such careless grace, he'd only meant to be getting a quick anonymous idea of the way the house sat on the land, and maybe, as he'd told himself gruffly, as if answering a question even then, maybe he really was thinking of making a second, better offer on the land and house. Maybe, who knows, Rosie'd like to live out here, more space than she's got in town, now that there's the baby. Though why he wouldn't bring that up to her, or at least to Julia, he wouldn't be able to say. Now he knows but wouldn't be able to explain to anyone he's ever known why he wouldn't make an offer: now he wants the house and land never to be sold away from Jacob, wants Jacob never to leave this house and land but to remain here forever for him to come and look at, wants it so strongly, with such a sense of shame, that it's almost erotic. The way Jacob comes out the back door, for instance, as he's doing now, carrying a tray that holds a blue coffeepot and two cups. Dan can't remember ever having seen such a thing as a blue coffeepot anywhere else in his life, but Jacob is clearly both familiar with it and fond of it. Fond: maybe that's it, what makes Dan come out here every day for far too long at a time: the fondness with which Jacob touches everything, so that Dan can see, at least as long as he watches, that the world is a place of beauty and peace.

The back door opens again, more certainly, just as Jacob has taken his place in one of the chairs, and Rachel comes out. Dan is startled: it is the first time he has seen her here, and though he is fairly sure he is well hidden, she would, he knows, call his watching by the name of spying, which is what, in her presence, he remembers it really is. But he can't leave now without being seen. He closes his eyes but feels both silly and dizzy, so he opens them again. If she saw him standing here with his eyes closed, would it make any difference? But he knows that isn't the point at all.

Rachel, moving more lightly than he remembers, takes her place across from Jacob, and says something. Dan can hear the voice but not the words, for which he is grateful: eavesdropping would be worse even. She pours the coffee and leans back. Jacob nods, benign as an old king, and they talk, slow answers or not-answers, back and forth. Now and then Rachel rocks, lifts her hair from her neck; her full skirt fans out a deep emerald color under the table, where Jacob's feet lie flat and parallel in soft black slippers. Jacob speaks again, raising his arm away from the table in a wide sweep that covers his whole patchy but vigorous garden.

Rachel seems to protest, but mildly, and nods.

Jacob leans forward, rises and turns; still speaking, softly smiling, he approaches the side of the yard beyond which Dan stands hidden, stops and turns, his arms wide again. Rachel watches him, and his movements are like a dance. She speaks again, and the strained care of her smile takes Dan by surprise—he remembers such a look from other women's faces, a kind of sorrowing sympathy. She reaches her hand out to Jacob, who lowers his arms slowly and takes a step toward her. Even from behind him, though, Dan can tell that he is not discouraged or disappointed. Then, swiftly, thrillingly, Jacob dips down and touches the air six inches above the grass, as if there were low plants growing there for him to be caressing.

Rachel nods, and she is the one who is discouraged, Dan can see. She speaks, gathering the two cups and spoons into one hand, the blue coffeepot into the other, as if to keep Jacob from noticing her face. She seems to ask a question as she moves away from the table toward the house. She looks back at Jacob as if for an answer.

And sees Dan. He feels her eyes meet his as if the contact were blunt with muscle. She pauses, looking, her face widening with surprise and then closing, sharp. He cannot look away.

Even after she has nearly nodded and turned and gone inside the house, and he has sense enough to feel a chill of panic at what she might do next, he is reluctant, ashamed, to look again at Jacob, until he must, in order to escape, and then Jacob has disappeared. Dan steps slowly backward out of the hedge and tramps fast and heavy-breathing to where he's left the truck on the side of Town Line Road.

The screen door shuts behind her mother and Dinah lets her breath out. She's been afraid for the past half hour, sitting rigid in her bedroom, that today of all Fridays her mother might not go over to Mrs. Cullinan's. But she's gone now, and Dinah takes the full skirt (which had been put away, too big for her this year, in a bag in her closet) out from under the bed and pulls it on; she overlaps the waistband and fastens it with a safety pin. The skirt swishes against her calves with a gratifying weight as she goes down the stairs, her kerchief in her hand, and out the front door. It's a quarter till one and heavy out, so Dinah walks slowly, enjoying her skirt, and passing her dreams before her eyes as she goes through the village and down the dip toward the bridge. Just to be safe, she passes the post office on the far side of the road.

But Mary hasn't gone to Julia's at all. She's gone to the parsonage to play her trump card with Ellen Parsons: the fact that there seems to be something peculiar going on with Dan Cullinan and Rachel Cavanaugh, and given that fact, any effort to try to convince Rachel to stay in town would be unkind, at the very least. Her own opinions of Rachel aside. And Ellen isn't at home, no one is at home, so Mary turns away from the door and steps back onto the side of River Street, and sees Dinah sashaying toward her.

Her first severity is for the skirt, that Dinah would walk through town in a skirt as wrinkled, as outsized, as peculiarly rucked up around the waist as that. "Dinah Aldrich!" she exclaims, in her shock almost missing how Dinah freezes and goes white around the mouth at seeing her.

They stand facing one another on the soft dirt of the shoulder. Dinah is almost as tall as her mother, but hopelessly, helplessly childish at this moment in her suddenly heavy skirt, in her nausea of guilt.

"And just where do you think you're going in that getup?" Mary says, because the words, the questions, have a kind of inertia, although she knows, already, that it is something else that is wrong.

Dinah shrugs, looking down.

And then Mary looks in the direction her daughter was heading, as if for a clue, and sees the bridge, the rise of Bridge Road across it. Impossible.

"Well, you'll just march back home and get out of that and into something respectable," she says.

"But I'm supposed to—"

"Speak *up*, Dinah. Supposed to what?"

Desperately, "I'm supposed to meet Janet at one o'clock."

"Janet? Out here?"

Dinah nods.

"Well, then Janet will wait, or she'll come by the house for you. I won't have you seen in that."

So Dinah starts hurriedly for home, half believing her mother will allow her to go after she changes, half terrified she will meet Janet Tolli in her mother's sight and their estrangement will be apparent. Half afraid her mother, coming along more slowly behind her, will meet Janet and tell her that Dinah will be right along.

But Mary, coming along more slowly behind her, sees now and must believe: Dinah in her drooping skirt is a perfect parody of Rachel Cavanaugh, and Mary would laugh if only her throat weren't seized by grief and fear.

"Hey, Timer?"

He can't move, can't answer, clings to the hope that he's invisible and whoever it is will go away.

"Timer, hey—wake up. Wake up!" He's shaken by the shoulder. "We got visitors, sockhead."

"Ungh," he manages.

"Come on, come on—there's three guys waiting to see Dan and we can't find him, so you got to talk to them. Come on."

Timer manages to sit up, rubs his face. "What guys?" His tongue feels weighted.

"I don't know, but two of them are wearing suits."

"Damn." He gets up, trying now to wake up, pushing off the sleep he was cherishing. "Time is it?"

"About one—they been sitting there about half an hour—we couldn't find you either."

"Okay, I'm coming." He walks slowly toward the light of the doorway, forcing himself not to close his eyes.

"Almost thought you'd taken off wherever Dan goes."

"Very funny. Now get back to whatever you were doing."
Across the hot gravel, into the hot shade of the office. Three
guys, two in suits and one in clean work clothes, sit stiffly on
the bench outside Dan's office door.

"What can I do for you gentlemen?" Timer says, his voice still
low and soft with sleep.

The three men eye one another uncertainly, but the man in
work clothes finally stands up. "You Mr. Cullinan?" he asks.

Timer shakes his head. "Timer Darcy," he says.

"Foreman?" the man asks. The two in suits are watching like
it's a movie.

"More or less," Timer says. "You looking for work?"

The man nods.

"We don't start picking for two weeks, but I can take your
name and Dan—Mr. Cullinan will get back to you."

The man shifts his weight. Clearly, he doesn't want to start
in two weeks, he wants to start now, and Timer runs his hand
up the back of his neck in irritation. He doesn't want to make
this guy look bad in front of the two suits, but for crying out loud,
nobody hires picking crews this early. "You got experience?" he
asks roughly. The man is older than Timer. He nods, but he
doesn't look Timer in the eye. Timer blows out a quick breath.
"Look. Let me take care of these fellows and then I'll see what
we can do." The man nods again, takes a step back and away
from the bench.

One of the suits looks at his watch and glances at the other.
"Who's first?"

The watch stands up; he's got a briefcase, too, and Timer
scowls. The man holds out a card. "I'm with Rinehart Distribu-
tors," he says, and Timer feels relief. "I had a twelve-thirty
appointment with Mr. Cullinan."

"He's not here," Timer says.

"I gathered," the man says. "Do you know when he'll be
back?"

"No idea," Timer says, worrying now about the other suit,
who doesn't seem to be in any hurry.

"Well, I've got to be at Hammond Orchards in about half an
hour, so I can't wait any longer. I'll leave my card."

"Yeah, he'll call you. Sorry about the inconvenience." Timer takes the card and looks at the other guy. The other guy smiles, friendly, calm. *Trouble,* Timer thinks. "Your turn," he says.

The guy doesn't stand up. "My name is Howard Andersen," he says. "I'm from the State Department of Agriculture and Markets."

Trouble. Timer nods.

"When do you expect Mr. Cullinan?" Howard Andersen asks pleasantly, as if he hadn't heard a thing, and as if he plans to wait, no matter how long it takes.

"Like I said, no idea." Howard Andersen's smile continues unchanged. "Hour, maybe two."

"Timer!" from outside and work boots crunching gravel at a run.

Timer whirls; one of the high school boys bursts around the corner of the shed, scared. "That damn wagon axle gave and fell on Wink!" Timer's running across the gravel before he can think, heading for the wagon where two of the men have already lifted the bed and swung it aside.

"Bad?" Timer yells.

"Broke his arm!" somebody yells back. "Better call—"

But Timer has already turned and is running back to the office. He passes the three motionless men and bangs open Dan's office door.

He calls Dr. Emmons's office, listens to the doctor's first-aid instructions carefully; the doctor says he'll be right out. He grabs a couple of slats from the back of the pickup on his trot back to where every man on the place except the two suits is hunkered down around Wink.

Twenty minutes later the doctor arrives, checks the splint, and drives off with Wink in his car, and still Dan hasn't showed up. Timer sighs as the men slowly move off, back to work, and he glances back toward the office building. Where the guy in the work clothes is still standing, and Timer can tell by the way he's standing that Mr. Ag and Markets is still sitting just inside on the bench.

"You are nuts," Timer growls through clenched teeth, glaring at the office building where Dan isn't and should be. "Nuts!"

Without even a deep breath, he lunges for the pickup and swings the door open, and he's inside, driving along the edge of the orchard like he hasn't driven since he was sixteen: fast and hard, aiming straight away and ignoring the ridges and dips except for a grim pleasure in keeping control of the bucking wheels. He heads east, the sun through the windshield hot on his chest, and then wrenches the wheel around and guns the truck out onto Town Line Road. He goes past the intersection of Town Line and Bridge and pulls the truck off the road to a stop a few inches from one of the scrubby trees, in the shade. He's not getting back into the thing until it cools off, either. He gets out, feeling young and righteous, and shades his eyes.

From here the only sign of the house is the stand of trees, and Dan's truck is nowhere in sight. Timer stands looking toward the trees, with nothing, after all, to do, now that he's here.

"I'll wait," he mutters, but the fury is gone, leached away by the relief he feels at not having discovered Dan and not having had to walk up to him and say *Where the hell have you been.* He hunches down to sit in the truck's shade.

When Susan goes into the store, Amos is nowhere in sight. Alone, she hums quietly as she walks back to the milk case and draws the door open to take out two quarts. Amos comes hurrying out of the back room, wiping his hands on a cloth and smiling expectantly toward the front of the store. Susan shuts the door and tilts her head toward him. "It's only me," she says. He looks and his smile changes just enough to make her laugh. "You were expecting someone else?" she says. She cradles the two quarts of milk not quite suggestively, one in each arm.

He laughs too. "I was just cleaning up some in the back," he explains.

But Susan still feels him listening past her for someone else, and the feeling makes her shy and cross, so she turns away and walks to the front of the store, speaking straight ahead, but cheerfully, jokingly: "You've interrupted your cleaning just for me, then? I ought to buy a rib roast, at least, to make it worthwhile."

He comes behind the counter, smiling, and tucks the cloth into the little space between the cash register and the jar of fireballs. He puts his hand on one of the quarts, a gesture that makes Susan feel hurried along, so she says, almost challenging where she had meant to be charming, "So, Amos, how much are my good looks worth today?"

He scowls over his smile, not understanding.

He makes her so impatient in this heat and after her row with Timer that she could slap him, although she has never, in five years of daily flirtation, touched so much as the outside edge of his thick hand. She laughs instead. "Timer went off and left me penniless," she says. "What am I to do?"

For a quick instant his face nears concern, and she wonders if he's going to force her to say the actual words, plain, ordinary, humble, but then his brow clears. He seems finally to have focused on her, realized that this is Susan in the afternoon. He smiles wider and says, "Well, I should think this is the perfect day for a rib roast, in that case!"

But still, after he has weighed out her pound and a half of ground beef and written the milk and meat and a package of rolls and a sack of potato chips on the charge pad, she feels his absence, that listening past her. She lingers, the bag on her hip, missing something she has come to depend on from him. She is jealous and hardly knows it, until finally, too sharp, too shrill, she says, "I surely hope your special customer doesn't disappoint you today—it would be a shame if you did all that cleaning for nothing."

But he only smiles. "See you later, Susan," he says, and by the time she's taken her two angry steps to the door, he's on his way back through the store, and whistling.

Susan stops with exaggerated courtesy to let Mary Aldrich's daughter pass, heading toward the post office with two letters in her hand, and Susan doesn't notice how blotched and swollen with tears the girl's face is, but as she looks after her, spiteful of the girl's easy slenderness, her mind is on what's gotten into Amos, and maybe it's the way Dinah moves that puts Rachel Cavanaugh into her mind. Susan almost laughs aloud in triumph: of course that's what it is. And by the time she reaches her own front porch, she's found room for a little pity for Amos. Half the town thinks Dan Cullinan's after Rachel Cavanaugh, right under Julia's mild and kindly nose, but only a man could believe that it could amount to anything even if it were true. And only a man could believe that that woman would ever be interested in a paunchy country storekeeper with hair in his ears. If Rachel'd take anybody around here, it wouldn't even be Dan Cullinan with his big orchard; it would be somebody young and muscular, narrow in the hips, somebody worth her trouble. Like Timer, Susan thinks, not without pride.

What Timer wants, walking home with his lunch box in his hand and his shirt slung over his shoulder, is never to get home, never to have had to leave the apple sleep of the storage room. As he turns onto River Street, though, he hears a lawn mower vibrating the late afternoon air, and that seems a possible solution. When he gets home he'll drop his shirt and lunch box on the back steps. He'll walk across the yard to the dirt-floored garage and get out the mower, which will start on the fourth measured pull of the greasy rope, and he'll mow, thoughtless and protected under the noise. Nothing will have happened. No smiling Ag and Markets man, no pale Bobby Wingstrom sweating in the shade. And no Dan Cullinan sitting at his desk when Timer got back, no Dan Cullinan to look up at Timer, close his eyes, and pinch the bridge of his nose as tears, unmistakably tears, try to escape, no Dan come back at all, especially not to say, clearing his throat three times in the short sentence, *Thanks, I should have been here.* None of that, and Timer hawks and spits to keep from thinking about it, and the sound of the mower gets louder. Mow. He'll mow out back and up the side yards, and then he'll kill the mower and walk it down to Mrs. Phoebe's and do her yard. He'll tell Susan to wait supper, and he'll get his boys out there to rake, and he'll rake Mrs. Phoebe's himself. He can already feel the strong sting of the blister he'll get in between his thumb and his palm from the rake handle, the cool green pleasant pain of the moist flesh uncovered as evening comes down. The thought lets him worry for a second about whether the Ag and Markets thing means anything, though Dan said not, after he got ahold of

136

himself. Routine check, he said. And by the time they both left for the day Dan seemed back to normal. Until Monday, at least.

Mow. Rake. And then a hot bath and sneak to bed early. Sleep, alone between cool sheets.

He knows before he gets to his house but he goes out back anyway, lunch box and shirt, to see that it's true: the mower he heard was his own, Susan out there with the damn throttle wide open, starting in now on the last bit back by the garage, the smell of gas and cut grass heavy to suffocation.

The roaring motor covers the slam of the screen shutting behind him, the clang of the lunch box on the counter, the thump of the chair he pulls over to the refrigerator, and the ring of the silver bowl that falls out of the small cupboard over the refrigerator and bounces onto the floor as Timer reaches far back for the bottle of Christmas whiskey. Even the intimate sounds of ice cubes in the glass and liquor cracking them is hidden, and he takes only bitter pleasure in the first sips. Then he goes through the house to the front porch, where the mower might belong to anyone on this side of River Street.

Because months have passed since he drank hard liquor, and because he is sipping as quickly as he can stand it, the whiskey hits fast, so fast that he almost relaxes, the noise and the booze working toward the full silence he's after. Before she shuts the mower off, and Allen appears as sudden as the emptiness of the noise stopping.

And Allen is carrying his father's fishing pole, electric blue. And Timer sees the boy and that pole soon enough and surely enough that he's ready when Allen comes up the steps, his face sullen and unaware.

"Been fishing, Allen," Timer says, and enjoys in a way the boy's startle and recovery, and his caution.

"Yeah," Allen says.

"With my pole," Timer observes, after a pause and a sip.

Allen lowers the pole and looks at it. Timer waits. He hears Susan come in the back door, pick up the bowl from the kitchen floor and put it on the table, and come down the hall. Now she's standing behind him, just inside the screen door.

Allen looks away from the pole, the door, his father, off up River Street. "Momma said it was all right," he says simply. Timer nods, almost smiling. "Catch anything?"

"No." A pause, in which Allen doesn't move, Susan doesn't move, and Timer alone is free, sips, the ice clinking solidly. Then a burst of complaint from Allen, "Some stupid girls were at the good place, and me and Chris didn't even get to cast there, so we went on down to the other place by the old dam and there was two big guys there, so we came on back—I didn't get to even *fish!*" He takes two quick disgusted steps past his father, steps in absolute imitation of his father, steps that only Susan recognizes, before he stops, turns. "Daddy?"

Timer smiles, tips his glass to hear the ice clink, looks kindly out past the railing.

"Can I use it tomorrow instead?"

Timer laughs pleasantly, and then there is only waiting in the air. Allen hunches his shoulders and goes in, angling the pole carefully in front of him. And Susan comes out, stands between Timer and the door. Between Timer and the invisible boy.

"You're home early," she says.

She smells, even from here two feet or more away, of mower exhaust, sweat, clean hair, and grass, but Timer has other ideas. He swallows what is left in his glass as if it were water. He smiles just past her shoulder, pointedly, as he goes by her and inside, where the silver bowl, dented, sits next to the whiskey bottle on the table. He pours more whiskey over more ice, and swirls it around to cool it more quickly. He can feel a faint smile still holding his face steady in front of the whiskey in his brain. The cellar door stands ajar: Allen is down there, replacing the blue pole. Timer smiles a little harder as he rejects the impulse to close and hook the door.

Susan has settled cautiously in her rocker on the porch, and smiles carefully as he comes out. He smiles back, raises his glass to her.

"I didn't think you'd mind," she says, her hands a caricature of modesty in her lap. "About the pole."

He drains his glass. "I am going," he says, "to take a bath."

"Timer," she insists.

He hears her with the back of his neck as he goes slowly up the stairs. The door slams, her steps follow his. "Timer," she protests. In their bedroom he lifts clean underwear from his second drawer. Pretending she is invisible, he moves straight through the doorway back into the hall, and she steps back out of his way. His hand is on the knob of the bathroom door when she gives a short, thin laugh and says, "He didn't even *use* it, for crying out loud."

He can feel his smile still mysteriously firm on his face. He turns that face to her. "I know," he says. She is holding out to him a folded towel and facecloth, which he would accept except that the bathroom door is opening inward, pulling him with it and turning him around.

Kneeling on the sink, Tony balances himself with one hand on the mirror, into which he stares intently as he applies lipstick carefully and firmly to his lips. Timer thinks vaguely of the sink separating from the wall, of the probable size of his white handkerchief that is tied crooked as a pirate's around Tony's head. The boy turns his face, perhaps slowly but certainly open-mouthed to his father and mother in the doorway. His bright red lips stretch further, a smile dawning in his eyes, a little Aunt Jemima on the sink.

Timer nods, weary, smiling, carefully relinquishes the doorknob that has brought him so far. He reaches his curved hand toward Tony. "You're nuts, kid," he says gently. "You're nuts just like my boss and old man Wilcox."

And the boy seems to have seen something worrisome over Timer's head, because his smile, so wide and red and foolish, is shrinking like a leaking balloon. Timer remembers Susan behind him, so he turns around. Her face is very white and still, as if he were about to do something very violent. She seems to have missed the joke. "Don't you think so, honey?" he says. "Don't you think he's as crazy as old man Wilcox?" Her face stays still. He tries again, with the whiskey already rising chilled through his chest toward his throat. "You sure fooled me, honey," he says, and he feels his smile has grown sick so he takes great care with his voice, keeping it level and clear. "This pretty one here—I thought all this time that he was my son."

Without any more warning than a warm nudging past his thigh, Timer is alone in the bathroom with his clean underwear balanced on one hand and a folded towel and facecloth on the other, like two soft trays. He considers for a second, hearing steps going downstairs, then presses his hands together and lets all that cloth drop to the floor. He vomits effortlessly into the open toilet bowl, thinking how handy it is but Susan really ought to teach those boys to put the lid down when they're done. By the time he crawls into bed, he's enlarged that thought: if boys were taught to put the lid down, there wouldn't ever have to be scenes like the one at work today.

CHAPTER 13

onight Jacob has gathered a huge bundle of cornflowers, and he sits in the still heat of his garden
working them into one long, thick braid for his drying shed. In the first moonlight the pink and white blossoms
glow along the dusty gray stems, and he is fanciful, leaving many
of the darkest blue flowers on longer stems so they will hang
and curve, as they dry, away from the thick plait of paler flowers.
He works carefully, his hands pleased with the tough flexibility
of the stems and the abundance. Twice he looks up and sees
Rachel through the window, washing up the supper things at the
sink, and his pleasure grows. After supper she brought out a box
from the house.

"I found some interesting things while I was cleaning," she
said, and lifted from the box first a papier-mâché doll. "Remember this? You brought it to me from Mexico." The colors were
still gaudy in the dusk, and he remembered the smell of the
shop, dry and hot as an old piano, somehow, and then it faded
off, as she took out a pair of little girl's shoes that he remembers
far more sharply, though where he bought them he doesn't
know. So many years of traveling, traveling alone, and so long

ago. Mostly pleasant times, the safe pleasure of architecture, guidebooks, shopkeepers who spoke languages that seemed to have no words, and they asked so little of him. So long ago now. "These?" she said. "They didn't fit, and I was so terribly disappointed, but I tried not to show it—I was only seven, though. I bet you knew, didn't you?" And he had remembered instead of a little Rachel a tall woman who wept over a thin baby, maybe in Egypt? Had he ever been to a place called Egypt, and how could that have been? But she took more and more from the box, and that long-ago season of travel became realer and realer, he could feel oceans beneath him, trains, and the company of an occasional young man like himself, and only rarely the times of terror. And then, last, she lifted out the brooch: a circle of simple golden roses as big as a child's ear, the pin their mother had worn at the throat of her day dresses nearly every day; clearly they both remembered the rasp of that pin now and then in a hug, the glance of light off it every night, every night at supper, every night after prayers.

"Mother's pin," he said, simply.

She smiled, and he thought she looked sad.

"Put it on," he said. "It should be yours, of course."

And she did put it on, pulling the lapels of her blue blouse into something like their mother's collars and fastening the pin with the same tucking of the chin he remembered from terribly long ago, from before this house, even, which he had forgotten had ever been.

The air holds the quiet as it has for days now, the rain-wait that is hope for relief rather than hope for sustenance: the air is heavy with moisture, and no plants suffer the lack of rain, the soil is not dry. He weeded carefully this afternoon, all around the flowers and vegetables. And again this evening, as Rachel sat with the box of things at their table, he pulled the bindweed from around the shed and off the drainpipes of the house.

He looks up a third time, thinking vaguely of the dryness of grasshoppers in the air over a meadow as he walked home, the dryness of sand on a wooden floor some place he has forgotten even as he remembers it, and the dry color of these cornflower stems. At the window Rachel is still for a moment, and then lifts her hand to rub her forehead with the back of her wrist: her hand is briefly the shape and color, in the yellow kitchen light, of columbine blossoms, yellow dancers in some past mountain sunlight. He smiles alone in the dark, free and almost unthinking, his hands slowly busy with the long stems, which seem, every August, to wish to be braided and hung in long garlands in the shed.

Rachel, the smells of her own evening's meager cooking, omelet and coffee, unpleasant in the kitchen around her, forces herself to keep on with the cleaning up, though she has worked all day sorting and listing in preparation for the auction-house man who will come on Tuesday, worked all day without the help she thought she wanted and ended by being glad not to have to put up with, the heat has been so unbearable. She is weary, and there is no promise of rest or pleasure soon, silent in the back with Jacob where she can say none of the things she thinks, especially not the things that fill her mind tonight: the face of Dan Cullinan, motionless in the hedge, even though that may explain Julia's cutting of her at the store; Dinah's failure, probably forbidden by her mother, who is the only person in the whole town that Rachel as a girl had ever tried to become friendly with, Mary de Marco never to return after that one embarrassing day of play; Jacob's clear refusal to hear her when she says that she has been sorting things but these special things she will keep, he will not hear that the people who have come around four times now have come to see about buying the land (and house, though she has not yet found a way to explain that to Jacob, who has not objected to the sale of the land, saying it is hers, of course, and better it should be used, of course); that boy she believes was peeping in at her today as she cleared out the ancient and useless papers from the old, dark desk: the form of the whole ugly little town spying and sneaking and naming her brother mad, probably naming her mad as well, by now. She knows they thought her mother mad, or (as they now think Rachel is, or Dan wouldn't have dared come so close) immoral. And although the whole stupidity of the lives and opinions of people in this town is no threat to her (Dan's face was sullen, but not threatening, she has been more frightened in fact at

143

cocktail parties with her husband within sight; she is accustomed to unwanted approach, though not like this, not this sneaking silence), the air and the day's work and disappointments (for she sorted and sorted, and found only the little silk shoes that sent a shaft of memory clear and cleansing through her, a bit of regret) and the mere presence of that town combine in oppression. And despair, of a kind she knows is temporary, because Jacob will not be told that he and she must leave here, that a better life can be lived far away. Tonight, in the kitchen, knowing he sits in the dark happy, as happy as he was when she arrived but no saner, less sane perhaps, because she has relieved him of the little responsibility he had (well discharged: the house hardly needs cleaning in order to be sold), she cannot imagine a life with him in her house. He won't eat inside here, and winter will come eventually to the city. And now she cannot get the cheese off the edge of the pan, and it puts her close to tears, and memory without detail comes over her and with it the old wish for rescue.

But then it is done, the pan clean, the counter clear, and she goes to the back door drying her hands on the towel.

There in the dark Jacob's hair is pale with moon that hasn't risen yet above their own trees.

There in the frame of the door she is an easy silhouette in the gentle old kitchen light.

All up and down River Street at just this moment people peer at one another secretly and believe what they see, but, like the density of the heat and the days-old thrum of heat thunder, their vision is a deep distortion, outlines and textures false. And for this moment every heart but Jacob's is afraid that nothing will ever change from exactly this, which seems so clearly permanent and hopeless.

So all over town people choose to try to sleep again instead of watching, and Rachel, rinsing out her stockings in the bathroom sink, chooses sleep, too, and resolves to be back in her own house with her own washing machine and her own clothes in plentiful supply in a month or less, no matter what, with Jacob or without him. For two weeks the nights have been as hot as

144

the days, and everyone is exhausted. Everyone but Jacob, who sleeps his days away.

No breeze comes up. Her bedroom is stifling hot, not one of the three antique fans she has discovered in the house works, and at nearly midnight by the little travel alarm's glowing dial, Rachel gathers up her pillow and sheet and carries them down to the parlor. The room is stripped of its heavy curtains, stripped of the pictures and bits of bric-a-brac that loaded its several small tables and its mantelpiece, and even before Rachel opens the windows this room seems cooler than her own. She spreads her sheet on the sofa. The open windows let in the night sounds, and the air, though still sullen, seems fresh in this room that has been for so long closed. Rachel lies down on the couch and wills herself into a drowse that is something like sleep, shallow but drifting, enough like sleep that the first she hears of the sweet singing voice comes mysterious and beckoning from far out front, somewhere in the meadow where she first cut the daisies and chicory, only a month ago, a life ago. She lies still in a real purity of delight and listens, until the voice begins to soften with distance, not quite a loss but a leading. Rachel makes to herself no excuse or plan as she imagines herself rising and walking out onto the deep front porch to listen, imagines a small place next to the high privet where the grass seems gentler than in the meadow beyond, a small place just the size for a woman to lie down in and feel the earth's coolness as she waits for the man who could sing such deep magic to return and rescue her, make her again young and precious.

For the voice is nearly gone now, a light echo Rachel imagines as something visible skimming slowly over the river's slow chuckling, and even before her hand has given her body release, she drifts toward sleep again, wrapped in vague memories of romance and tender accident.

And now it is past midnight. Susan sits on her porch. Timer is deep asleep, the boys are deep asleep upstairs. Susan sits waiting on the porch, vivid and still. But Jacob is singing far off tonight, out toward the farms on the other side of the river, far, far off from Susan waiting to claim him tonight.

145

So nothing happens on River Street. Another hour rolls past in cicada-laden silence, and another, muffled in heat lightning and its soft thunder. But no one comes to love or rescue Susan, who is certain just before she sleeps that Timer has always known that Tony is not his and that he will leave her, with two children and no money, or he will stay right here, and despise her and punish Tony, and her whole life will be one long misery either way. She wakes, stiff and chilled in her rocker, at dawn.

At dawn Rachel comes awake to the crunching of footsteps on the roadside gravel, and an image of Dan Cullinan's face is before her. But it is not Dan outside. The voice raises one last note in the garden and flips it gentle and soft, sky high, the note dancing like a pale flower in the heavy, rumbling dawn, and desire sways through her again like a long, narrow stem.

CHAPTER 14

*R*achel sleeps again and wakes sweaty and stiff-necked after ten o'clock, the sheet shifted into ridges beneath her, and the first thing she must do, gathering the sheet into a bundle and climbing slowly up the stairs to dress, the first thing she must do is decide and accept and require that the voice, early and late, was a most unsettling dream.

The second thing she must do is walk into town to the post office as soon as she is dressed, because this is Saturday and the post office closes at noon, and she is expecting letters, from a very good residential facility less than a mile from her home, and from the real estate agent in Livingstone, either of which might well have arrived yesterday, either of which will require, probably, her immediate telephone response.

One of the three envelopes is from the rest home; the other two have local postmarks, but in the heat and in her dread-filled eagerness to read the first she isn't even curious about them. Standing beside the long, high table in the post office, she opens and reads that a place is available for Jacob, pending an interview to be arranged at her earliest convenience and an examination by their medical and psychiatric staff.

So Rachel is relieved, she supposes. She walks down to the phone booth outside of Amos's store and makes the call, sets an appointment for a week from Monday. Surely all this will be taken care of by then, the house, the auction. But her stomach protests all the long dully hot walk back to the house: Jacob must must must be told without more delay, made to understand, so he can get used to the idea while he's still here, still within whatever comfort the house and garden offer him. Oh, and maybe, if she can just finally find the right words in which to present reality to him, maybe it won't be necessary at all, maybe he will come home with her, kindly and gentle. The thought of it brings tears stinging along her eyelids, and again she denies her memory of the night song, but still her stomach knots and falls away and knots again.

Coffee. That's all it is, certainly, an empty stomach and all this tramping in the heat after sleeping so poorly. A cup of Jacob's good coffee will set her right, and they can talk over the coffee.

Jacob is invisible when she gets home, and making the coffee herself seems far too great a task. She opens the refrigerator and discovers the other two letters in her hand. And knows she doesn't want to open them at all: there is no one in this town to write anything to her that could give her pleasure or comfort. She puts all three pieces of mail on the table and pours herself a glass of cold tea.

The tea fortifies her, as her mother used to say. Still, she opens the first envelope in dread, though she has to grin in relief as she reads Ellen Parsons' childishly round handwriting inviting her with a repeated sincerity that is nearly hysterical to join the Dorcas Society and make her home if it should be convenient right here where an active community of concerned neighbors can share and lighten her burdens. By the time she gets to the signature Rachel is in danger of giggling, her mood is so brittle this morning, so preposterous an idea of this town does Ellen Parsons put onto paper, and *Parsons,* for heaven's sake, doesn't anyone else see the humor there?

She finishes her tea, for her unlaughed laughter has made her weak.

And vulnerable, she realizes, reading the one sentence of the letter from Mary Aldrich. *My daughter is not allowed to come to your house, and I must ask you to have no more contact with her.*

As if I were a leper, or worse, Rachel thinks, but she feels defeated, not indignant. Just what she'd expected after all, just more overtly than she'd predicted, but the same message she'd already guessed at and thought she'd made her peace with yesterday.

But. She forces herself not to reread the sentence, rips both letters into pieces and puts them into the wastebasket under the sink. So much still to be done in the house, heat or no heat. And since Jacob's not around to have the important talk with, she might as well get to work.

She goes into the dining room where she stacked boxes last night in readiness for today's packing. She opens the bottom drawer of the buffet. It is full of table linens, untouched, she is suddenly certain, since some eternally lost morning when her mother, still young and still in some measure hopeful, starched and sprinkled and ironed and folded them here, and Rachel Wilcox feels the threat of tears again. She could sit right down on the floor and put her head down on her arms on the open drawer and sob, for her dead loving mother who meant so well, for her brother she is betraying, for the cruelty of this town that has taken from her the small pleasure of her distant affection for something she thought she understood in Julia Stone long ago and thought she had met in her again that morning in the rain-thrummed car, taken the possible pleasure of a mild friendship with young Dinah, who seemed to like her, perhaps even to admire her. She could cry and cry for her brother's terribly mistaken gentle trust of her, for the pure white hope of the starched and folded napkins in the drawer, and, at last, for her widowhood stretching before her, no tender accidents, no brother she can devote herself to, no return to revise all that all of them have lost and missed. She could just cry, and she can almost see herself doing it, almost feel the eventual discomfort of the drawer edge against her forearm. Instead, exhausted, she

149

releases the drawer, pushes it shut, and goes into the kitchen. It is too, too hot, she has slept too little, and been made to see too clearly: tomorrow she will do the things she must do, the packing and inventory and Jacob, but today she will rinse her eyes and cheeks with cool water to drive back those useless tears, and she will go up to her bed and sleep.

She is drying her face with the hand towel when Amos Brown at the back door says, "Hello?" For almost a second, the damp towel held loose over her mouth, she thinks he might just go away if she doesn't answer. But the water is running; he knows she is here. "Mrs. Cavanaugh?"

"Why, Amos," she says, stepping to where she can see him and slipping the towel through the drawer handle. "What a surprise."

He smiles and comes in. "Hope you don't mind my stopping. I was just going over to Livingstone and I thought I'd check in on you—didn't see you at the store yesterday or today." He hands her a small paper bag, which she accepts helplessly. "Some ice cream," he explains.

She is grateful for the reason to move away from him: he's much larger and warmer here in her kitchen than in his store. "How kind," she says. "Thank you." She's about to put the carton into the freezer when the idea of offering him some passes across her mind. No. Absolutely not. She closes the freezer door on the idea and turns to smile at him vaguely. "And, as you can see, we're just fine. I've been very busy getting things in order for the appraiser. And it's been *so* warm." She keeps her eyes a little averted from him; he has noticed, she knows, her strained face, and his own face is suffused with sympathy she cannot bear.

"Well," he says, and pauses. "Well, don't you work so hard in the heat," he says in a rush. "Exhaust yourself—that won't help anybody."

Rachel makes a small laugh. "Oh, I won't," she says. "In fact, I was just on my way up to take a nap when you came."

"Good," he says, hearty approval. "Only sensible thing on a day like this." He clears his throat. "Actually," he says, and Rachel hears a peculiar thrill in his voice, the tenor of courtship, a sound she hasn't heard in years but a sound that is unmistakable and always unbelievable, and she looks directly at him in astonishment. He smiles back shyly, boyishly, for a flash and then goes solemn again. "I stopped by to ask if you might go out to dinner with me tomorrow afternoon at the Crystal Restaurant in Livingstone."

Nothing about this heavy, balding man, earnest and hardworking and consistently kind as he is, is attractive to Rachel, and she doesn't even try to imagine sitting across a table from him in a restaurant. But she is vulnerable this afternoon, hot, tired, heartsick, and exhausted by tears withheld, and for the space of several heartbeats Amos Brown could rescue her from it all, marry her, admire and cherish and never demand, accept Jacob as a matter of course into their home, where the three of them would sit evenings around a table, he would buy a better store in a better town and keep her and Jacob safe in his homely, friendly, workaday aura: he has the power to make them normal, make all those people accept them as he does.

So when she says, "I'm sorry, Amos. It's very kind of you but I won't have the time, I'm afraid. It's only a week until we leave," her voice is not carefully, kindly, recognizably neutral. However great her regret, she can see that the tone was unpleasant, dismissive, superior, because Amos's formal face of invitation spreads in surprise and hurt and then contracts and solidifies again, changed, bitter edged.

He nods. "Well," he says, "I'd better get going."

"Thanks again for the ice cream," she says, wishing very much that she had offered him some—a cool visit here in the kitchen would maybe have let her do better at the last—wishing it so much that she sounds cold again, in keeping the entreaty out of her voice.

"Welcome," he says.

And then he is gone. As she goes up the stairs (for there is nothing to stop her now) she tells herself what she has told herself before, but not for so many years that it is as if she is discovering its truth for the first time, that she would have lost his friendship anyway, however she had managed her voice and words. She'd have lost his friendship even more certainly if she

151

had accepted, let it move on nearer the impossible conclusion. Still. He's the only one I'll miss, she thinks as she lies down.

In the first moments, before the pillow is heated through and the sheets crushed, Rachel slides just out of full consciousness, but she can go no deeper. She believes her clock has stopped, but then she discovers her mind busy over the sizes of the four hall runner rugs, and after a bit the clock's crisp ticking reminds her that the Dutch oven of her stove at home needs repair and she'll have to call someone about that right away. She comes wide awake to what she thinks is the sound of a car door slamming shut; even though she doesn't hear any car pulling away, she hurries downstairs in a panic that the real estate man came and thought she wasn't here. The sense of having missed a desperately important connection takes her all the way out through the empty garden to the roadside, but no car is in sight as far as she can see from here to past the bridge or up the road to Town Line. Even so, she can imagine no other reason for the sound that woke her. *Maybe Jacob heard,* she thinks.

"Jacob?" she calls softly, and isn't surprised at no answer. She can feel the creases in her face from where she lay on the pillowcase that refused to stay smooth, and her blouse clings damp and uncomfortable below her breasts and across her back. Sweat prickles in a pattern across her forehead. She hasn't seen Jacob all day. "Jacob?"

She thinks she hears an answer from the drying shed, and so she waits a moment in the air that has not altered its color or intensity for hours.

But Jacob doesn't come out, and the dread that has accompanied her this whole day solidifies around the thought that he may be lying stricken in the shed. Her sweat stands cold on her skin; she runs awkwardly the seven strides to the door on the far side, lifts up the latch and looks in.

Jacob lies as composed as an effigy on the neat pallet bed. In the instant she believes he is dead, her relief is enormous.

He sighs without stirring and the whole interior of the shed becomes visible to her: the bed, the chair, the oval table, the round-topped trunk, all set on the wide dry boards of the floor, the mad garlands and hanging bouquets of the thirty years' gardens, the half-broken basket of soiled clothing. He lives here. His silence about the house has been absence. She cannot breathe.

Now she is outside again, suspended in the weighted air. She has stolen her brother's home and never noticed he was gone. She is no savior, no good angel; she has accomplished only harm. And wished him dead. The topmost leaves of a thousand trees tap against one another with a sound like fine tissue paper crumpling and tearing as a wind passes far above, leaving the ground and garden and housetops untouched. For the briefest instant, sunlight appears, yellow, unhealthy, and disappears, gone like a shriek.

Jacob comes out of the shed into near dusk. Rachel is dressed in blue; she sits in the rocker, but she has moved the rocker back from the table, near the house. He smiles across the little distance as he moves toward his own chair, which remains in its usual spot beside the table where they take their dinners together and have their morning coffee together. By the rhythms Jacob has so gladly and simply accepted, Rachel should speak now, and after a few moments she should begin to bring plates and silverware from the kitchen.

So he is still smiling as he takes his place, but the count of moments passes and he feels something like unease. He looks over at the tomato plants, so heavy with tomatoes, then back toward his sister, who still sits in the rocker, looking away now from everything here. She begins to talk so carefully and with so much breath in her voice that Jacob is surprised and pleased that he can hear her.

"Jacob," she says, "I will be leaving on Monday, to go back to the city. I will be leaving just before lunchtime."

"Yes?" he wonders, aloud but unalarmed. "Monday. Today is Saturday." He feels unwilling to ask what her business in the city will be; she had a life there, he knows, a few friends, property. Any number of things, he supposes. "And when will you be back?"

"I will— No. No, Jacob, I won't." She rocks once, but the chair is too close to the house. "Jacob," she says, sternly, "sometimes things don't turn out the way we think they're going to. Sometimes we plan things, and even though the plans seem sensible, things just—change."

Once Jacob cut the long grass behind the drying shed and found an old board lying on the ground, and he picked it up. Underneath, the white tangle of rootlike grass stems had been blind, almost like a sound in their patterns of searching for light and air. His mild heart hears such a twisting in little Rachel's squeezed voice this heavy day. He wishes his chair were closer to hers. She sounds afraid. Perhaps of travel, which is such a pleasure, sometimes a pure relief. He should travel again, himself. Mexico. The western mountains.

"Sometimes we think we can change things, improve on the way things have come to be by accident," she's saying.

Among the stems, white grubs had lain, fat and unafraid, while tiny dark ants had fled from the disruption.

"I thought, you know," her voice easier now, the words burred a little in her throat, "need for me," the ants of course had moved off with a kind of confidence, "so very neat and in a way," not as if his moving of the board had caused any kind of panic, "actually better for both of us without me here, quite able to take excellent," as he understood the minister's bees also had actually been gathered and ordered by some, "of course I will contact them and the sale will be prevented. Which," almost a laughter in her voice, almost tears, "I suppose, is what everyone meant for me to discover."

Jacob rocks steadily in his unmoving chair, but he smiles. "Of course, and everyone is glad you are here," he whispers. "Home again."

Her hand on his shoulder is too light to turn his head to. "No, Jacob," she says, all steady, all heavy as this unbreathable air. "My home is back in the city now, and yours is here. All this," she lifts her hand to indicate all of something, and the light contact disappears, Rachel disappears.

But the white, hopeless stems had had no form at all, a wild mat of terror, mute and still. He rocks, he can feel it, a net of wild muteness spreading from his chest.

A voice bright with relief, brisk, about supper, but he raises his hand to catch at something that flutters near his face. Her hand. Her voice. Rachel. He struggles harder than he has in years of drifting to stay quiet and hear her. Harder than since before Mother died and there were doctors, and no matter how afraid he was and he had to listen to them and. He catches her hand and hears himself humming a sound that wants to be a word. Though she stands still he can feel how she has receded from him, so he draws his breath deep, deep, into quiet. "But, my dear," he hears at last, what a gentle voice, what can it say when this clutching of blind white grub hiding, "this is your *home,*" he breathes again so slow that finally the husk of polite disbelief, dry and exterior, rattling.

She pats his holding hand, she folded the socks so and stayed and lights on and off as Mother would and he needn't, you see, and away from even this kind garden into the dimness of drying and age of beauty. "Oh, Jacob, don't you see?" She is crying now, he has made. "I thought I could come here and take care of you and take you home with me but just look at this! Here you are, out here in this *shed,* and how do you wash? And everybody in this town, this nasty little," and the tears in her voice are terrible, he cannot look at her anymore so bent and helpless back in her chair somehow when he'd thought she was dead this long time, all unmoving and so sad about things, somewhere is the clock, the medicine time.

"No no no," he hears his voice all gentle reminding, "not Mother, this is Rachel, Rachel."

The cold roots and stems that won't ever go green suddenly struggle in his hand and he trembles with pity and revulsion as he throws his hand open to be rid of their terrible mute screaming.

There is a bruise, he can tell, where the keys have hit his thigh again and again and again and again, but he keeps on running with his head down, over the tops of hills as if they were waves, his breath groaning the only sound, on and on until the heat explodes into thunder and he stops in a clear space to feel its impact. Barely stops, and the hair on his head and arms prickles and lifts, and the lightning reaches down to him and through him, welds the keys in his pocket into an intricate uselessness. Jacob feels himself rising and quivering into the huge white electric brilliance and for a long instant he is held, more helpless than even he has ever feared, and suddenly he struggles, wrestles against this shaking of his limbs. All noise disappears and he is dropped, relieved, into silence, as huge water falls in drops as big as open hands on his face and throbbing body.

PART III

CHAPTER 15

*T*he rain brings the windows down on River Street in a hurry, the women flying up and down hallways and stairways to struggle with the swollen casings and frames. They wrench out the sawed-off mop handles and odd bits of board that have held the windows open for weeks; they snatch out the sliding screens, they breathe hard through their noses as they battle the little pins that hold the windows open. Thump thud all up and down the street the windows bang shut, and the curtains stop snaking and whipping on the wind out into the rooms and fall limp. The women stand for a moment breathless in their suddenly quiet houses, counting their children in their minds, and then hurry out the front or back, emerge to shout against the wind, which is already cold with rain.

The children come at a full run, hoping for and fearing the cleansing violence of the cold rain through their clothes, and collapse on their porches and just inside their front doors, their heads and the skin of their backs chilled and beaten by the rain, wetter than they think they've ever been. Their mothers yell at them for the wetness, scold them off the floors and into the bathrooms, out of clothes miraculously heavy, but the children are in a state of stupor, savoring the meeting of their cold skins with the month's heat that remains trapped inside their skins and inside the airless houses. They rub their heads with towels, suddenly laughing and breathless; where there are brothers they bump against one another in confused delight. *Wet to the skin,* their mothers scold, *chilled to the bone.* They run half naked to their bedrooms and leave their wet things in heaps in the bathroom, the bedroom, the hall, on their beds, anywhere; their dry underpants slide on warm and smooth. Downstairs their mothers make angry preparations for supper in kitchens that are hotter than ever, robbed of the cooled air by the wildness of the wind. Three times, four, half a dozen, the women leave the food on the counter and go to the stairs to scold again, loud over the tumult that is outside, up the stairwell and force the children to reappear dry and still ecstatic downstairs, and then they scold them back up to drape the wet clothes on the towel bars and bathtub edges, *for heaven's sake.*

Hail begins just at five, drumming the car roofs and lunch boxes and shoulders of the home-coming men: the ones who walk to work are crowded into the cars of those who drive, who are furious that they left their windows down as they have for days and now sit in wet seats trying to see through walls of rain, trying to hear past the huge barrage of hailstones on hollow metal, driving out of their way to take these others home. Three different cars all traveling the same road in the same direction narrowly miss hitting the same miserable black dog who wanders, helplessly crying, off and on the shoulder that is suddenly winter in painful pebbles. The men gallop heavily from the road to their porches, wanting to shout but with nothing to say against the monstrous unfairness of such a change in the weather, when all that was needed was a steady soft rain, a drop of say ten degrees, nothing like this useless assault. They remember and curse their tomatoes as they reach the front doors, remember and curse the wheat and corn and hay of farmers they know only by rumor, the farmers who probably prayed for rain, and now this.

Which hasn't even cooled their houses, where their children wait with hair awkwardly plastered on disturbingly round and

160

narrow skulls, for daddies to make this a holiday in spite of the sullen mothers, who call everyone to supper immediately, as if supper can't wait, as if the men had been out carousing instead of struggling to get home.

And then the electricity goes out, of course, but every man is honor bound to find the damned flashlight and make his way down cellar steps, intentionally cluttered for just such an emergency, to check the fuses and bang his forehead on a beam before he tacitly accepts what the children shouted at the first darkness: the power's out!

Somehow the candles lit and stuck into blobs of their own drippings on saucers and set on the kitchen tables generate the critical degree of heat that drives the temperature of the kitchens, after all these days of heat and this, by now, hour and a half of airlessness, past the bearable level, but the supper is there, and all up and down River Street and along the two other streets and across the three false avenues, families take their places and hate their food. The hail gives out, but the children aren't allowed to run out and gather up the already melting spheres of ice to save in the freezers until they become indistinguishable from the fuzzed frost: *sit down and eat your supper, your mother didn't spend half the day for you to run,* and so on. Four children in four separate houses sneeze, and their four mothers accuse the four fathers: *he'll have pneumonia now,* the women say, and their men stab guiltily at the fish sticks or boiled hot dogs on their plates.

The wind diminishes, but the rain keeps coming hard and steady and won't let up until after midnight, and won't completely stop before noon tomorrow. The houses begin to lose heat to the rain, and children begin telling each other the two worn ghost stories they all know, just because the houses are dark. Their mothers, now that their first anger and then their private worry about tornado (after all, there was a tornado in Clayborne three years ago, only twenty miles away) have passed, remember their electric refrigerators and freezers, and grudgingly give the children ice cream before bed: it would be soup by morning.

Out at the parsonage Ellen remembers the lemon sherbet and

mentions it to Jim. He's carrying their two bowls from the kitchen back to the living room when he hears the knocking at the front door, and assumes the wind has pulled the screen door open and it's banging.

"Here you are," he says and hands Ellen her bowl of pale sweet ice.

She accepts it, but her face is distracted with listening.

"Probably the wind—" he begins to explain.

"Shhh," she says.

Then they both hear it almost plainly, the shout almost drowned in the rain's noise. "Me IN," the voice shouts, and then the banging again. And Jim remembers distinctly Ellen latching the screen door hook just as the storm started.

They both hurry to the door, ashamed and eager, and open and unlock and open doors to admit Rachel Cavanaugh, though it takes a moment to recognize her, wet to the skin in spite of a dark raincoat, her hair plastered about her head and face, as she stands shivering and breathless but already talking faster and more urgently than they can understand there in the dark front hall.

"Wait, wait," Jim protests, reaching out to draw her farther into the house, toward the living room where the candles are lit. "Is your brother *hurt?*" Because the need to help him is all that has come through her words so far.

Ellen hurries to the living room and back with the afghan to put around Rachel, who has resisted Jim's hand, but Rachel pushes the blanket away. "I have no idea, but he could be—he's just gone, you know how he just goes off, so fast—we quarreled and he ran—and then the storm broke and he hasn't come back. I've looked all around our place, he's just not there anywhere, and I've got to use your telephone—the sheriff's department—"

"Sheriff?" Ellen says, pallid.

Jim is nodding vigorous agreement. "Yes, exactly—they'll have someone, probably, trained . . ." He gestures and Rachel follows him now into the living room. Ellen smooths the afghan back in its place over the back of the sofa.

Jim looks the number up in the front of the phone book, keeps one finger on the boldface number, and lifts the receiver to his ear. Slowly he turns to Rachel, who stands hugging herself, trying to stop the shivering. "The line is out," he says sadly.

As if she is prepared for this (as, Jim realizes, he also should have been, after all), she breathes deeply, says, "Well, where do *you* think he might have gone?"

Jim, taken utterly by surprise, just shakes his head.

"Listen," Rachel says, almost wild herself, "you have a car—we could drive out to the house and then in the direction he went—he started off toward the orchard land. Don't you see? *Any*thing could have happened to him, all that lightning and wind, there were branches all over the road." She draws another wavering breath.

"Now, Mrs. Cavanaugh," Jim says, still startled by her appearance, and now by her terror; although he will do whatever he can to help, he has been dry and comfortable, and did not see Jacob flying off across the grass in the queer green light. "First of all we have to get you warm and dry, or you'll be ill."

"Jacob is certainly as cold and—"

He touches her shoulder. "Quite possibly not," he says. "Jacob knows this area very well, and quite possibly he found shelter when the storm began." He clears his throat; in trying to calm her he has gone well beyond his certain knowledge of Jacob, which, after all, is little more than the most common knowledge of him, despite the dozen nights a year he spends talking to him across dark grass. "And we can do nothing until daylight—"

"Daylight?" she protests. "He's already been gone four hours!" She turns away from him and then back, trying for control of her voice. "I know you're being sensible."

"Mrs. Cavanaugh," Ellen says, a meek imitation of soothing, and then she has nothing more to say. Rachel looks at her a moment and then hurries past her to the front hall again. "Jim?" Ellen says.

"All right," he says. "Let me get my slicker."

And in two minutes he and Rachel are out the door, hurrying hunched through the rain to the long beige car. Ellen watches them pull slowly out of the driveway and head slowly toward the

163

dip that will lead to the bridge. In the living room the sherbet has melted.

Out on Pearl Street Alice and Elsie Reese look up at one another from their plates of cottage cheese and canned peaches, across the light of the two candles in the low silver candlesticks. In confusion, and, as their eyes meet, away, embarrassed. Alice thought for an instant that she'd heard something out back. Elsie thought for a second that she'd heard someone out back. To avoid having to say how silly and old that mistake makes her feel, how terrifying this flicker of senility is, each of the Reese sisters hurries a small forkful of cottage cheese from her plate to her lips. Her lips, so thin now that she hardly recognizes herself in the mirror anymore, this woman whose face is becoming tinier and less accurate with each passing season, though she remembers (and she is certain again, abruptly, that she knows what she knows) how times like this violent passage from summer to the threat of autumn used to invigorate her physically, used to make her eyes brighter and her skin firmer.

First Elsie and then Alice, in order of age, turns farther aside from the candlelit table to hide from her sister the thin silly tears of age and regret that come clouding her eyes. As if she could hear so much as a fork against a plate, much less a shed door. In the midst of pouring rain and thunder so close you can feel it through the furniture.

Neither Jim nor Rachel says a word when the headlights of the Pontiac show the bridge invisible under rushing water, only the rounded tops of the zebra-striped posts visible, nothing between them but the end of the pavement and the turgid water. Rachel begins to cry, but silently, and Jim puts the car in reverse and backs all the way home; the fields and shoulders are far too soaked to support an attempt at turning around.

In the Reese sisters' shed Jacob, breathless and drenched, stands in the dry smell of empty wooden walls and wonders less at the pain he still feels than at the utter silence he hears.

CHAPTER 16

*I*n the moment of waking, Rachel fumbles with the possibility that she has lain sleeping in the hotel room in Livingstone, all her efficient intentions about her brother (for the moment still a man of just past thirty, troubled but still endowed with all the mysterious potential of her childhood) and her life to come still bright and beckoning before her, if only she can shake this heavy veil of sleep and dream from her and rise. The room is quiet, unfamiliar by the gray light of early morning, and the bed warm and comforting. Rachel moves; in motion she regains the present almost without intervening memory, and she's out of bed in dismay and hurry.

The rain has slowed, light has come, they must hurry now. She finds her clothes, dried, a little stiff, wrinkled, lying across the chair, and she listens for sounds of the minister and his wife as she dresses, but all is quiet. She will leave without them: the car is unnecessary, probably worthless. If the bridge is passable she'll check first at the house—no, she corrects herself, she'll check at Jacob's shed, for she remembers (and is almost proud that she remembers) that he won't, of course, be in the house no matter what—and then follow out toward the Orchards the way she saw him go. Or, going quietly down the stairs, should she try the telephone again first?

By the time she gets to the bottom of the stairs, she recognizes the house's silence as emptiness, remembers that this is Sunday, sees by the living room clock that it's nearly ten, the Parsonses will have gone to church; in fact, she hears now the occasional car turning in next door, people arriving, a child calling. She lifts the receiver, but the phone is still as dead as a toy, and Rachel is slightly relieved: she'd rather not call anyone, at least not until she's sure Jacob hasn't found his way back by himself.

The water is down off the bridge, and Rachel crosses, feeling the river still rumbling its back along the underside. Probably she was more worried than necessary last night: probably she will find Jacob lying comfortable in the shed, or moving slowly through his garden, vaguely touching the rain's damage.

The garden is wrecked, of course: tomato plants flattened, their split fruits and tangled stems crushing flowers, only the zinnias still upright, tough stems bearing tattered petals that a day ago were crowned and gaudy spheres.

Rachel is chilly, standing at the shed door, and though clearly Jacob is not there and has not been there, she steps inside for a minute, just for the utter dryness that is some cousin of warmth. The smell of Jacob and of the old trunk blends with the fruitiness of this year's roses.

She leaves, pulling the door tight to protect and preserve all that, and finds the house as empty as she had expected. She puts coffee on to perk while she hurries upstairs and into clothes better suited to walking and searching, brushes her hair and ties a scarf over it. The church bells are beginning to roll out through the morning as Rachel comes out through the garden zipping her jacket and heads off past the hedge for the Orchards, her feet already drenched by the cold wet grass.

Some of it could be saved, but Dan, standing a few feet from the mess of tattered plants, skewed stakes, and burst and bruised tomatoes and cucumbers and zucchini, can't seem to make himself bother to gather up what's merely fallen and carry it into the house. It hardly matters. Or it seems only right, this cool damp ruin of his neat garden. The root vegetables will be all right, the beets and carrots, and they couldn't have eaten all the rest anyway. And now he'll have to go out to the Orchards and see how bad it is out there. The five minutes of hail probably did no harm at all, being small and so brief, but the wind may have. He hears Julia start the car. She'll be going to church now, and though he's aware that probably he should drive her there and take the car, he's glad it's almost too late for that. The walk out to the Orchards will be cool and quiet, and whatever he finds there he'd rather find and decide about alone, without having to hurry home or talk about it beforehand. So he stands a minute more, and she drives away. He's fleetingly grateful: all this past couple of weeks she's kept a kind distance, for which he's proud of her in a confused, pitying sort of way.

He walks the orchard by every third row. The wind brought down enough apples to make it worthwhile to put the men out tomorrow to collect drops: if it stays coolish they shouldn't lose too much. But his real worry seems unfounded, since the trees and most of the apples in the main part of the orchard are safe, hardly disarranged. He finds nothing really amiss until he gets to the southeast corner: as if a tornado had come by and nicked the very edge, four trees are turned and lying completely uprooted, as if they'd been kicked over. The roots rise up almost exactly the height of the branches, so each tree looks like a frayed dumbbell, a ragged baby's rattle. Nothing to be done about it, he knows, beyond picking what they can (and these are Macs, maybe not even worth picking except that he's got the crew that can do it) and hauling the wood away. But their symmetry, lying there, gives him the first pleasure and relief he's had in what seems like weeks, since the first time he saw Jacob in his garden at twilight. He walks around the trees, touches the roots thicker than his legs, thinner than his fingers, some of them washed clean as bone and pale, some of them bark-callused where they were raised aboveground. Then he walks back around to their tops and sights along them to see if he's right, that the roots and branches match, a desirable miracle of blind agreement, cooperation that denies the forces of soil, rock, sun, pruning.

Through the leaves and high standing roots he sees Rachel Cavanaugh walking steadily toward him, looking regularly to her right and left. When she sees the uptorn trees she stops, touches her knuckle to her lips swiftly, and then hurries forward, her arms stiff and a little away from her sides, as if she meant to raise them up. He cannot imagine what she will say or do when she sees him, but even as he waits he can feel the earth below him filled with roots, as the sky behind him is filled with fruited trees.

She says a word but not to him, and very softly, and then again, louder but still suppressed, tight held in her throat. "Jacob?" she says.

The quiet terror in her voice makes him weak, and then the terror and a guilt squeeze at him: Can he have walked, dreaming of branches and roots, past the crushed or mangled body of a man beneath one of these neatly arranged trees, tangled in branches or roots? He can almost believe he has seen it, a leg, a mud-stained black slipper just visible, and he moves with a lurch of panic to go where she is.

She cries out and her hands fly up.

"What is it?" he shouts, though he is only eight feet away, and her face goes from white to scarlet in one instant, and she wraps her arms around herself, and Dan can see that she remembers.

Her face is sullen. He comes on anyway, to face her, his fear greater than any embarrassment, and he's beginning to be impatient with her face even before he asks again, "What is it?" His voice is bullying, he knows, but he'll be told why she said her brother's name here among the ruined trees.

Right during the processional, at just the moment she sees Mary Aldrich in her choir robe leading the others down the aisle, Ellen feels the first swoop and lift of pride in knowing the secret, that Jacob has disappeared and Rachel Cavanaugh of all people lies sleeping in her own guest room. Not another soul in this church, not another soul in this town, knows. Except Jim, who, for some reason, seemed to want not to even mention it over their quiet breakfast, and she suspects, rightly, that he's not going to mention it during the service either, though that would certainly be the most efficient way to get people out looking for the poor man. But Jim even insisted that they let Rachel sleep; though Ellen had thought it rather unfair, since they knew how very worried she was and that she'd want to get out there as early as possible, she had nodded, submitting if not agreeing, but in fact she'd already started to savor the secret. Poor Ellen! During the collection she'll begin to be a little uneasy, and long before the benediction, after Jim has given a shorter sermon than usual and the choir has sung only two verses of the last hymn instead of four so that everyone can get back to whatever near-emergencies the storm has left them, she'll be in despair again at this petty pridefulness of hers. It's happened many times, almost every time she's known a thing that not everyone knew. But it always surprises and disappoints her, the way she moves in apparent innocence from care to concern to a peculiar possessiveness about whatever the trouble is. She knows, standing beside Jim at the door, smiling and nodding and patting shoulders, that she'll be a little disappointed when Jacob's found, and she won't be able to resist telling someone that she has known since way last night that he'd been lost.

All this, and wondering whether Rachel will still be there when they get home, and if she is, what there is special for dinner, or if Rachel will have Jim out raising a search party and there will be no dinner today, and wondering why, after all, Jim didn't mention that Jacob would need finding: all this half distracts Ellen, but as she's walking home (along the roadside instead of across the lawns, because the grass is so wet) beside Jim she's not at all sure the Reese sisters were in church today, which isn't like them, unless they were ill, or something had happened.

"Jim," she says, "I think the Reeses weren't with us this morning."

"Probably," he says. "Lots of people weren't there. Wet going."

"We must call on them tomorrow," she says, vengeful, for

she knows he hates going out there, dear as the two old sisters are.

Jim drives the Pontiac carefully across the bridge, wondering whether it's wise or not: maybe the bridge disappeared under a mere sheet of water last night, but maybe it was inches, and maybe the bridge is so weakened now that the weight of his big car will be too much. Of course, by now he's across, safe and sound, rolling up the rise to park beside the stand of privet.

No sign of Rachel, no answer when he knocks (for the first time since the first time he came out here, seven years ago, and was not answered then, either, though Jacob was home). He stands a moment beside the back door and looks back to the break in the hedge where he usually stands when he comes here. It is years since he's been in this yard by day, and he's never been just here, way in next to the house. The break in the hedge is a comfortable distance away; anyone coming through would be well recognized, even avoidable, before he came too close. A swallow swoops and dives from behind him down and sudden into the hedge, and Jim smiles. He's half ready to walk quietly to where the bird disappeared and see what he can see, just as if this were his own yard and he had dominion, but at the first step Jacob's rocking chair is moved by a breeze and rebukes him, so straight and composed is it in every line. Jim hurries back toward where he came in through the hedge and then turns and hurries around the other side of the shed, just in case, and opens the door.

What Jim sees (though he has no idea what he expected, perhaps a dimness of old rakes, cobwebs, broken lumber): the neat pallet, the domed tin trunk, the kitchen chair and the small table, the shaving things lined up on a rafter from which hang armfuls of drying roses and bachelor's buttons, makes him nearly groan: with recognition, yes, he admits it as if it were a calling, with love and without shame, his groan is composed of desire: here is all he could want: silence; and safe, dim, dry, softly scented solitude.

As he drives his long car back home, where he will leave it and walk up River Street to begin in earnest the search for

Jacob, he's aware of his own shame: at wishing to have another, longer time alone in that shed before it is restored to Jacob.

For days now Julia has resisted as best she could the rumors she's felt brushing past her about Dan and Rachel Wilcox. Not that he hasn't been as silent and accusatory as if he were guilty of something at least that bad, and not that she's forgotten (or disowned) that first flutter of suspicion she felt when she saw Rachel in the store that first morning. It seems to her that suspicion has been borne out, what with Rachel's plan to put Jacob into a madhouse and sell the house and land at a high price, and what with her trying to get Dinah out there to work for her for nothing, and probably get the innocent girl to tell things just as well kept from outsiders. But surely, Julia believes without even making inventory, surely twenty-five years, a daughter, a grandson: early this morning, while she was dressing for church, she saw Dan out the window standing with his arms folded, looking away from his ruined vegetable garden, and sympathy welled strong and sure within her.

So now that she has come home and found him gone, she doesn't hesitate (longer than to turn the potatoes off so they won't cook to a mush, and to turn the oven down on the roast even further) but drives right on out to the Orchards, which is the only place he could be, checking for storm damage and preparing work plans for the crews for tomorrow. She drives out there with the very simplest of intentions: she means to bring him home, and he'll be wet and chilled by now with walking through the high grass around the trees. The roast will be done in an hour, and Rosie and the baby and Arnie will be there. Julia has the car. Of course she drives out to the Orchards, with no more intention of checking on him or spying on him or even of getting out of the car unless she has to than she'd have had a month ago, before all this foolishness. She pulls into the parking area and sits with the motor running for a good five minutes before she thinks he must not be in the office yet, and before she thinks how it might be good (though this is as vague as her wondering whether she's ever seen that second shed behind the office building) for her to show more of an interest in the Or-

171

chards, as her father used to urge her to do (that had been, after all, the point of her year's training over in Livingstone, to teach her to keep the Orchards' books, which Dan has done himself ever since Rosie was born, and why didn't she take that work back, she wonders now), and before she feels a swift nostalgia for walking with him. How long has it been, she wonders. And so, in spite of her Sunday shoes (though she did leave her hat at home) and the wet ground, she gets out of the car and walks across the gravel of the parking area, down one of the paths between storage buildings, toward the rows and rows of plump trees; she goes cautiously, as if at any step she might decide to go back, as if she had no real right after all to be here in the orchard she brought to her marriage.

Dan, hurrying back down the wider aisle between the greenings on his left, unscathed, and the Granny Smiths on his right, heavily dropped, is at first uncertain even what she is, moving so slowly two or three rows over, and he stops to get a better look. And when he sees and recognizes the person of his wife, he doesn't move but lets her go on past him. His instant of furious defensiveness passes almost at once, though: she won't find a thing here.

And so, because he is thinking more violently of Jacob, and willing him to have fled far beyond harm and far beyond finding by anyone in this town, most especially that sister of his who would have denied him on grounds of privacy, as if a lost man were a private matter, he lets Julia go, and at the far eastern edge of the orchard, she sees the figure of Rachel Cavanaugh walking steadily away.

If Timer were awake, he'd tell Allen to stay away from the river, as if he'd never been a kid excited about high roaring water in the trough he's known as a flat rocky stream. Susan slides another plate into the rinse pan. If she lets Allen go, she should let Tony go, even though Allen's far the more cautious. And Tony would never cry foul if she kept him home and let Allen go; all the more reason.

"No," she says.

"Oh, Momma, *please*—I promise hope to die stick a needle in my eye I won't go down the bank *please?*"

"Stop teasing, Allen." She submerges both hands in the rinse water and lifts the plates one by one and sets them into the drainer.

He sits heavily into his father's chair at the table behind her.

Tony, leaning against the counter, floats a glass on the soapy wash water. "We wouldn't go down the bank, would we, Allen?"

But Allen doesn't answer. Susan pushes Tony's hand aside and puts the rest of the glasses into the dishpan.

"We'd just stay up on the bank and then we'd throw in some stones or something," Tony says, not even asking really, just pretending. "And if somebody *else* went down that old bank and fell in that water we could throw them a rope and pull them right out!"

"Or you could just stay right here and read the funnies," Susan says. In the interest of peace, and because she actually wants both of them to stay home so she won't be alone here waiting for Timer to wake up and be silent and accusing, as if she were to blame for his hangover, she offers, "And maybe we could make popcorn later—or popcorn balls."

"I hate popcorn," Allen growls.

"No, Allen—you hate squash," she says, and Tony giggles. "You hate liver, and you hate cauliflower, and you hate—matzoh balls!" Tony laughs out loud, disbelieving there could be such a food, but Allen sinks farther forward on his folded arms. Can she let just Allen go? He is cautious. And it isn't really a flood. She rinses the glasses and begins rubbing the silverware piece by piece between her fingertips underwater.

"*Chris* is going," Allen says.

She nods. "You're sure about that?"

He shrugs, she knows it as if by feeling the disturbance of air.

"Honey, it's really pretty dangerous. Why don't you just find something else to do—"

"I don't want to do anything else!"

"—and don't interrupt—" He slumps heavily onto the table. "—and when your father gets up you can ask him. You could even ask him to go with you." She plunges a handful of forks and spoons into the rinse water, lifts them dripping into the drainer cup. Tony moves the serving dishes down the counter toward her one at a time, a fleet of bowls and plates on the move.

"Well, can I go over to Chris's?"

She blows out slowly. "Well," mimicking his whining complaint, "will you be back in half an hour?"

"Yeah," he concedes dully and drags himself upright.

"It's two o'clock now. You be back here *by* two thirty."

"Yeah," he says.

"Can I go?" Tony asks, but without either hope or fear of disappointment.

"No!" Allen comes slightly alert.

"No," Susan says. *"You* don't hate popcorn, do you?" He grins. "And you," she half turns, her hands still deep in the dishpan, to Allen, who is already only a grouchy back receding down the hall toward the front door, "Allen, don't you dare go anywhere else, you hear?"

"Uh-huh," he says.

"I mean it," she says. "And wear a jacket," though she doesn't expect him to obey that.

She hears the door open and then a man's voice, "Is your daddy home?"

She hurries down the hall drying her hands on a dish towel. Allen stands mute and resentful inside with Mr. Parsons on the other side of the screen. *Oh Lord,* she thinks, imagining her pleasant popcorn party with Tony disappearing into a tense hour of pastoral chat.

"Why, hello," she says cautiously, and pushes the screen open to let him in. "Go on then, Allen," she says.

"Hello, Susan," the plump minister says, barely stepping in, which she takes as a good sign. "Is Timer here?" He glances into the empty living room.

"He's asleep right now," she says, but she can feel panic creeping up through her chest: something is wrong or he wouldn't ask for Timer, of all people the most distant from the polite church and all that.

"Oh. Well, no need to disturb him. I'm just—well, it seems that Jacob Wilcox disappeared during our storm yesterday, and though he's probably all right I'm just asking people to keep an eye out for him, or if they have the time—"

"Disappeared?" Susan wonders aloud. It is the last word she heard, and the image in her mind is of a magical puff of smoke.

He clears his throat and shifts his body. "Well, he was out— away from home—and then, when the storm was over, well, he hasn't come back. His sister, of course, is very concerned."

"Of course," Susan agrees vaguely.

"Well then, some of the men are thinking of organizing themselves to have a thorough look," and his voice goes on, explaining as apologetically and evenly as if he were asking for contributions to something. Susan can feel Tony's slight warmth behind her in the hall.

She nods. "Well, I see—that's—bad, isn't it."

"So if you would just let Timer know—it's probably not terribly urgent, but his sister is, as I said, quite upset, and it seems little enough—"

"Yes, of course." She's as lethargic as if some minute brightness had caught and held her vision, what her brothers had called the blind stares. "I'll tell him. Right away."

And then she's standing alone in the hall as if she'd just wakened.

"That old Jacob Wilcox," Tony says in the kitchen. She hears the discomfort in his voice. "That old Jacob Wilcox," he repeats. "Probably he went and got drownded in that river," he says softly.

Susan hurries secretly down the hall and bustles Tony out the back door with her, and hurries across the back yard and through the wet, hanging, mildew-whitened leaves of the lilacs and past the Deerys' house where the baby cries and down to the riverbank to see if it is true; she takes Tony's hand and rushes out through nameless meadows and sees Jacob standing sweet and tall beneath a spread solitary elm and takes the boy and runs breathless with relief, almost laughing, tears upon her eyelashes, to stand before him.

"Who was that?" Timer says from the top of the stairs.

"Jim Parsons," she answers.

175

*

On Sundays, when they eat always at two and always in the dining room, Dinah is open to the sober delights of heavy silver and starched napkins, as open as she is closed to any delights in the daily table setting and clearing that is her chore. Her only dissatisfaction with the whole process, from silencer cloth to flowers in summer or candles in winter, is that she knows no fancier way to fold the napkins than a simple triangle under the forks, and her mother, who decreed long ago this formality of Sunday dinner, is no help at all.

Dinah does love the table, but she loves equally doing this family chore on Sunday after Sunday school and church and feeling it an act of fealty and devotion. Sundays, moving carefully from china closet to table, cherishing thin dishes with intricate edges between her thin hands, Dinah is aware of herself as the daughter, obedient, a comfort, a helpmate.

And beautiful: Sundays this year, because her mother has allowed her stockings and a garter belt for Sundays, which pull taut along her thighs and redefine her body to herself, the slide of her slip against the stockings, the firm clasp of the garter belt low on her spine. And today, because it is cooler, she's wearing the green dress with three-quarter sleeves that was a little too big last fall but now fits perfectly; as she sets the glasses, two at each place, at the correct distance off the tips of the knives, she's aware of the wide plain neckline and the pearl buttons on the shoulders, and their simple beauty pleases her so that she forgets to keep her voice formal and cold when she says into the kitchen, "Will we want the gravy boat?"

And her mother says, "Yes—would you bring it out here?" just as naturally as if yesterday had not been silent, even through the excitement of the storm, between them; just as easily as if her daughter had never turned on her a face of righteous suffering and said through strangling tears *Because you hate me, I know you hate me;* just as if she had never felt such a furious and magnetized revulsion that she had had to physically hold her hand down from striking out at Dinah's face of secrecy and guilt. "We'll need the small compote, too, for the cranberry," Mary says.

In the living room Nobel and Brian read the Sunday paper in white shirts, neckties, and an easy silence of exchanged sections. Their jackets are laid side by side on the back of the chair nobody ever sits in, and when Mary calls them to dinner they'll fold up their parts of the paper obediently and immediately, already an hour tantalized by the smell of chicken browning and rolls baking, put on their jackets, lifting their shoulders to shrug the jackets into place, check their ties in the hall mirror, and enter the dining room.

But this Sunday, after Dinah and Mary have allowed their bodies to brush one another casually at the shoulder or forearm as they pass back and forth from kitchen to dining room, after that but before Mary calls the men, while she is still stirring the golden chicken gravy, scraping the fork's side so vigorously over the pan bottom that her curled and arranged hair trembles slightly, Dan Cullinan is at the front door. Mary in the kitchen finishes, pours the gravy into the silver boat, her jaw tightened against Dan's lack of consideration, even though she can hear him apologizing for the interruption; a month ago she'd have hurried out there to try to get him to stay for one of her hot rolls. She carries the gravy as far as the door, where Dinah meets her and takes the gravy and sets it on its saucer.

Because Dinah is proud of how much the table with its steaming dinner and pretty china resembles a magazine illustration of Sunday dinner, and because she is relieved that she and her mother have stopped being angry with each other without having to say anything, and because she loves stuffing and cranberry, she looks up from the table to her mother with a shy smile, asking for her approval of it all.

Mary feels her whole body flushed as suddenly as if she'd stepped onto a heating grate.

"I imagine," Dan goes on, "he's holed up somewhere and'll show up at the house sooner or later, but"

Nobel's voice overlaps, agreeing, both of them calmly concerned, responsible.

Dinah sees her mother tilt quickly forward and catch herself almost violently, as if she'd been about to fall, or as if she'd dreamt she was about to fall.

The two men's voices separate, resolve into Dan's, "About three, we're aiming for, if people can get there, at the store," and Nobel's, "Soon as dinner's over, and Brian here can help too," his voice a little cautious because Mary's listening and has that unreasonable thing about Rachel Cavanaugh, but after all this is an emergency, a thing that's got to be done no matter who it is.

Dinner, Mary shouts, dinner, when he's floating already twenty miles from here rolling over with his mouth full of mud, dinner! She'll have you out there as if there were saving him, don't you know, I know her, to prove she loves him like a child, dinner! Mary turns from their male blankness to Dinah's face of question and she must sob once in grief and rage, how Rachel could have managed this is beyond her, and she cries to Dinah in defense, in apology, I don't even know! What difference could it make, you never even spoke to him!

"Who're they talking about?" Dinah whispers.

The door closes behind Dan; Nobel comes to the doorway with Brian solemn and important behind him. "You hear?" he asks Mary, who nods, and he nods in return.

Mary goes into the kitchen and takes off her apron; the gravy was all that was needed.

"Jacob Wilcox," Nobel answers Dinah in the dining room.

Mary sees Dinah's profile become, barely, politely grave before she lifts her napkin from beneath the heavy-handled forks and spreads it on her lap.

And so the men gather at a little after three on a gray, damp Sunday afternoon on the long, narrow wooden porch of the building that once held an insurance company, a diner (or before that a drugstore), and a dry goods store and now holds only Amos Brown's store and home. They come together back in their working clothes, Sunday ties laid off sooner and with more anticipation than usual, and they fold their arms and talk quietly, agreeing about gardens and how high the river is and the chance of more rain. By three thirty, about twenty men stand around, and almost as many cars or trucks sit in the parking area, and at last, by curious default created more by impatience than urgency, Arnie Deery speaks in a public voice, saying they'd better get organized and get going, and the other men, most of them older than he, mutter agreement and begin to volunteer. This one says he'll drive out toward Livingstone as far as Galpin's, and he'll take Bob here with him, and they'll look both sides of the road maybe half a mile, and work their way back. This is such an admirable pattern that more than half of the searchers will adopt it. Dan says he's already had a good look around the Orchards, no need of repeating that, but he'll go north on Town Line a couple miles; Tom Douglas says he'll do the same south on Town Line. And on they go, until it sounds like they've got the likely area pretty well covered when there're Jim Parsons and Jack Haines left.

Jack clears his throat. "Well," he says, "why don't I just go out Town Line to Covert and start stopping at the farms out there, see if anybody's seen him." There's a nodding acceptance around, and then a pause, men wondering who's left, men wondering what the minister's going to do.

"I'll stay close in, then," Jim says, as if agreeing with some suggestion, "take a look through that little woods up between Pearl and Spare."

Relieved, they stand another minute, scratch their upper arms, and then, settling caps or jackets or just hunching their shoulders, they take the first steps toward their waiting cars and trucks, and with something like a sigh, the search begins.

Tony and Allen and Chris sit on the Darcys' front steps, Tony on the top one and Allen and Chris two steps down, and watch them go.

"What they ought to do is get some dogs," Chris says.

"Dogs?" Tony wonders.

"Too wet," Allen says.

Tony wriggles, waits until the last truck has gone out of sight, and scampers into the house to pee.

As if he had waited until Tony was gone so as not to scare him, Allen says confidentially, "He's probably in the river."

Chris nods casually, though the idea is sudden and new and delightful.

"They ought to drag it," Allen says softly.

"Yeah," Chris says, and stretches. "Get a big net or something."

Alice saw him first, right after breakfast when she went to set out the plate of scraps for the nameless cats who come to the back porch. He did startle her, coming out of the shed that way, as if unfolding, he was so tall, and there was something a little menacing about the sharp smear of dirt all along his left shoulder. But then, the shirt itself had, she thought from here, French cuffs, and he was, indisputably, in his stocking feet, which was at once so pitiable and so comical that Alice wasn't the least bit frightened, for all the ruffianness of the dirt. She set the plate of scraps down and let the screen door shut; for maybe five minutes, before she went and got Elsie to show her, Alice watched the white-haired man through the screen.

Not that he did much, poor fellow, but stand there quite near the shed, and look slowly about. When he finally turned his face toward the house, he was frowning just a little and Alice was almost convinced that he looked familiar. And she hadn't forgotten the sound she thought she'd heard last night during that storm, and her gratitude at finding that she wasn't crazy or at least wasn't completely mistaken probably added to her feelings of generosity toward this lost soul. That was when she went to get Elsie, feeling vindicated and excitedly responsible, to see if Elsie recognized him, too.

Elsie was running the carpet sweeper slowly under the breakfast table and Alice had a job getting her to understand, shouting and gesturing, that what she wanted to show her might not wait until she'd finished and was important enough to bother about. But he was still there when the two tiny sisters returned to stand a little awkwardly side by side at the screen door. They both saw him turn, still slowly and apparently unaware of his feet, which must be wet to the skin, and touch the wood of the shed wall lightly with his slender palm, and nod.

That nod was what convinced Elsie, the way it made his longish hair swing a little. She turned to Alice and mouthed (for Elsie never forgets that she and Alice are the only deaf ones, whereas Alice sometimes acts as if people can't hear her when she shouts at Elsie) *Jay-cob-will-cocks,* and Alice nodded, that was the name, wasn't it, and here he was in their shed.

By the time he actually went back into the shed, and Alice and Elsie sighed each to herself in something like satisfaction and went back to finish the morning chores, it was too late to get to church on time, which secretly pleased them, though both fussed about it almost as if it were the other's fault.

They've spent their Sunday, then, like children who are nursing a nestling found upon the ground. One or the other is nearly always at the back door or at a sewing room window to see whether he's come out again or not, and Alice spent her whole hour's nap time upstairs at her bedroom window watching for him.

He comes out twice more around the middle of the day and takes that same puzzled and slow look around him. The next time he comes out he's barefoot, which Alice points out to Elsie (they're both in the parlor with their faces close to the cool glass of the window) with approval; Elsie, with more complicated gestures and a deeply worried face, shows Alice that he doesn't seem to be using his left arm at all. They both look, and wonder whether he injured it in the fall he obviously had on his way here, or if it means something more fearful, a paralysis, a stroke.

Still, they try to go on with their routine, and they set the table in the dining room for their Sunday dinner, and Elsie lays out the bone-handled carving set before she takes her place. Alice bows her head and asks the blessing they learned from their mother and have taken turns saying at every dinner for as long as either can remember.

"Dear Lord, we thank Thee for this food. Bless it to the strengthening of our bodies, and lead, guide, and direct us through life and at last bring us safe to Thee in Heaven. Amen."

Elsie says her amen exactly on the heels of Alice's. They open their eyes, and Elsie pushes back her chair and stands. She takes up the carving set and slices each of them two thin pieces of white meat from the little chicken and lays them on their plates. Then she sits again, and they both unfold their napkins and lay them in their laps. Elsie passes Alice's plate to her. They both glance half guiltily away from their plates toward the window and then back, in a kind of pleading, as if each were asking Mother for dispensation of the usual rules in view of the extraordinary circumstances, to one another. And after a second, they both nod.

Alice gets the plate and silver from the china closet while Elsie stands again and cuts off one whole thigh and drumstick. Alice dishes up a boiled potato (although that leaves them only one to share, and it is the larger one she puts on the plate) and two large spoonfuls of peas while Elsie splits two of the biscuits (leaving them only one apiece, and they both are very fond of Elsie's biscuits) and puts a generous pat of butter into each steaming middle. Alice considers for a moment, watching Elsie tuck a cool bit of cranberry jelly in next to the joint of chicken, and then she goes to the buffet and takes out of the drawer a large napkin and wraps the silverware in it, knife, fork, and spoon held snug.

At the back door they hesitate, Alice with the silverware and a tumbler of ice water in her hands, Elsie carefully balancing the ample dinner on the plate, and perhaps if either of them were alone she would lose courage here and leave the plate on the porch railing, at the mercy of any wandering cat. But together they go on, walking balanced and self-conscious, out the back door and across the small porch and down the still sodden back steps.

At the closed door of the shed they realize that neither of them has a hand free to knock, and that nearly undoes them until Alice, who is the younger by nearly two years and has always been more inclined to excitability and impatience, kicks the door three taps with the toe of her black oxford. After a second, each of them blushes slightly in the cool air, afraid he'll open the door, and then remembers that they cannot hear a response should he choose to call out instead of coming to the door. A few more seconds pass before Elsie begins to despair: she can almost feel the food cooling, and how pitiful to be carrying a plate of cold food. She nudges Alice with her elbow and nods as clearly as she can toward the latch. Alice looks so startled she almost looks young; they haven't shared such a pother at a closed door since they were in their early twenties and invited to a Christmas dance in Coville. But she obeys, and setting the glass carefully on a piece of old cordwood that stands handy next the wall, she lifts up the latch and pushes the door gently inward.

Inside the shed, where neither Alice nor Elsie has been in any number of years, since they have a boy who comes to do the yard, stand two old metal lawn chairs with shell-shaped backs, the lawn mower and its gas can, and farther back is the last third of the last cord of wood they bought before they agreed, sadly, not to trust themselves to have fires in the parlor anymore, after the one they both forgot and the carpet was scorched. Off to the right, in the darkest end of the shed, is the old porch glider, rusted motionless, and by the watery light of the one far window they can make out the form of Jacob Wilcox sleeping there, his left arm held tenderly across his chest by his right arm, and his long, thin legs bent at the knees. He doesn't stir as they step inside carefully and set their offerings on the seat of one of the chairs, but they can see (each of them checks, delicately, looking only at his chest and not at his face, as if that would be an intrusion) that he is breathing regularly and seems comfortable. They watch him for a moment before they turn and leave; Elsie draws the door gently shut behind them.

They walk back to the house hand in hand and don't feel the least bit silly until they get to the steps, where they must let go and go up one at a time because each needs the support of the railing to steady herself.

At a quarter past four the telephone lines are back in operation and Rachel's third trip in to the telephone booth outside Amos's store is rewarded with a dial tone. By now she has the sheriff's number memorized and she dials.

The line is busy, but Rachel has learned in the past twenty hours a new kind of patience. Fifteen times she dials and fifteen times the line is busy. *Five more,* she thinks, *and I can call the operator and have her check the line.* Across the road a little boy stands watching her. She no longer cares about that; even this morning when Dan Cullinan appeared so suddenly, she'd been upset not by a memory of his spying face but because he was witness to her half-theatrical leap of hope and terror that Jacob lay within the prostrate trees: already she had stopped caring about the rest of them. She dials again, her dime ready on the little rounded shelf. Busy. Since that first moment of waking confusion in Ellen Parsons' guest room, she's cared only about getting the very next thing accomplished: getting home, then walking to the Orchards, then walking back to the house, then here to the telephone, then back to the house, and out again. She has walked almost fifteen miles today on that one cup of coffee. Dial. Busy. This last loop out to the south of the house and back she hasn't even looked around, almost forgetting why she is walking. She dials.

This time the phone rings.

She is dumbfounded for a second and then hurries her fingers after the dime so quickly, her fingers so suddenly stiff, that the dime skids away and almost falls off the shelf.

"Hello, sheriff's office," a woman's bored voice says.

"Hello," Rachel says hoarsely, her dime tight and cold between finger and thumb.

"Sheriff's office," the woman insists.

Rachel fumbles the coin into the slot, hears the jangle of the machine's swallowing.

"Hello," Rachel says. "Hello. May I speak to the sheriff, please."

"Sheriff Elliot's busy right now may I help you."

"Yes," Rachel says, and then she can't imagine how to begin. "My brother is missing."

The woman doesn't answer, as if she were waiting for more from Rachel, who cannot tell her any more. Finally the woman says, "And where are you calling from?"

Rachel tells her, and gives her name and address when asked, Jacob's name and address as requested, an explanation for her presence when asked.

Maybe it is the relief of finally having reached the authorities, her day's goal, or maybe it is the recitation of her familiar street and number and city carrying the hope of home and ordinary life again, or maybe it is having to say *I've been visiting* as the only possible design within which to identify her experience of the past weeks, but something brings tears pricking along Rachel's eyelids. She inhales slowly through her nose to relax her throat so she can go on answering the questions.

Missing since, last seen, description (which might have been impossible for Rachel with her tears so close but that "description" is only the heading the woman reads and goes quickly on to the rest): age, race, height, weight, hair color, eye color, identifying characteristics or marks.

"He," and Rachel has to pause to clear her throat, how to explain Jacob's identifying characteristic to this woman, "he often is quite—confused. He. He shouts, sometimes."

In the background Rachel can hear voices, another telephone ringing. She flushes as if the woman were visible, looking up at her from the form on which she is not writing anything because what Rachel has said has no place on the form. Across River Street the little boy seems to be singing to himself as he pushes a stone slowly along the edge of the pavement with his bare foot.

"I think I know the one you mean," the woman says, her voice suddenly and unpleasantly personal and animated. "I got a cousin who lives over on Covert."

"Oh," Rachel says. But she doesn't care about that anymore. She closes her eyes.

"What they'll probably do is send out a deputy," the voice as cordial as a nurse's. "There a phone number they can use?"

"Oh—we don't—well," she forces herself to think calmly, a telephone number where she can be reached. "They could leave a message with James Parsons. He's the Baptist minister, I'm sure his number's in the book. I'm at a pay phone—"

"That's fine. James Parsons. All right, Mrs.—Cavanaugh. We'll be in touch."

"Thank you," Rachel says.

"Goodbye," the woman says.

Rachel hangs up. Her coin moves on to another stage within the machine. She sits suddenly, absurdly drained and grateful for the little bench that duplicates the little shelf in the opposite corner of the little glass-sided booth.

As Jim Parsons approaches, in concentric trapezoids from the edges, the young blue spruce that he considers the center of the grove, because it was from a branch of this tree that his swarm of bees finally hung and a day later disappeared, he walks more and more slowly. Because he is an honest man at heart he stops before he reaches the tree itself, before he can be quite certain that it is within his sight. He is not even completely certain he would know the tree if he came to it, but he has been certain since before he entered the grove that he would not find Jacob here. So he stops.

He doesn't go so far as to accuse himself of anything. He doesn't go so far as to wonder whether he would know Jacob if he found him. He stops, so he won't have to go so far as all that.

He stands among the trees with his hands in his pockets and finds himself thinking about how this day's searching is to end: they made no plan for signaling or even reporting if Jacob was found, no agreement on whether or when or where to come together after they each have done what they said they would do. Nobody really took charge; nobody will watch or know.

He breaks off the still soft tip of a fir twig and crushes the needles between his thumb and finger. Christmas for a moment. Snow, long evenings, candles in the church, the church full, children's faces. Men singing. Snow on the roof and undisturbed a foot deep around that low building of Jacob's, Jim himself booted and mittened, sitting in that straight chair in the snow-lighted dark and silence, his breath hanging in the air before him as the dried and brittle flowers hang all around

A long cool moment for Jim to the near melody of spent rain falling off branches and leaves with flat splats onto the wet ground: a sweet aching victory of longing, of loss accomplished, as if Jacob gone were the one thing necessary to the perfection of the life of James Parsons, to the life of every other man, to the completion of their collective manhood, so that that one grief can stand tall and straight at their center, to be saved, to save them. So that they can live with that as their emblem: Once there lived a man in solitude of his own making, and that solitude was a beautiful and comforting thing. He was given to us in our need of him, and he was taken from us in our need of his absence, that we might cherish our loss of him. So be it.

He checks his watch, less than an hour since they all met at the store. He tosses the bit of fir trash away and rubs his fingers down his thigh as if they were soiled.

And Ellen deciding not to fix a large dinner, though there was clearly time; *she* should have come out searching. He scowls at her eagerness about it all, she hardly knowing Jacob. Or knowing Rachel either, any better than he does, but making all that bother this morning, and then of all things insisting as he left this afternoon that he be back in time for their usual Sunday call on the Reese sisters.

He kicks at the thick years of needles and then, slowly, forces himself on to the center of the grove; afterward, hardly looking even where he is going, much less about for signs of a lost man, he walks more and more quickly out of the woods onto Pearl Street and along it until he is well past the village, alone out on the side of one of the country roads that has no name he knows of. He walks on until he has come to the tenth tree since he started counting, and then he crosses the road and walks slowly but steadily back into town.

He arrives at Amos's store just before five, and there's no one in sight. Still, he goes up onto the porch and pauses, as if a gathering were about to begin, and glances half accusing about him. The parking area is empty.

Jim knows one thing, stalking on down River Street for home. He's not walking out to the Reese sisters'. He's done his walking for today.

The other men have done no better: they have done the same as Jim. Like their pastor, they are heading home, and not a one of them even wonders whether anyone else has found Jacob or not, as if their own failures were prophetic and sure, as if they all knew that Jacob is more lost than ever by not having appeared in any of the places they already expected him not to be, as if that is what they wanted all along. And yet they have, most of them, spent more than an hour walking in the wet of some grass or other, standing hidden and to themselves nearly revealed as searchers with no wish to find, rescuers sullenly glad not to rescue: their feet are uncomfortable, their thighs a little tired in the coolness, their fingers weary and irritable from too much time in pockets feeling the thin lines of lint in the seams.

So they go home and try, by taciturn and boyish devices they cannot imagine failing because they learned them from their fathers, to gain a welcome of some kind from their wives, whom they know they have somehow failed, and who therefore should comfort them. Their wives, who have spent now a couple of swollen Sunday hours also out of rhythm without even walking to do, with no family of the missing man to visit or prepare covered dishes for and thus atone for their own greedy fear, with only the restless and resentful children to vent it all on: the women have spent the hours in exactly the urgency of a swollen injury that throbs and aches but is no danger and cannot be treated except by time, an urgency finally as false as the men's searching, and as true: from these women, nearly exposed by their own terror, these men, nearly exposed by their own satisfaction, attempt to gain a comforting welcome in their own homes: supper, sympathy. But the women don't even ask, except by a secretive glance immediately knowing, and from that knowledge that the one man of liberty and passion among all the world is still and probably forever lost to them dead or alive, and from the unsurprised knowledge that their men have exhausted neither their bodies nor the fields and roadsides in their game of search party, the women feel how useless all of this has ever been, and will not be satisfied. They prepare supper, banging pans and almost deliberately rushing, so that the stuffing and the potatoes are still cool at the center.

Jacob is brought awake by the sweet delight of cold water washing down the rich brown savor of roast chicken that has nearly melted from its bones at the greed of his hunger.

He is brought awake kneeling on the dirt floor before an emptied plate that is not familiar, which lies on the seat of an old metal chair.

Because there is no table.

He begins a small rocking where he kneels, cradling his arm, which has waked with him to its aching.

No table where a table was.

188

Not in this shed.

Which is the only shed. Outside, across wet grass but he has no shoes, is the house.

Not the house, but the only house.

And then he is barefoot.

And not Rachel there and not Mother. And he, also, not there but here.

But food, rich smelling, napkin rolled.

He looks around quickly, almost crafty, to catch the looped and bunched and secret flowers hanging in the dim, hiding light.

Gone.

He sneers, stands himself up tall to meet it. The failed arm, dropped, lurches pain again across his neck and back and he shouts.

Unhearing.

The noise will not gather, and his throat, astonished, pauses.

Roast chicken. And—peas.

The napkin, unused, is disarranged, the spoon angles awkward and unpleasant off the plate's rim.

Table?

He turns.

An old porch swing he has no porch to remember upon, but must be his, his back and legs still knowing its hard coolness. He steps to it and nudges it with his bent knee. And knew already it does not move. So.

His hand slides habit-bound into his pocket for the keys, almost happy; habit-forced, his mouth and throat begin. But the keys refuse to slide, somehow are become one patterned mass in his pocket, their chain stiffened.

And silence.

The silence of his throat sits him sharply down and bends him over his arms, which tend one another and warm his chest.

No tin-covered trunk, no light blanket inside it.

He pulls air in deep, deep, but only his own smell and the smell of metal and a dirt floor, no old kind smell of softened colors. When the air flows back out of him, it draws a stinging of tears behind.

Then he can sleep again, lost.

Supper over, dishes done up, day bleak on the other side of the night that has come steadily upon them this whole broken and stalled afternoon, the women resist still; they draw forth baskets of mending they have neither wish nor need to do, fumble clumsied fingers in the pointless messes of tangled thread, stab their fingertips and make no startle of pain. They put the baskets by, take up some part of the Sunday paper that lies abandoned on a table or couch or chair arm, and open it studiously.

The men wait, sullen, cheated.

The women sigh, take suddenly energetic looks around the disheveled front rooms, step out into the kitchens and flip on the light switches, reveal tables cleared but some way left unclean, and they wring out a cloth at the sink.

Come to bed, a man says, his voice hard and level.

The cloth hesitates, and then smooths onward across the tabletop, counter, down the cupboard door. Across the seat of one chair and then another, around the plate of the light switch. *Go on up,* she says. *I'll be up as soon as I finish.*

A man walks quietly to the doorway. *Let it go,* he says. *It's late.*

She stacks the sections of the newspaper deliberately, squaring the corners. *Yes. I'll be right up,* she says, and glances around to find the funny papers.

All up and down the street that nearly follows the river, at this distance of almost a quarter mile, the river that follows minutely the weak and strong places in the earth that holds it and is molded, discovered, and revealed by it, all up and down River Street, the men and women have begun this, the women stalling, resisting the men waiting, challenging with plain-voiced factualities, their voices a near chorus from house to house, their words and tones are so nearly identical. *Time to go up,* the men say. *Come on, then,* they say, biding their time. Neither patient nor impatient, only steady, tepid, undeterred by the women's business. And the women, not yet seeing just what they should fear, distracted by the wish for a few moments alone downstairs, the women go on with their tidying until the men acquiesce, almost ironical, undeceived and still undeterred. *All right,* they say. And they go on upstairs in their heavy-soled shoes. But not good-night. No goodnight yet between man and wife.

The women go on a few minutes more, emptying ashtrays and wiping them out, setting throw pillows straight in the corners of couch and chair, unpinning and smoothing and repinning doi-lies on the arms of chairs and antimacassars on the backs of chairs, all the unnecessary chores of deliberate delay. Upstairs water runs, toilets flush, floors creak, and then it is quiet.

The women turn out the kitchen lights, turn out the lamps in the living room one by one. In rooms that are dimmed, lit inescapably by hallway lights that must burn until the women too climb the stairs for the whole night, the women stand still at last and wait in something like solitude, like invisibility, to be taken. They wait, for something they cannot wish or even pray for: something large and unmistakable: terror maybe, or, missing that, grief, something to move them like grief, at least some clutching worry that would prove their loss, and in proving the loss prove also that once they have held its opposite.

But here they are in their own homes. Smells of dishwater, the sourness of the damp dishrags, their own soaps and powders and shampoos; outlines of furnishings familiar to shabbiness, curtains, the false images visited on wallpaper patterns by the nearness of dark, the shine on bare edges of floors in the light from the hall; from the kitchen the ticking of the floor and dishes settling in cupboards, a refrigerator humming or clicking quiet, from upstairs a body turning in bed, their own too calm breath-ing; the static insincerity of their shoulders, a slip skewed at the waist to a bias, a crumb beneath a thumbnail; the late taste of pot roast with onions.

And so, finding nothing that will move them, they retreat slowly from anticipation back into resentment, and go on up the stairs, brush their teeth and wash their faces, avoiding the mir-rors.

In the bedrooms they are half undressed, their hands already busy with garters, before they feel that the men are awake and watching them in the dark. They blush and hurry into their nightgowns, shamed. They slide quickly into bed, pretending not to disturb the sleepers.

Who lie still until the women seem quiet. There will be no mistaking.

All of them lie still, breathing as if naturally, and wait.

The men's hands come down firm and quiet and undeceived on hip and breast, and the women don't move. Not one says a word, no sigh of protest escapes, neither thigh nor shoulder slides or jerks away in recognition. For one terrific moment in the dark a test is made before the hands, calm and uninviting, unrequesting, deeply unseducing, insist.

And every woman allows herself to be turned onto her back, allows her legs to be opened with her mind as cold as damp stone, her heart thudding against her ribs in shame.

Outside only the bats scream above hearing and swallow convulsively the scarce insects of darkness.

And every man lowers himself into his wife in cold distaste, and can scarcely stay strong enough against the weakening power of shame to go on to the finish that is less climax than expulsion, before he pulls out and turns heavily with his face to the door, away from the woman who lies unmoving, letting the wet ooze out and make a cold damp beneath her.

In less than fifteen minutes, then, from the moment the first of the men started up the thirteen-step staircase, less than five minutes since the first of the women slipped her shoes off her swollen feet in the dark bedroom, all these husbands and all these wives have betrayed one another and themselves in the silence of Sunday night on River Street. And now grief can begin, for Jacob is lost, lost, washed away.

Of course the children wake all night long in noiseless suspended dream-screaming, sit up in narrow or shared beds too afraid to cry, their eyes in the dark seeking some shape to relieve the shuddering image of mud-filled mouth and white hair floating in tangles: of course they do, and lie back down shocked and emptied by terror, smelling their own briny sweat.

But upstairs on Pearl Street Alice Reese sits on the edge of her bed in the dark for a full minute and then goes to the window and looks out. By the light of the back porch light she sees her sister go carefully down the steps with a blanket over her arm and her thin white braid down her back, and pause at the bottom. Then Elsie goes slowly across the dark grass to the door of the shed, where she stops again and half turns to the house before she moves the blanket to the other arm and knocks. Alice counts the seconds from Elsie's disappearance: four. And then Elsie comes back into the night and pulls the door shut behind her and comes more quickly back toward the house. Alice can see her shoulders breathing hard and the empty plate in her left hand as she pulls herself up the steps, her hand rigid and frail on the railing. Envy and approval make Alice say aloud, "And your slippers are completely wet— you'll catch your death," and stay a minute more looking out where the dewed grass shines dark.

Every room in the old Wilcox place is alight. Famished for sleep, Rachel moves light and attenuated about, checking every noise, and the noises do not cease. He will come back, she insists, he will come back, harmed, afraid, and she must not sleep. Images of Dan Cullinan satyrlike beyond leaf masses, of Amos Brown insinuating and resentful at the back door, of cold-eyed James Parsons accusatory on the front porch, move her dry-mouthed to lock doors and draw curtains and shades. She has made tea, now tepid and nauseating; the water makes such noise rushing from the faucet that she fills her glass before it has run cool enough to drink. She spits into the sink and her own reflection in the window terrifies her: for an instant she thought it was Jacob staring in.

She sits on one of the white chairs and clasps her hands on the cold white enamel of the kitchen table. Her hands tremble. She watches them and agrees she must sleep: absurd to sit here feeling so afraid, shaking.

He will not come to the house. The lights are no beacon to him who has shunned the house, shunned her presence; the lights are for her own fear, and will send him away, proving as they must her alert presence deep in the night. If he comes, he will return to his drying shed, the neat pallet, the hushed garlands.

And could have come any moment of her sustained and silent

panic since dark forced her in. Could lie out there now, safe home. Or could lie out there now, injured and confused.

Stealthily, still terrified of what she cannot quite force herself not to imagine stands hidden by the reflection of light on windowpanes, Rachel moves back down the hall to the parlor and snatches the light coverlet from the back of the couch. She swirls it through the air and around her shoulders like a shawl, hugs it like a refugee's blanket around her shivering body, and trembling, her fingers turn off one lamp. In the kitchen again she stops and draws her breath in deep, moves the switch down with a loud *tunk,* and stands in the dark with her back to the wall.

Such distillation of silence. She could almost sleep standing here, the soft, dry smell of satin rising warm.

What she will do is go out the kitchen door and across the grass to the shed. She will be hidden by the darkness, and she will leave the kitchen door open to receive her back should she need to flee from anything out there.

She does it, wondering, at every step across the worn kitchen floor, how she dares move at all, wondering why she is so afraid, and explaining like a mother to herself the facts of her worry and exhaustion, this nervous terror a predictable result to be borne if not transcended.

If only the bolt were not such a terrific noise drawing back, if only the door would not shriek so.

But at the first step off onto the wet grass the night's calm absorbs her, and again she feels sleep prepared to enclose her. Smooth as shallow water she moves away from the house, past the ruin of flowers, the flattened garden, to the shed. Holding the quilt at her chest with one hand and touching lightly along the rough wall of the shed, she floats around it to the door and pushes it open and goes in. She feels the empty space of it, dry and gentle, and she pretends to wait in here for Jacob, pretends she kneels on the pallet only to be sure in the blind darkness that Jacob is not here yet. The smell of the dried and drying flowers confuses itself with the gentle scent of Jacob himself that permeates the pillow beneath her face. As sleep gains on her in this sudden docility, she can almost feel that dry, warm cheek, and her lips nearly purse in a kiss against the cool cloth of the pillowcase.

Rachel's grief will wait for morning and the least of the sheriff's deputies, a tall nervous boy who fears the appearance of cadaverous resolution. Even before the boy tells her in his flat pretense of police voice that communities downstream have been alerted to the probable drowning, Rachel knows that Jacob is dead, swept away in the one-night flood. She will wait until the stupid tall uniform pulls its car away up Bridge Road, and then she will begin to rage, shouting, the spit webbing the corners of her mouth. By nighttime tomorrow, she will be able to sob herself to sleep in her own bed, with nothing to be afraid of anymore. She will begin to mourn, but her rage will remain, and she will believe she can never forgive the narrow chill of this horrid town for robbing her of all that might have been her life with Jacob. Already she will begin to forget her own dismay, her own despairs. But that is tomorrow, and the day after. For now, she lies overtaken by sleep.

And in town, the men and women sleep; out on Pearl Street, Alice and Elsie have settled under the light cover of aged sleep, and Jacob, alone in the dark of a strange shed, covered by a blanket that smells of camphor and, vaguely, of lavender, sleeps and wakes to the rhythm of the pain in his shoulder.

CHAPTER 17

veryone is careful on Monday morning. The heat is returning, seeping slowly upward again, and no one is rested, but the men eat exactly what their wives set before them, and the women are careful to set everything on the table in pure neutrality. No one looks at anyone else, except the children: after the men have gone off to work, the children come to look for their mothers' faces, to see something comforting. They are shown only that same plainness, calmly determined ordinariness, and one by one they give it up, wander out to find one another. Allen is kinder than usual to Tony, and they pointedly exclude Chris, who wanders by without a plan and then wanders off again. Dinah simply wanders, up and down stairs, out onto River Street and back again, until Mary, irritated in spite of herself, puts her to sorting the clothes in her dresser, making room for the school clothes that must be brought down and tried on before the end of the week. September is close now, school, everything must continue and revolve, again and again without change now, without hope for anything but endurance. All day Julia catches herself listening for geese, winter seems that close now, in spite of the growing oppression of late summer heat.

After lunch, which Jim and Ellen eat in silence, politely, Ellen asks, "Had you meant to call on the Reeses today?"

And although Jim had not, had hoped somehow to become and remain invisible for the day, especially from the discomfort of that old house and the deafness of those old women, he answers as courteously, "Of course."

But once they are there, Jim is too warm even to try to understand the peculiar conversation his wife is having with the two old women, and he feels subtly tricked. Like a boy forced to remain indoors by people he cannot find a just reason to hate, he struggles to keep his eyes open, and must eat a tiny cucumber sandwich from the pretty tea table every few minutes just to stay awake. And yet he is irritated: the flurry of voices seems intent on confusing him, preventing him from discovering something he has no interest in.

"Our mother," Alice says, "would dress us in fresh cotton nighties and let us play in the parlor all through the heat of the day."

Ellen nods, smiling.

"Just outside the window our father sat alone on the veranda, because she'd never allow his cigars in the house," Elsie confides, keeping an eye on her sister, who is struggling to pour a spot of tea into a cup.

Ellen makes her mouth into a sympathetic *ooh* shape for Elsie, and doesn't glance at Jim.

"All the doors and windows were kept shut through the day, to keep out the heat, and the draperies were shut, against the heat. The sun would come in stripes on the floor."

"She bathed us twice a day, sometimes. Though I never understood just why, since we rarely moved even from room to room. Sometimes the second bath came so soon the talcum from the first would float off my skin and sit on top of the water in patches."

"Probably once a week she'd say it, 'Alice can't be trusted with scissors,' long after that was true in any way."

Jim forces himself upright again, sure he has missed something, but there is Ellen, nodding solemnly between the two old ladies, who fuss over the things on the table as they talk, never both at the same moment, but he cannot tell why not. Clearly neither can hear a word the other says.

"And he would tap at the window sometimes, to startle us."

"I suppose we were lonely children, separated from others that way."

"We had a kitten, of course—all the girls had kittens in those days."

"We never quite understood, and she died rather young. She said he was our uncle, though he came only that once, and was so surprised at the heat, as if he had expected we lived in an arctic area."

Jim smiles and passes his cup, which he had forgotten he held, and feels himself leaning forward like a plant in the heat as Elsie or Alice slowly chatters the spout of the teapot against the rim of the thin cup.

"And Mother would sometimes sit with him, before he died, and I believe he would not smoke while she sat with him, out of respect for her."

"He was weak in many ways."

"But things change, they say, and I remember her best as a grieving woman, still young and passionate."

The hands of Alice and Elsie bumble against one another suddenly over the plate of cookies, and they look up into one another's pale eyes in surprise. Their sudden silence alerts Jim, but he doesn't know to what, and then, as suddenly, they nearly smile at one another, and Alice speaks again.

"Of course, one year we were sent to the mountains, by train, and Elsie was ill."

Jim can no longer tell, in the dim parlor where the heat sits somehow completely on him, because the women have denied it or because it spares them intentionally, Jim can no longer tell which woman is speaking, Alice or Elsie or his own wife, or whether the voice he hears comes from the thin moving lips or one of the silent faces. He makes a desperate motion toward Ellen, who looks at him from a far distance.

On the walk home Ellen says, "They seem well."

And he nods, lying, as he always does but with more anger and more frustration than usual, and says, "My, but it *is* humid today." He almost pats her hand by way of apology, but then doesn't. For the rest of the day he feels himself spying on her, as if she had understood and taken part in some plot out there while he was in the dizziness of the parlor.

Next to the broken radio on the middle shelf in the back room of the store sit eight cans of cling peaches, ordered by Amos ten days ago in the time of his optimistic generosity: cling peaches in cans have been bought in this store in the past three years once by Julia Cullinan and three times in the past month by Rachel Cavanaugh. And Amos had thought how pleasant it was always to have on hand, but in the back rather than on the shelves, the peaches that Rachel liked to buy. He had, several times, considered taking them on out to her, perhaps some Saturday as he returned from Livingstone freshly barbered and Saturday free, cooled by the breeze created by going forty miles an hour along Town Line Road between the farms.

And now, early afternoon on Tuesday, the cans, which he is only distantly grateful he never made a fool of himself by delivering, have become part of the ominousness of the day, the day of the sheriff's man's stiff acceptance of Amos's report and (Amos imagines, for he saw him go into the post office and come back out) Nobel's report and who knows what other reports of Jacob Wilcox's absolute disappearance, of the probability that the crazy old man is dead, drowned, carried off downstream. Amos works on in the heat, allowing himself visions of the discovery of the drowned man with an almost vicious revenge. Amos has not quite forgotten, though he doesn't bother to remember it vividly, his own pleasure at the idea that Rachel was going to do something about Jacob. Take care of him, somehow. He pushes boxes aside on a middle shelf with bitter carelessness, not real anger. The air is too heavy for even anger. But there's a threat in it, hanging from the solid gray sky, and the threat seems to have to do with time: Amos has had, he suddenly feels, this impression before in his life, on a train long

199

ago, sometimes even lately in quick disturbing flickers, as he's driving along some distance—this feeling that time doesn't actually pass, that somehow all change has ceased and he and the world are now suspended in a misplaced eternity, where nothing matters because nothing actually happens. This morning he forced himself on and on, stacking Jell-O boxes, counting change, washing the front windows, every small task as much as he could force himself to do, his energy barely kept up by the goad of those eight cans of peaches staring at him every time he had to go in the back. The first two children in this morning, for milk and for bread, had clearly been crying, and they were barely awake. The swollen eyes and reddened noses seemed to have arisen without tears enough to wash away the sleep crumbs and last night's creases. Along with hope, grief, even gentleness, seem to have been pressed out of the whole world. And it's only Tuesday, and there's actually no proof that anybody's dead: Amos tries to remember and convince himself of how little he actually searched on Sunday, tries to pretend there are a dozen places the old man could be. Each time Amos sees those peaches now, now that the first impulse of the day has passed and the heat rises and rises, he feels fate heavier and heavier. The cans prove it all, somehow: the only thing that will ever change is that this dull lack will deepen, the gray sky will go black again and lighten again without meaning, and the cold of winter will keep everything as numb as this heat does.

So Amos isn't surprised when Susan Darcy comes in with dark rings under her eyes and her hair lank down her back. She looks at him obliquely, as if raising even a shoulder would take more strength than she has to spare; she and he nearly nod but can't dredge up more greeting than that. Amos stands behind the counter and waits, while Susan goes aimlessly down the center aisle.

Rachel has not been in today, and Amos feels that she will never come in again, in soft shoes or not. Surely she will leave now that Jacob is gone, but something leaps in his belly at the thought of the shoes, and he almost sneers: foolish. The idea that she would not leave is foolish, and more, obscene. He feels the sweat wrinkling its way along his skin in half a dozen places, and the waistband of his undershorts begins to wilt and roll. Susan lets the milk cooler door swing shut, but it bounces back, refusing to latch without the pressure of a hand. Poor kid, Amos thinks, and even before she turns and comes back toward him down the aisle and he sees that the second button on her blouse is undone and he will be able to see in a moment through the gap the white cotton of her brassiere, before all that, and just from the utter droop of her young shoulders as she reaches heavily to push the door shut, he feels his lips go loose with desire.

She sets the quart bottle and the pound package on the counter and leaves her hands on them. It is true: he could reach slowly forward and slip his hand into the opening of her blouse. She looks up from her butter and milk, a face of sullen defeat, lacking even a plea, and she looks terrifyingly, thrillingly delicate and doomed.

"Can I charge it," she says.

He could keep looking right into her face and put his hot, damp palm anywhere on her body. His breath comes shallow and thick as she lets her eyes drop from his, and he cannot tell whether he believes she has seen what he feels and submitted. They stand a long moment in absolute stillness. Years from now, after all that will follow has become simply part of the lives they each will live, a kind of weather will drop Amos back into this moment, and he will wonder, always in a kind of horror of intensity, what might have happened if he had dared, if he had whispered, "Susan," there over the counter, before the boy stepped through the doorway in his bare feet and broke the stillness.

"Sure," Amos says, his voice brittle almost to breaking.

"Thanks," Susan says. "Hello, Tony."

The boy smiles, giving Amos a jolt of pure hatred.

"Hello, Momma," Tony says.

Amos feels Susan watching him; he smiles stiffly at Tony, who looks only at Susan.

"Can I carry the bag?"

"Now," Susan says, and the mockery in her voice is unmistakable, though Amos cannot imagine what she means by it, "isn't this a very polite young man, Amos?"

Amos nods, still unable to look at her.

"I mean a very unusually polite and gentlemanly young boy, to come here and be so thoughtful." She reaches out and smooths the hair back from Tony's forehead. Amos stares at her hand as she holds her palm steady with the boy's forehead revealed. "And handsome, too—*fine.* You know."

Amos nods again, confused, hearing an intimacy in her voice that he knows is not for him. And Tony just smiling calm and gentle beneath her hand.

"Aristocratic," Susan says flatly. "Like he came from some old noble family." She lets his hair flop back down. "Like he hardly belongs in this town."

"Can I, Momma?" The boy's voice is smooth, sleepy.

"Of course you *may,*" Susan says, and then, leaning the least bit toward Amos, "Not much of Timer there, is there?"

Amos is shocked. He looks her full in the eyes. She smiles. "Would you put those in a bag, please?"

He nods, snaps open a paper sack for the milk and butter that are now beaded with moisture. As he lifts the butter it slips a little in his fingers and thuds clumsily into the bag: he glances up at Susan as quick and guilty as if it had broken.

She is smiling viciously, her mouth tight and her eyes cold. Slowly, holding his eyes, she brings both hands to her bosom and does up the button. He feels his face prickle with new sweat.

"Thank you," she says.

So Amos is almost wildly grateful for the sound of footsteps as Mary Aldrich comes in. He grabs his dustrag from beside the register and wipes the wetness from his hands.

"Mary!" he says.

She nods to him, says, "Susan," touches Tony's shoulder lightly and smiles toward him.

Susan half turns. "Hello, Mary. Another hot one."

So Mary stops to say, "Yes, and I'm sick of it."

Susan laughs.

Amos takes a deep breath. "I'll say," he says.

Mary moves as if to pass on but Susan says, her voice enormously casual, "Now, Mary would know what I mean," so Mary stops again, and Amos sees her politeness and impatience. "I was just telling Amos," Susan goes on, still slow and too easy, "how sometimes you wonder where your kids get their good qualities." She lifts the small bag, folds its top with a delicate sound and hands it to Tony, who looks a little surprised, as if he had forgotten all about the grownups and their groceries and their talk, as if he had just waked up. "For instance, my Allen— now, he's no mystery! He's the image of Timer, you know? Temper and all, but he's got my coloring. But then Tony here— he's just a whole different case. Dreamy," she says, smiling at the boy again, "musical. Like a little prince."

Mary smiles down at Tony, too. "*Are* you musical, Tony?" He grins.

"And graceful," Susan insists, "and small-boned, but tall—just a very different kind of boy, not like Allen much, not much like my family either, except his hair."

Amos is sickly afraid she will caress the boy's forehead again; he feels Mary's discomfort, but he doesn't look up from the rag in his hands.

"Both your boys are good-looking," Mary says.

Susan agrees with a sharp laugh. "But you have the same kind of thing with your two, you know? So you'd understand what I mean. Isn't it funny," and she's talking faster now, "how Dinah's so tall and—oh, kind of elegant, you know, even at her age? Like a real lady. I mean, when Brian's built just like Nobel—"

"They're not that different," Mary says, and her tone, Amos feels more than hears, has taken on the same elaborate casualness that Susan's has. They sound like they're talking a secret language. "They both have my father's eyes. And my mother was quite tall."

"Was she?" Susan says.

Amos hears steps on the porch again and hopes without energy for rescue. Susan has paused to see who it is; the steps have stopped right at the door. "Well," Susan says, her voice suddenly diminished and cautious but not friendly, not defeated, only deferred, "I didn't know that." Amos looks up and sees that Rachel stands in the doorway, a Rachel so changed, aged, simplified, he would hardly know her. Susan taps the counter with her fingertips. "Well, Tony—we'd better move along now. 'Bye, Amos." And more elaborately, "Mary."

Rachel moves back to let Susan and Tony pass, and she stands just outside the door. Mary, looking toward the rear of the store, past where Susan stood, takes a deep breath; Amos would hear the quaver in it if he weren't so astonished at Rachel. And in less than a minute, he would notice the tremor in Mary's habitually firm hand as she accepts from him her eleven cents' change. Only when she turns to leave does she see Rachel, unmoving out on the porch.

"Hello, Rachel," Amos hears her say, and this he does notice, the uncertainty in her voice. And Rachel makes no answer, no sign she has heard a thing.

After a long few seconds Rachel comes into the store.

"Excuse me," her changed, aged but something more, furious and controlled face says, with less familiarity than when she spoke here first, weeks ago. "What time does the bus for Livingstone stop here tomorrow?"

Amos tells her, understanding that "here" is some town that she has found herself in by unpleasant accident.

Mary forces herself to walk up River Street at a normal pace, to hold her sack of two quarts of milk normally in the bend of her left arm, to look straight ahead as if Susan Darcy had not named herself Mary's sister in secrecy. She wills herself toward calmness, and after a dozen strides the heat helps: it will not allow more than dullness, of hate or of fear. When she comes almost even with Julia's house (her own only two doors more, two more wide porches and narrow side yards, and across, attainable after all so quickly), she glances toward it purely for habitual comfort, but there is Julia standing at the top of the steps. Mary recognizes sharply the discomfort of Julia's arms, straight but crossed just above the wrists over her abdomen, the way her feet are wrong, and she feels how Amos was all awry and helpless the same way, and she feels the ache across her own neck and shoulders. For a flick of an instant she could just cry for them all, as if they were all children abandoned, astonished and helpless even to struggle.

But she shifts her sack instead and, "Julia," she says, and stops at the foot of the steps.

Julia looks slowly to Mary from where she had been looking, back toward the store. Julia begins to speak, but her voice is muffled and she clears her throat and begins again. Maybe it is the false start that makes her sound so artificial and distant. "How does she seem?"

Mary is startled, looks back toward the store herself before she answers. "Tired," she says. "She didn't speak."

Julia nods and looks again away from Mary. "She's gone back already."

Mary nods, stiffly, offended that Julia would accept the slight so easily.

"I wonder what she came in for," Julia says.

"There hasn't been any word," Mary agrees.

Julia shakes her head regretfully, and the two of them stand looking through the heat at the bridge.

"Susan Darcy was in there, too," Mary says.

"Oh?" Julia asks, as if Mary had interrupted.

"She's odd today," Mary says.

"Well," Julia says and shrugs slightly.

As if I deserved it, Mary thinks, and feels sun hidden but hot on her shoulders and her head, and Julia stands in the shade, uninviting, as if they were strangers, too. "Well what?" she snaps before she can help it, but in this eternal heat, exasperation is slowed and emerges sounding like challenge.

"Well, she has a perfect right to be *odd,*" Julia says in a rush, resentful, tears behind her voice.

Mary snorts a bitter half laugh. "I suppose she does," she says, and her voice seems to mean something she herself doesn't know the secret of.

The friends glare at one another, each accused and defensive, and the moment for retraction passes. Julia stands her ground in the high shade of her own house's front porch, the house where she was born and raised, the house she will own until she lies down and dies because that's the way her father wrote it in his will. She stands and watches without regret as Mary turns her whole body away and walks rigidly home. Julia stands, in fact, as if guarding against her return and invasion, breathing faster with the knowledge of her kitchen behind her, its floor littered with the broken plate and cup of Dan's breakfast lying where they flew from her hands hours ago.

Alice and Elsie sat for a few minutes after the minister and his wife finally left, checking to see whether they needed to rest from the effort of keeping the man in the shed a secret, but they both found themselves energized rather than wearied. So the clearing away was quick and cheerful, Alice carrying the tray carefully from the darkened parlor to the kitchen and Elsie extricating the carpet sweeper with less trouble than usual from the hall closet. When they had both finished they met in the dining room and smiled an agreement: they had certainly earned a peek.

From the dining room they saw that the door of the shed stood open, the interior a dark rectangle, but the back yard was deserted in the dull heat. Alice reached out to touch Elsie's arm so she wouldn't be alarmed, just as Elsie made the identical movement, and their thin, dry fingers met and tangled briefly in the air between them, such a surprisingly different thing than either had expected that they nearly missed Jacob's reappearance around the end of the shed.

"Now where do you suppose," Elsie muttered, taking her hand back, though as soon as the words were out she knew where he'd been, of course.

Alice supposed he'd been to Answer the Call of Nature, but since she hadn't heard Elsie's question she was under no obligation to find a way to mention it. She nodded instead, and Elsie felt a small flush upon her cheek, thinking that Alice was thinking what she was thinking.

Because neither of them has quite recovered from the fact that Jacob Wilcox is in the back yard, and is a man, and is at least as mad as their mother's madman, who used to eat the peonies so frightfully when they were very small and timid.

Elsie pointed, and they both watched with approval as Jacob

stopped just outside the shed door and stretched his left arm out a ways, gingerly but not apparently painfully. He went in out of sight and they turned to each other almost congratulatory, as if they had in fact had something to do with the natural easing of his bruised muscle.

But then they began to fix a lunch for him, Elsie thinking that surely it was her turn since Alice took it wholly upon herself to slip out there with, of all things, Cream of Wheat and coffee, early this morning while Elsie was still dressing, without consulting her at all. But apparently Alice had other ideas because there she was, right in the way, as Elsie tried to get a nice sandwich made. And Alice, who could see that Elsie believed the poor weak man ought to be fed like a lumberjack, and who hadn't forgotten at all how Elsie sneaked out there last night with a blanket, was only trying to get a bowl of nourishing soup heated up for him before the day was completely gone.

And now they lie, cross as two sticks, on their separate beds, thinking hard thoughts each about the other's selfishness and foolishness, how she's just silly about this man, just as if she were a silly girl again and jealous, for heaven's sake. Each of them stops even in her thoughts before she reaches the point of thinking, *instead of an old woman, both of us old enough to be his mother,* for in fact they remember him a young man, and remember his mother.

By the time they get up to begin preparing their own dinner and his, they'll each have already half agreed that things can't go on like this, for Alice's sake, for Elsie's sake, and heaven's, they certainly have enough to do to take care of themselves and one another, not to mention how awkward it would have to get after a while to have a man living in the shed. Perhaps they should have told Mr. Parsons in the first place.

Sitting comfortably with the blanket beneath and behind him in the old metal chair, Jacob eats both the soup and the sandwich, no longer, with this third meal, surprised at the silent appearance of food. His arm has stopped throbbing, and a while ago, around the end of the shed, he found an old crimson glory climber almost totally choked by weeds. After he eats he will go out and begin to free it: there were buds for the fall bloom despite the shade and the long coarse grass grown up around.

He searches again, having forgotten his earlier searches, under the glider and chair for his other slipper. If only he could find that, he might begin to hum, and feel the warmth of it in his chest. But the slipper is not there, so Jacob stands bemused awhile in the dimness and strokes the three days' growth of beard on his face before he goes out at last into the heat with his socks and one slipper on, which is why he limps as the Reese ladies watch him from the window.

CHAPTER 18

ll day Dan has worked in the harsh droning of chain saws, cutting and hauling the four fallen trees, so for the first while at home the silence is welcome almost physically, and he pretends for that first hour that it is quiet rather than silence. After all, he asks Julia what's for supper and she says ham; then after he washes up he asks has there been mail and she says on the hall table. He looks at the bills and the newspaper, and when she says supper, he comes right away, which he means as goodwill—yes, even as some kind of apology—though he won't blame her for not noticing, or for not seeing what he means by it. But now that their meal has passed without a word from her, hardly a sound from her at all, and she has taken food on her plate but has only picked at it, now Dan makes a real and conscious effort. They cannot go on like this, really, and he knows the breach is there but who could have words for it?

He clears his throat, and Julia stops utterly.

"Well," he says, "how's young Master Deery today?"

She shrugs, her glance off from him at a low angle, as if she were lying.

"Didn't you go over?" he asks gently.

She nods.

He waits.

She sighs. "He was asleep."

"Hm," he approves. "And how's Rosie?"

After another frozen pause Julia says, "She's exhausted!"

"Exhausted?" In his surprise he hasn't quite kept the disbelief out of his voice.

Julia's face goes red in ragged patches so he has to notice how pale she was, and her voice too is ragged. "Yes! Exhausted, exhausted! The baby, the house—all of it on her, day and night—and he doesn't lift a *hand!*"

Dan wrinkles his brow, searches for a pacifying idea, sure he wants to avoid talking about Arnie, from the sound of things. "Baby still waking up?" he says.

"Yes," Julia admits, subdued as suddenly as she was aroused, and drops back into dullness, her eyes off again toward a far corner.

"Well," Dan says, meaning still to lead them somehow to peace, but Julia interrupts.

She pushes her chair back from the table and stands, bumping the table so the silverware chatters. "And he comes home and does nothing! Nothing to help her—dark under her eyes, her skin all drawn—!" She's hoarse, as if she's been shouting all day. "And he comes home and he just sits and expects her to wait on him!"

"Well, now, they're young—"

"*He's* young! Yes, *he's* young, and she's old before her time!"

"Now, Julia, he puts in a full day's work."

"Oh!" She stacks the two plates blindly.

"Arnie's a hard worker," Dan says, placating, searching madly for another thing to say.

"He doesn't know the meaning of hard work," she says, so low it's almost a growl. "Somebody ought to tell him what hard work is, with his little desk at the insurance office."

And despite her strange mood, despite all he intended when he first spoke, despite the fact that he actually agrees with her in a way, and despite his sorrow at all that has been growing so sour between them, Dan can't stop himself. "I wouldn't interfere," he warns, his voice as low as hers.

She looks at him with such eyes he nearly believes he can see the print of his hand on her cheek. "No," she whispers. She turns from him toward the counter, the plates in her hands. "No," she says so loud it is almost gay. "Interfere?"

She drops the plates and turns back to the table as if she had set them normally beside the sink.

"You wouldn't, would you?" she accuses. "You want her forgotten, as if she'd never been born! Because you're jealous, Daniel Cullinan! All of you—you're just jealous!"

Across River Street and down two houses Nobel Aldrich peppers his macaroni and cheese before he tastes it. "Rachel Cavanaugh was in for her mail today," he says.

"Dinah, don't slouch so," Mary says mildly.

"Pass the mustard," Brian says.

"Please," says his mother.

"Gave me a change-of-address card."

"Did you take any broccoli, Dinah?" Mary says.

Nobel is encouraged, and goes on. "I imagine she'll be leaving in a day or two, once she's made arrangements." *And we can all get back to normal,* he thinks.

"For what?" Mary says, but with a kind of challenge or warning at the edge of her voice.

Nobel glances at Brian and Dinah, who eat steadily, looking at their plates. He supposes Mary's right, no point in bringing up the drowning and all that in front of them, at the supper table. So, "Oh, I imagine she's got—affairs to settle."

"Affairs?" Mary says, mimicking surprise.

And Nobel scowls a little, puzzled why she'd want to bring *that* whole business up in front of the children. "Business affairs," he says. "House, insurance—funeral. All that."

"All that?" Mary says, and now the mockery is clear in her voice.

"Yes," he says, as if it's the last word. "Broccoli, please."

Mary purses her mouth. "All that—yes. She certainly would need some time for *all that,* wouldn't she?"

Dinah stops chewing; Brian chews faster, wolfing his food, the bulge in his cheek huge. Nobel decides not to answer.

"Let's see—she'll have to tell the madhouse there's nobody coming, and she'll have to go ahead and sell the house or leave it for haunted, and then there are all the wedding plans—"

"Mary," Nobel says.

"Well, she *hasn't* found anyone to marry. Or has she? Did I miss something?"

Nobel shakes his head, tired.

"Oh, well, maybe I'm mistaken—I'm not up on these *affairs,* not being at the *center* of town."

"Let it go," Nobel says.

"Certainly," she says. "Although if we peasants are to attend the royal wedding—"

"Mary—"

"We'll need new frocks. Or maybe she's not planning that at all—maybe she'll have a big auction, though—wasn't there talk of a big auction, Dinah? And we could all go and buy a souvenir of the golden age—"

"For Christ's sake!" Nobel says, putting his fork down on his plate with a clatter.

"Don't curse," Mary says evenly. "Brian Aldrich, don't stuff your mouth!" she barks.

Brian snaps his head up but looks at Nobel, not at Mary, and his eyes focus with indignation. Nobel flushes. "Sit up straight, Dinah," he says sternly.

"I have already spoken to *her,*" Mary says, haughty and defensive, her voice indicating that he has no right to speak.

Susan dishes boiled potatoes and string beans from the saucepans on the stove onto paper plates. The kitchen table is, for reasons Timer decides not to ask about, covered with the confused contents of the highest cupboards: outsized serving dishes, the tarnished creamer and sugar bowl on the little silver tray, a basket of paper napkins decorated with Santa Clauses, various small paper sacks that contain things like batteries and pots of paste and extra hinges, a box of rat poison. So tonight they'll eat out of the kitchen, the boys on the back steps probably, and he'll sit in the living room and read the paper. And he is purposely not complaining, not even mentioning it. She slides a cookie sheet out of the oven and pokes fish sticks off it with a fork onto the plates.

Tony howls from the back yard and she leaves the sheet balanced on top of the potato pan to rush out and see what it is. Timer follows more slowly, so he meets her on her way back, holding Tony's arm while he hobbles on the heel of one foot up the steps.

"What's the problem?" Timer says.

Tony sniffs. "I got a splinter," he says.

"On what?" Timer says.

"Sit down here," Susan says, pulling a chair out for him.

"On the dumb old cellar door," Tony says.

"Told you to stay off that," Timer says, but not really scolding. "Let's have a look." Susan has gone upstairs for a needle, tweezers, peroxide, iodine, whatever, but lots of splinters you can just catch hold of and pull out without making a big medical disaster of it.

"No," Tony whimpers. "It'll hurt!"

Timer takes hold of the thin ankle and looks at the ball of his foot. "Where?" he says.

"Ooh, right there," Tony whines, pointing at the whole, evenly dirty, sole and tries to pull his foot away.

Susan is back. "Here," she says, and holds out a wet washcloth.

Timer takes it. Tony wails. "If you can point to where it is," Timer says, "maybe I can just pull it out."

"Don't yell at him," Susan says, setting peroxide and the box of Band-Aids on the table.

"I'm not yelling at him! He's bawling so loud he can't hear. You're not killed, you know."

"Well, it hurts," she says.

"It hurts! It hurts!" Tony cries.

Timer takes a deep breath and lets it out. "Okay. I'm just going to wipe it off," he says.

"No! No!"

"—so I can see where the splinter is."

"No! Momma! Momma!"

"Hold still," Timer growls, and touches the cloth to the heel of the narrow foot.

Tony screams and jerks his foot violently.

"Here," Susan says. "Let me."

"Hold still!" Timer shouts.

"Don't *yell* at him!" Susan shouts.

Timer wipes the cloth firmly up the bottom of the foot and throws the cloth on the floor. "Give me the tweezers," he says, though he still can't see a thing that looks like a splinter.

Tony's sobs come like retching, and Susan says, "It's all the way in *now*—you'll have to use the needle."

"No! No!" Tony screams.

"Then give me the damned needle!"

"Let me do it," Susan says.

Timer lets go suddenly and the boy's chair rocks. "If you'd put his damned shoes on him like decent people—"

"He doesn't have any damned shoes!" she shouts. "He doesn't have any damned shoes because I haven't begged you for any damned money for any damned shoes!"

"Oww!" Tony wails, rubbing his ankle.

Timer's chair slams to the floor as he leaps up. "Shut up!" he bellows, and as he turns, his wrist knocks the cookie sheet off the stove, scattering pale brown fish sticks in his path, and he kicks them aside as he leaves.

With darkness, a chill motion of air arrives, just enough to set the heaps of broken tomato plants and cucumber vines fluttering where the men flung them from the garden spaces between the ruined suppers and comfortless sleep, just enough to make Dinah curl more tightly around her secret weeping in her bed, just enough to make Tony scuttle in his sleep closer to Allen's side of the bed. Just enough to make men and women on River Street aware of their cold backs, bitterly aware of the unavailable warmth of one another's bodies, as if the other had taken all the covers, which are, in fact, halved with painful precision.

Just enough that Rachel goes on with her packing with a lessening of the nausea that has accompanied her for two days, and with a growing certainty that she can and will carry both suitcases and the overnight bag by herself to the front of the dank, ugly store tomorrow and get out of here with no help from any of them. The bus arrives at 10:20; she sets her alarm, at last, for nine, and lays herself down on the long sofa at a little after two. She has not decided not to return, has not planned further than immediate escape from this house and this ugly parody of a deathwatch and the night terrors that will not let her rest, but everything she brought with her, and only what she brought with her, is packed in her bags. The air moves faster and more insistently, not quite enough to make the windows answer but enough to lull her with the rushing noise into sleep without any of the startling at small sounds that has kept her awake so long. Tonight she sleeps determinedly, not moving, not pretending or imagining or even hoping that she hears Jacob outside.

C H A P T E R   1 9

$\mathcal{T}$he town wakes to a steady chill drizzle, and Rachel, her face aching with this final insult to all decency and fairness, doesn't pretend not to believe that the rain is willed upon her by the people whose roofs she sees shining across the river as she begins walking, the suitcase handles already burning her palms. Her nausea has returned; for two days now she has eaten only a few crackers, and this morning the last of them were limp and sickened her even more. The scarf tied tight over her hair and knotted under her jaw leaves her face exposed, a face thinner and more like her dead mother's than the face that came with such certainty up the rise a few weeks ago. As she walks down the side of the road, her eyes steady on the bridge-side posts, where she will allow herself to put the bags down and rest for a count of fifty, her mouth moves, whispering, counting steps.

At the other end of town, Alice and Elsie Reese walk, too, one rusty black umbrella over the two of them, held by Alice's right hand. They wear small, neat hats, Alice's navy blue and Elsie's gray with a small pheasant feather, and their cloth coats, and they place their feet carefully between the puddles and miniature rivulets as they lean together, arm in arm. Without having had to agree, they know that Alice will do the explaining, and they did talk, this morning, with simple gestures and some shouting, and decided that they would go to Mr. Brown rather than to the pastor. After all, they have deceived Mr. Parsons, but they also told one another that Mr. Brown is very *practical*, and will know exactly what ought to be done. But neither of them is thinking of their errand just now, the store still a dozen houses away. Both of them are thinking of Jacob Wilcox: Elsie sees him as he lay that first night and smiled in his sleep like a boy when she covered him with the blanket. She's quite sure that the Mrs. Wilcox she remembers vaguely was his mother; she hasn't mentioned it to Alice and gotten confirmation, but she's sure enough of it that she goes ahead and feels maternal toward Jacob. Alice sees him as he was this morning in the lawn chair when she went in with the plate of hot biscuit and fried ham, and though she was startled to see him awake and sitting, he seemed to have expected her, and he smiled and stood up like a gentleman to accept the plate. And so she is sorry, as they walk along, that she had forgotten his coffee, and sorry that she had been suddenly too shy to go out again once she'd gotten back inside the house.

Jim Parsons is thinking of Jacob, too, this morning, though he'd rather not be. At breakfast Ellen broke the silence of a day and a half to say firmly, "You must go out and make arrangements with Mrs. Cavanaugh."

"Arrangements?"

"Today."

He stirred his coffee. "There's been no word," he objected mildly. Dishonestly.

But Ellen didn't argue.

And so he is pulling his big car out of the drive and has already decided that if Ellen asks later, he will tell her Mrs. Cavanaugh wasn't at home. The rain on the windshield is melancholy, and Jim sees his life roll out ahead of him like the wet pavement, a life of fibbing to a wife who has suddenly and, now that he thinks about it, predictably become the kind who declares what he must do and when he must do it. Still, as he heads down River Street for the bridge he means to think of something else, while he drives for a decent, believable interval, of how utterly he failed to be a friend to Jacob Wilcox or to his sister, of what he truly believes a minister should do who has discovered himself without faith or charity or, as the windshield wipers chunk endlessly back and forth, hope.

He slows for the bridge and there is Rachel, heavy laden and shiny with wet, standing back from the other side to let him pass.

"No," she says.

He looks away from her sullen face to say, "Well," and sigh, and, "At least let me take your bags, then." He doesn't look back to see whether she nods or hesitates.

"No," she says. And then he sees that she is moving past his car, the two suitcases bumping the door as she passes. So he thinks, *There's nothing I can do,* and she walks past his long car and he waits until she is on the other side of the bridge before he drives on.

There's nothing I can do, he thinks, and, *At least I won't have to lie to Ellen.* But when he gets to the privet trees around the old Wilcox place he stops the car and makes a laborious turn in the road and drives slowly back into the village.

He pulls into the parking area in front of Amos's just as Rachel lets the suitcases drop to the porch floor. She sets the small case beside them and stands rubbing her palms slowly and hard together.

By the time Alice and Elsie reach the long porch of the store the umbrella has begun to tremble and Alice is relieved to be able to lower it. She pauses and Elsie waits while she works at the mechanism, which is so stiff and difficult she doesn't at first realize that Elsie is intentionally patting at her arm. Then she looks, and Elsie points surreptitiously at the woman standing at the other end beside a pile of luggage. Alice doesn't understand, and as she looks back at Elsie again she notices Mr. Parsons getting out of his car.

"Oh dear," she breathes, but Elsie doesn't hear.

Elsie points again, more insistently, and Alice is doubly embarrassed, at the minister's approach (although she supposes

they'd have to face him again sooner or later) and at the rude-
ness of Elsie's pointing finger, but she looks anyway, and back
at Elsie.

Elsie leans close and Alice smells her dry tea breath.

"That's the sister," Elsie says, and flushes. The woman beside the luggage, clearly, has heard; she stops moving her hands
against one another and puts them into her pockets and is still
again. Elsie pulls back to see if Alice has understood this time—
she had no idea, suddenly irritated, that Alice was so unobserv-
ant. She'd give her a shake if that wouldn't just make everything
worse.

Alice makes an *ooh* silently with her thin lips and nods, ready
now, relieved in fact, and, forgetting Mr. Parsons, takes Elsie's
arm and moves the two of them down the porch to speak to
Jacob Wilcox's sister, such a stroke of luck to find her here.
Though a mystery why no one has told Alice a thing about a
sister.

"Miss Wilcox?" Alice says.

Oh Lord, Jim thinks, believing that the two old women have
come, called by some instinct of the aged for death, to pay their
respects, and lurches forward to prevent them from dealing
Rachel this one last and gratuitous blow. He comes onto the
porch as Rachel turns her whole body stiffly to face the two tiny
women, her eyes leaden, and his impulse divides with the desire
to protect them from her hatred, and he stops. *Let the bus come
now,* he prays.

Elsie smiles a tight little smile that still burns with how loud
her voice must have been, and she nods encouragement in spite
of the younger woman's unpleasant face. Her nod is com-
municated through their linked arms to Alice, who scowls the
least bit at being rushed.

"I'm Alice Reese, and this is my sister, Elsie. We live out on
Pearl Street, you know. We would have come sooner"—she
can't help it, Elsie keeps nodding so, she gives her a little nudge
with her elbow—"but we just don't get around so easily anymore. Especially Elsie," she says, dropping her voice just
enough, but Elsie has heard her name at least and Alice feels her
gather herself to begin another nod. "She can't climb stairs, you

know." Alice sighs, and finds herself uncertain what the point of it all was.

On the other side of the big front window Amos stands watching Rachel's profile, miserably aware that she looks more like Jacob than he had ever noticed, that she must be leaving and probably forever, and that for all the weariness and sternness of her face she is the most beautiful woman he has ever known, and his bitterness of the past few days is utterly dissolved.

"It would be different if we were younger, you understand. Our mother, in fact, often had gentlemen boarders—Mr. Hotchkiss boarded with us for almost fifteen years while he was superintendent; I believe it was almost fifteen. So it's not a matter of propriety!" Alice smiles, and if her eyes are more sad than merry only Elsie would know, and she's not looking. "It's just that we're not able to do much more than take care of ourselves, though he certainly hasn't suffered any real neglect." She straightens a little, thinking with sudden pity and pride of Elsie struggling back up the porch steps with the empty plate in her hand by the light of the porch light. "We've made sure he's had good hot food, blankets—of course, I had no idea you were so close. But we've done what we could, and his arm seems better already."

Elsie sees Rachel speak, and when she feels Alice go on again she thinks it is in answer, that things are being arranged.

"Though there's the limp, too; that ought to be looked at, I'd imagine," Alice goes on.

"What are you talking about?" Rachel repeats, louder, not because she sees that the woman is deaf but because she cannot bear to listen to her go on anymore. A person might expect not to have to be lectured by an old lady (for poor Alice's tone has been that of a scolding teacher, all unknown to herself, and no one to tell her or teach her anymore how to modulate to a ladylike and kindly pitch).

Elsie tilts her head toward Alice to make sure she hears the rest of it; Miss Wilcox seems to have taken their news rather crossly.

And Alice blushes, because it's true, what with Elsie nodding and the hostility in Miss Wilcox's face from the first, she has forgotten to start at the beginning and explain carefully. She drops her eyes from Miss Wilcox's perfectly reasonable anger and clears her throat before she says quite softly and apologetically, "Why, your brother, Mr. Jacob Wilcox."

Miss Wilcox quite lunges forward, and Alice startles, pulls Elsie's arm by reflex tight against her side; Miss Wilcox puts her hand tense on Alice's shoulder and speaks.

"I'm sorry," Alice says proudly. "I'm quite deaf—you'll have to speak up."

"Where is he?"

And although Alice can understand, she supposes, Miss Wilcox *does* look so nearly threatening that she wonders for a moment if they've done the right thing after all. And Elsie, feeling Alice jump so and seeing how this Miss Wilcox has come right up to them so—well, *fiercely,* as if they were to blame for something, Elsie wonders if they shouldn't have just gotten on as best they could; after all, if this is how Miss Wilcox is, perhaps her brother isn't so disturbed after all but quite sensible to stay away from her, where people are kind to him.

But Alice makes that kissing motion of her mouth to make sure her teeth are setting right, and says, "He's out in our garden shed," though she does wish Mr. Parsons hadn't had to be there to hear it.

CHAPTER 20

At some moment in the shouting confusion there on the porch of the store, between the minister and Amos and Rachel all trying to find out from the two ladies how long Jacob has been in their shed and whether he is injured seriously enough to need an ambulance and Amos rushing back into the store to call Dr. Emmons and back to see where to have him come and the minister trying to calm everyone down and find somewhere for the Reeses to sit down, the rain stopped. And when Rachel gave up trying to understand and got someone's attention long enough to find out which house on Pearl Street and started at a half run off the porch, she pulled the scarf off her head. So when she passes Mary Aldrich on her front steps without seeing her at all, her hair is loose and floating around her face, as straight as when she was twelve and went away, and Mary is startled at how much like Jacob she looks, moving so fast and unseeing, and Mary suffers a swift shock of horror that Rachel has gone quite crazy from it all.

But when Rachel comes around back of the Reeses' tall old house she is suddenly shy, and pauses for a second to push her hair behind her ears. "Oh please," she whispers.

Jacob has sat the past hour at the doorway of the shed, half dozing as he waited for the rain to stop, and now, in spite of the wet grass, he's outside pulling weeds from around a stand of foxglove and dropping them into a mound behind him. Already he can see that here too he's just in time to make sure the autumn bloom will have a chance, since at least four of the plants, old and vigorous despite neglect, have tall spikes of buds, and one is already half in bloom. He pauses to roll his trouser cuffs another turn higher, and to touch a speckled bell gently.

"Jacob?" Rachel says, coming slowly over the grass.

The blossom is pale yellow now, but in a week, he knows, it will begin to blush, and by the time the bells at the top of the spike begin to open, these lower ones will be fully pink and on their way to such a deep rose color that the golden specks will hardly be visible. He smiles at this, and then, solemn and regretful, because of their gay courage, pulls out a handful of tall sweet clover plants topped with tiny bright suns of flower.

And Rachel comes closer and speaks louder, hoping he only has not heard, weak with the hoping and afraid. "Oh, Jacob," she says, "Jacob—" Her voice catches near a sob at his slender ignoring of her.

Quite by chance he turns to drop the sorrel onto the pile of weeds, and there, only a few feet away, stands a woman. For a second he barely remembers a plate of food and wonders if he is hungry again so soon, but then, clearly, this woman is not the same. She is taller, and wears a long coat, and her hair falls like a girl's behind her ears. As he looks, already habituated to this new and utter silence that has given him, at last, the confidence of impregnability, her chin dimples and trembles, and Jacob sees with calm concern that she is about to cry, despite the smile that reminds him distantly of his younger sister, of whom he has dreamt so vividly. In his dream, however, he remembers without a struggle, the Rachel was a different woman and wore their mother's aprons over full dresses and her face was brighter, until the bad part of the dream. He scowls the least bit pushing that bad part back, the cold white groping of it that went suddenly so dark; it distracts him so that when this other woman lifts her hand toward him he starts back from it.

"Oh, Jacob," Rachel says softly, the tears hot down her face, "I'm so sorry—please! We thought you were drowned—are you really all right?"

While Jacob watches her face and mouth in such fluid motion, he is sure there is some meaning in it, though he understands only that the tears shine in the thin sunlight.

"And they said you've been here since Sunday—all that time! I can hardly believe you're all right, and here, we've found you—" And to be certain of it, and because she is so in need of the comfort and he has made no second motion to avoid her, Rachel takes the last step and puts her hand gently on his hand, beside the long weedy plant that he holds.

Jacob sees her hand and feels her skin against his, and the touch is just like his dream: without remembering that everything is silent now, his throat and lips have sent out "Rachel?" so gently and in such wonder that he isn't disturbed by the absence of the sound of it, and raises his eyes to the moving face again and sees that yes, this is Rachel. Little Rachel, so tall now! He moves his head to the side to see her better, so odd how different she is from how he dreamt she would be, so much thinner than in his dream, and softer somehow in spite of it, though still the recognition carries that uneasy darkness at its far edge. It is enough that he only stands and allows her touch. Rachel, of course—and she has come—but not home, is it? He looks away from her carefully, trying to see and remember, and he is nearly certain that this is not the right place. The soft touch of her hand on his free hand reminds him that someone is here, and yes, it can only be Rachel, Rachel who knows this is not the place, for she lifts his hand as if to lead him somewhere.

"Oh, you poor, poor man!" she cries, laughing almost in her relief, smiling to the aching point at his actual presence, pretending that he is transformed only by the silver growth of beard and the disarray and soil of his clothing, that a bath, a day, a week at most, will give back the gentle, eccentric brother of a week ago. She can nearly, in this moment of his resurrection, forget how she had found him at the last impossible, shocking; any memory of song is deeply lost in the nights of clarified fear, his life in the drying shed is clearly sensible to her now that she too

224

has lain in the smell of the ancient flowers, his caution about voices in the house is reasonable to her now; all that he was is so sweetly desirable, now that she has had in its place the cold fear and vision of her second and guilty widowhood stretching aimless before her, that she can forget she ever despaired of him at all. "Here you are in your bare feet! Oh, come home, Jacob— you'll have pneumonia!" she says, and draws him a step away from the overgrown flower bed, the weeds still dangling in his hand.

And if Rachel knew, leading him step by step over the grass where the rain shines in this new sunlight bright enough to dazzle them both, if she knew that in a day she will have to accept forever that he is deaf and speechless; that in a week she will wake suddenly knowing in horror that he was familiar and unshocking to her here beside the Reeses' garden shed because he was at last the helpless madman she imagined when she first rounded the tree-high privet beside their mother's house to save him; that her own words and ambition and the accident of storm and lightning wrecked his fragile balance and left him not empty but endlessly forgetful (each night he will forget her as he sleeps and she will bear each morning his surprise and faint suspicion of her presence) and locked away endlessly from her explanations and apologies, for he will look with no more comprehension at her carefully written notes than at her carefully speaking mouth: if Rachel knew in this moment all that, still she would lead him and tuck him over his mild reluctance into the back seat of Jim Parsons' car at the foot of the drive, and suffer them both to be taken home, and still she would offer him first the drying shed, and grieve a moment that he clearly does not recognize or desire that refuge now. Not for prideful sacrifice now, and not for penance, though she is deeply penitent, but at last, feeling his hands alive and warm where she holds them, at last for love of him, and for deep sorrowing joy at life remaining.

CHAPTER 21

*A*s Mary steps onto the far end of the porch Amos turns from the two old ladies with his face shining and calls to her, "He's found! He's found!" All thought of Rachel mad and haunting her life forever in grotesque caricature of the lost Jacob flies from her, a thought and worry she will remember only in the dim corners of dreams, and even the dreams are years away. She hurries up to hear from Amos the essential facts of Jacob's life and his safety, and she sees and is glad for the glimmer of tears in Amos's eyes above his sure and humble voice (how has she never noticed before that voice, the clear, simple brown of his eyes, his courtesy even in this excitement spreading over the Miss Reeses and herself?), and then she turns and pauses only an instant before she goes, with more grace than she has felt in years, across the parking area and down past the two houses to the post office. She will stop at Julia's afterward, time enough after Nobel knows.

He is sorting mail and she is beside him before he knows who she is, and even when he turns, her face is so softened here behind the wall of glass-fronted boxes that he has no time to recall their bitter division before she speaks, her voice as soft and infused with relief as her face, "Oh, Nobel, they've found Jacob Wilcox, alive and well!"

"Alive," he says, and though in half an hour he will discover with humorous chagrin that he has not a detail of who or where or how it could have come about, for this moment he is filled with a thrill of pure gratitude. He touches the corner of Mary's mouth with his fingertip and takes the full knowledge of the strength of her face, even of the fading caution in her eyes, for an instant before she steps close and her head is against his chest, the smell of her hair rising to him.

At the foot of Julia's steps Mary remembers that she never got the coffee she went to Amos's for, and it seems to her a good joke, a better one than she needs in this moment to carry her fearless up the steps and to the door, plenty good enough a joke to let her call out, "Julia!" as she knocks. She looks back toward the post office and sees that Ellen Parsons is heading toward the store where Mrs. Phoebe and Sandy Clark and two little boys without shirts are already standing, and Mary hears the faint voices of exclamation like bells on the clear air after rain. "Julia!"

Next year at picking time, as his grandson reels and staggers beside him late in the afternoon between the laden trees, Dan will wonder how different everything might have been if he hadn't had to stay that extra ten minutes in the office talking on the phone to Mr. Andersen from Ag and Markets the day Jacob Wilcox was found. If he hadn't looked up from his notes and seen Julia in the doorway with the sun behind her lighting up her hair, if he'd looked, say, down from the seat of the tractor or from near the top of a ladder instead. But as it happens, he is at his desk, and the sun makes a crown above her face, so that even before she speaks in the voice of the woman he knew so long ago, he is a young man again astonished and half disbelieving her attention is to him. "They've found Jacob Wilcox, Dan," she says, so quietly and evenly that he is sure Jacob lies now dead and bloated on stony ground, and he feels his head begin to roll back for grieving. "He's alive—not even hurt, they think—out at the Reeses'." Her voice is so calm and measured and so generous still that Dan is startled past the news she has brought: she is telling it to give him something else, and he feels his first new understanding of his wife in years. It's that business about Rachel Cavanaugh, he knows it now, Nobel's polite inquiry makes sense now, and he feels the relief rising sweet and smooth through his chest: that's all it was, that's all it was! So he uses the voice he has found for talking of Rosie's baby to her, and for the same reason, because there is no other voice in which to tell her his gratitude and his fear. "Well, that's good news!" he says. "Good news! A day for good news, I'd say— come look at this," he says, and pushes the yellow pad of figures a few inches to the right. "Looks like we're going to stay in business another year—state wants to buy from us for the school lunches."

And Julia hesitates only a moment before she comes into the cramped office where she has not been since her marriage, and looks at the figures. Which are so addled on the page that she smiles and more than half forgets that she meant to decide by his response whether he meant to stay with her or go to Rachel. "Why, Dan," she says, "I don't see how you can tell whether it's good news or bad, all jumbled like that."

The slap of the screen door removes the frail cover of sleep Susan has lain under for the hour since the rain stopped and released the boys from the house and her grim cleaning, but she doesn't move until she hears Tony sniffling as he comes up the stairs. She sits up without even pushing her hair back from her face.

"Tony, I'm in here," she says.

He comes into the dim room and climbs onto the bed beside her without a pause in the regular sniff-sniff of make-believe crying.

She sits with her elbows on her knees, the blanket to her waist, and can barely summon interest enough even in Tony to say, "What's the trouble," staring at the foot of the bed.

"Allen wouldn't let me go with 'em," he says.

She forces herself not to shrug, not to yawn. "Well, that's the way it is, Tone—sometimes you can't go." She takes a deep breath and pushes the blanket off, pivots to sit on the side of the bed. "How about you pull some carrots for supper."

Tony sniffs twice more, but it's only for credibility; he does like pulling carrots, and he slides off the side of the bed. "How many?"

And in spite of the weight she feels pressing her shoulders and arms until they ache, Tony has cheered her enough that she finds her shoes with her bare feet and stretches as she stands up. "About a hundred," she says, and he laughs a short sound behind her. "Really, about fifteen, middle-sized." He comes around her side of the bed. "Where'd Allen take off to?"

He's smiling about the hundred carrots and he says, "Out to see old crazy Jacob Wilcox I guess."

So Susan's hair and skirt look like she's slept in them as she stands across the counter from Amos and demands through dry lips, "Did you *see* him?"

"Allen?"

"No!" she says, a low cry. "Jacob—did you *see* him?"

"I saw the car go by with him in the back—"

"But *did* you see—is it true? Tony said he's all right, he's not dead?"

And *dead,* of course, is the one word even the children have not said in all these days, and it shocks Amos so that he sees, as he somehow had not until the word was said, that Susan is bedraggled, rumpled, wild-eyed, and out of breath.

"Why, no—Susan, really, he's all right—he's been in the shed at the Reese place since before the storm was even over. Here," he says, and comes around the counter, "here," he takes her icy hand and makes her sit down on one of the folding chairs he brought down for the Reeses. "Now, just take it easy," he warns.

But she sits absolutely still for as long as it takes him to get back behind the counter, where he means to pour her a cup of this morning's coffee, stale but all he has, and then she speaks in a perfectly normal voice.

"Well, that's a miracle, isn't it?"

"It certainly is," he says. "Take sugar?"

"Thank you—thanks, Amos," she says, and is gone off toward home again before he can turn around.

So at five thirty Timer walks into an utterly clean house and the smell of carrots boiling and dares feel for a second an edge of hope in spite of last night. He hadn't been sure what to expect, after she refused to even come upstairs. The house is clean and quiet, too. He leaves his lunch box on the counter and hesitates a second in the hall. Then, thinking she's either out or upstairs, he goes on up the stairs, unbuttoning his shirt. He draws a bath, and when, clean and comfortable in a fresh T-shirt and clean pants, he goes downstairs, the table has been set and he smells meat loaf. Then he hears a laugh in the back yard.

"Can not!" Susan calls.

He looks out the window over the sink. Both boys are running like crazy around the yard, chasing Susan, and all three of them are laughing, but *Jesus,* he thinks: there she is like a little kid in shorts twice as short as he's ever seen on a grown woman, and her hair is cut straight across just below her ears and straight across her forehead. She runs backward now, teasing the boys with the basketball in front of her, and then she heaves it straight up in the air. In a week she'll go into Livingstone for the day and come back with her hair curled tighter than a poodle dog's, showing the fine lines at the corners of her eyes and the tightness around her mouth, and Timer will be struck by how old she suddenly looks when she announces calmly on the front porch that she's got a job at the city clerk's office and she wants a divorce, but he won't be as surprised at any of all that as he is this very moment, staring at his wife transformed into a Dutch boy in the back yard. "Jesus Christ," he says aloud.

"They apologized," Ellen says over the sound of the bath water running. Jim stands in the doorway of the bathroom watching her pin her hair up for her bath.

"What for?" he says, barely thinking of the two little women.

She laughs in the mirror at him. "For not telling—Alice said she 'just couldn't think what got into her'!"

He smiles, and before he can overcome the warm brightness of Ellen here in this small, scented room and the sound of a waterfall and the certainty of Jacob safer than ever before, he says, "What do you think God's like?" Because his faith has returned, and he believes utterly and gratefully that God knew how afraid and alone he felt this morning in the rain.

She pushes in the last hairpin and shuts the water off before she turns her face to him; he's glad, through his astonishment at having asked her at all, to see that her mouth is still nearly smiling. "What do you mean—*really* like, or what I picture Him as?"

"What you picture Him as."

She pinks a little, not her real blush but a brightening really, as if she were about to sing or laugh again. "Promise you won't laugh?"

"Promise," he says. In seven months she will bear him a daughter and in two years a son, and he will love and honor her all the days of his life, but when she dics three years before him, this is the moment he will remember to comfort himself, her smile and the steamy smell of bath salts and her small hands busy with the buttons of her blouse.

"Santa Claus," she says, and they both laugh, soft and short. "Now you," she says.

"Promise you won't laugh," he mocks gently.

"*You* did!"

"So did you!"

"Be fair," she says, and steps out of her skirt.

It doesn't seem important anymore, now that she stands before him in the smooth white slip, her neck slender and inviting, and so he tells. "A giant beekeeper," he says.

CHAPTER 22

A week before the first frost, the maples on either side of River Street are in full color, and the street itself is dry, cleared of the first damp fallen leaves by the puffing breeze of this second day of sun and warmth, and the street is empty. The whole village is hushed: the men are at work, the children in school six and twelve miles away, the babies napping, and the women, invisible behind screen doors and windows propped open for maybe the last time this year, the women raise their heads from the hemming or the ironing or the letter being read or written, to listen:

Geese, high and faint, a jubilant mourning. The women listen for the long moment of their passage, until the sound disappears exactly as they all know the wavering line of black specks has disappeared. For perhaps two minutes their hearing is dazzled with the effort to listen further, just as their eyes would have been dazzled with straining to see, if they had left their quiet work and gone out to stand in their front yards or in the street itself and watch. And then the breeze speaks again in a shuffle, filling the houses with the sharp sweet smell of fallen leaves, and the women bend again to their work.

But it doesn't hold: maybe the geese have done it, or this spot on the earth has slid into some new magnetism, or it is only a shift in light or time or a drop of half a degree: whatever held these women at the small tasks of early afternoon lets go, and they push things back hastily, unplug irons and mark their places in cookbooks, and they go out. They gather stepladders, kitchen chairs, double window-washing buckets, rags and squeegees and piles of old newspapers, trowels and garden gloves, folded tarpaulins and splintery peck and bushel baskets with rectangular wire handles on either side, ammonia, vinegar, clean flowered scarves from their top bureau drawers, and they check one last time, at the doorways, on the sleeping babies before they begin on the windows and gardens that are their excuses for being in the breeze and the sun.

In an hour the babies are awake, talking quietly to the curtains and the shadows that rise and fall across the ceilings, and the mothers, always half listening, call up from where they've nearly finished, what a good baby to let Mother get so much done today, in just a little bit we'll come and get our girl and bring her out to see the pretty leaves, and soon Brother will be home on the big yellow bus.

So when the school bus comes to its halt in front of Amos's store and the younger children file out, sweaters tied by the sleeves around waists or necks or hung over shoulders or dangling out of satchels and dragging in the dirt, this morning's neat braids and ponytails wisping long strands that blow and catch across lips and eyelids and this morning's careful collars open and askew and rolled cuffs unrolled and trodden under heels, shoelaces clicking loose and harmless, River Street is already half full. The children swarm away from the bus, calling one another, ignoring or clutching the notices and workbook sheets the wind tries to snatch for a quick look, the socks of the little girls all falling down and the skirt suspenders slipping off shoulders, the pockets of the little boys' chinos half turned out and their shirts completely untucked; and then the older girls come decorously down the bus steps and stop in two clusters on Amos's porch to straighten their socks and touch their necklaces and bracelets, and then, from the very back seats, the four oldest boys each take the three bus steps to the ground in one lunge, their eyes averted from their feat and from the girls, their necks suddenly red as they walk away toward home silent and with a slow spring in their strides, until the bus starts again and passes them, and their friends from the farms out beyond Bridge Road stick their heads and shoulders out the small windows to call reminders and promises and small laughing insults, and one boy throws a sweater that spins to the ground like a giant leaf before its owner, the Clark boy, can snatch it from the air.

And it must be, the women think, waiting on the porches or beside the flower beds or standing at the half-done windows on kitchen chairs placed carefully among the chrysanthemums, that Rachel took him up River Street while they were all inside, for here she comes bringing him back down, through the generous freedom that comes suddenly upon them with the noise of the children and the *shush* of the wind and the sun lifting their hair out here, and they pause, leaving even their own children a moment out of their proud watchfulness, to watch Rachel coming along, and her brother leaning on her arm, the two of them upright and thin but strong still, their white hair burnished and her skirt dancing around her calves. A good-looking woman, the women think, but then here are their own, hands full of lunch boxes and notices and homeworks and twenty-four cupcakes for Friday, and the women are grateful, grateful and saddened, Jacob going so quietly by, nodding and smiling like an old gentleman at the boys who tear by, racing for home. Another line of geese comes by, but only Rachel seems to hear, the women all listening now to the children, and bouncing the babies on their hips: she pauses, and points for Jacob. They stand and watch until the ragged V is gone, and Jacob nods to her, and they go on, past the store and down the dip toward the bridge, for home.